CRAIG AND THE TUNISIAN TANGLE

CRAIG AND THE TUNISIAN TANGLE

Kenneth Benton

Chivers Press • **Thorndike Press**
Bath, England **Waterville, Maine USA**

This Large Print edition is published by Chivers Press, England, and by Thorndike Press, USA.

Published in 2002 in the U.K. by arrangement with the author.

Published in 2002 in the U.S. by arrangement with Juliet Burton Literary Agency.

U.K. Hardcover ISBN 0–7540–4840–3 (Chivers Large Print)
U.S. Softcover ISBN 0–7862–3944–1 (Nightingale Series Edition)

So far as I am aware nothing remotely like the occurrences described in this story is happening, or could happen, in Tunisia. All descriptions of Tunisian personalities, organisations and procedures are fictional. The Island of Sidi Abdallah does not exist.

The text of this Large Print edition is unabridged.
Other aspects of the book may vary from the original edition.

Set in 16 pt. New Times Roman.

Printed in Great Britain on acid-free paper.

British Library Cataloguing in Publication Data available

Library of Congress Cataloging-in-Publication Data

Benton, Kenneth, 1909–
    Craig and the Tunisian tangle / Kenneth Benton.
      p. cm.
    ISBN 0–7862–3944–1 (lg. print : sc : alk. paper)
    1. Craig, Peter (Fictitious character)—Fiction. 2. Intelligence officers—Fiction. 3. British—Tunisia—Fiction. 4. Tunisia—Fiction. 5. Large type books. I. Title.
PR6052.E545 C73 2002
823'.914—dc21   2001058476

CHAPTER ONE

It was shortly after five o'clock on a sunny afternoon, half-way along the causeway that crosses the Lake of Tunis, that Craig was kidnapped.

To the North, beyond the sandy edges of the dyke and the lazy cat's-paws skidding across the lagoon, the white minarets and villas on the distant shore seemed to be suspended in space, shimmering in the heat. South, on the other side of the Carthage railway, was the deep-water canal, with a freighter slowly gliding along behind a tug on its way to port. Then came the other protecting dyke and the southern half of the lake glittering in the hot sunshine and far away, the rugged outlines of misty mountains. There was little traffic on the road. It could hardly have been a more peaceful scene.

The Rolls was taking it quietly too, whispering along the smooth highway, very grand and elegant. The short chromium flagstaff on the bonnet carried a leather sheath with the Ambassador's standard correctly rolled up inside it. Craig sat alone in the back seat, idly watching two flamingoes fly past, looking for something juicy in the shallow green water below, the rosy plumage of their great wings vivid in the light of the westering

1

sun. Then things began to happen.

Peter Craig's view of the birds was interrupted by a man on a motor-bicycle, who rode slowly past, turning to rake the interior of the car with a penetrating stare. He was dressed in a dark grey leather jacket and breeches, white belt and holster and a white Sam Browne that carried a red star badge. Under the white helmet the square goggles faced forward again and the man accelerated and began to wave his hand at the chauffcur, signalling him to stop.

The driver hooted angrily. He wasn't exceeding even the low urban speed limit, and after all, he had a Corps Diplomatique number plate. He tried to pass, but the traffic policeman kept his machine in front of the gleaming bonnet and continued to wave furiously. The Rolls slowed demurely to a halt.

A black Citroën 127 drew up alongside, and two men emerged very quickly, with automatics in their hands. They wore dark glasses and black leather jackets above blue jeans. One thrust his gun through the chauffeur's window and shouted something in Arabic. The other opened Craig's door.

'*Descendez, Excellence,*' he cried sharply, the muzzle of the automatic pointing at Craig's head. Two other cars came up from behind, hooting angrily but squeezing past in the left-hand lane. Their drivers had no wish to get involved in what was obviously a police affair.

Craig didn't move. *'Qu'est-ce que se passe?'*, he asked, not unreasonably.

For answer the man fired through the floor of the car near Craig's feet. *'Descendez!'* he repeated, in a high-pitched voice that carried a note of strain. Craig complied, and was hustled into the back of the Citroën with the gun prodding his spine.

There was a third man there already, with yet another gun, but he was holding it by the barrel. As Craig tried to avoid the blow he was pushed violently from behind and fell forward. He felt a stab of pain.

When he came to his senses he was crouching in an attitude of prayer on the floor of the car, with his nose on the carpet and two pairs of feet holding him down. He twisted his body and stared up at the faces peering down at him through sunglasses. The big man who had used his pistol butt was obviously itching to do it again if he tried to rise from his undignified position, so he kept his head down and fingered the swelling bruise resentfully. It was painful. *'Qu'est-ce qu'il y a?'* he asked coldly.

'Soyez tranquille,' admonished the smaller of his captors, and continued in fluent French, 'We will explain all to you later. If you behave as we'd expect from an English gentleman you won't suffer. But remember, my friend here is very strong.'

Craig nodded—and even that hurt. He

allowed his eyes to be bandaged with a black scarf. 'Just a few more kilometres,' said the same voice, reassuringly, 'and we'll be able to make you more comfortable.' A hand patted Craig's shoulder. 'We have no wish to harm you, *Monsieur l'Ambassadeur.* You will be quite safe.' He was helped to sit with his back to the door, but leaning forward so that his head could not be seen through the window. *'Voilà!'* said the voice. 'That's better, isn't it?'

'*Merci,*' said Craig humbly. So that was why he had been called *'Excellence'.* They thought he was Sir John Radcliffe. He could see no advantage in undeceiving them. Presumably they wanted him for ransom, either money or—what? Political prisoners? Concessions? It could be anything, these days. He'd have to find some way of escaping, but with that big thug around and the car still moving along at a smart pace, to try to open the door and throw himself out would be suicidal. One way or the other. He wondered what had happened to the Ambassador's chauffeur, a grey-bearded, fatherly old boy who had served the Embassy for thirty years. He must have been scared out of his wits.

The car stopped, and Craig heard a gate swing open, squeaking on its hinges. Then the crunch of a gravelled drive, a sudden silence from the tyres as they passed over concrete—or could be grass—and finally the indefinable sounds of a car engine in a confined space.

Doors closed.

He was helped out of the car and through a doorway—he heard the sound of a latch. There was a short pause, and then his blindfold was removed and he stood blinking in the light of a single electric bulb suspended from the wooden ceiling of a small, oddly-shaped room. It was about twelve feet long by five, and furnished with a bed, a chair and table, and a bucket discreetly covered by a heavy wooden lid. The door through which he had been brought was in one of the long walls, and the thug stood in front of it, gun in hand. There was no window.

The thug was certainly big, with a chest like a beer keg, and the pistol looked small in those great work-hardened hands. He wore blue overalls. The other man was standing with the driver of the Citroën by the table. They were both dressed in coloured shirts, with half-boots showing below the legs of their blue jeans. The big sunglasses hid their eyes, but there was no doubt that they were young, probably in their late teens or early twenties. The wispy beards had never been trimmed. They told him to sit down, quite politely, and began to confer in low-voiced Arabic. The boy who had held Craig up in the first instance was slimmer than the driver. He was talking with an air of authority.

There was an involved knocking at the door, muffled by some kind of sound insulation. Two

5

taps, pause, two more, pause, then one. The thug opened it, and the motor-cyclist came in, still in uniform, his face radiant with satisfaction. The sight of Craig's brooding stare sobered him for a moment, but then he threw his helmet into the air, caught it, clapped it on his head at a jaunty angle and stood with arms folded, scowling the part of a stage policeman. Even the leader laughed, before calling sharply for order. The three younger men turned to face Craig, a half-circle of hidden eyes calculating, assessing, trying to foresee how he would react. Craig was reminded of the searching looks that children give a strange adult. The thug, much older than the others, maintained his malignant scowl.

Craig spoke in French, addressing the leader. 'What is the meaning of this charade, monsieur?'

'I regret, *Monsieur l'Ambassadeur*, that we have to inconvenience you, but I'm sure that our demands, which are reasonable, will be quickly met when the Government knows that we have you in our power. We shall then release you.'

'What demands?'

'The release of some of our friends, university students like us, who are wrongfully held in gaol. In the meantime we shall make you as comfortable as possible. You have something to read—' he pointed to some glossy magazines and a copy of Che Guevara's *Guerrilla Warfare* in its French translation, lying on the table—'and there will be food later.'

'And if I wish to relieve myself?'

'Er—*that.*' He pointed to the bucket. There was a suppressed giggle from the motor-cyclist. 'I'm afraid that's the best we can do at the moment, *Excellence*, but it will be emptied before meals. If you have to remain here longer than one night we shall make other arrangements, and also provide you with a change of linen.' He raised his voice menacingly. 'Don't try to escape, monsieur. The walls and door are sound-proofed and very solid, and there is no one near. You have a switch for the light here, by the door.' He paused, thought for a moment, and nodded. All points satisfactorily covered. 'We will leave you now.'

'I should like a bottle of wine,' said Craig. 'Dry wine. And a cloth and some cold water for my head.' He stroked the lump over his ear and showed the blood on his hand. A bottle could be useful in various ways, he thought.

The leader was upset, and threw a reproachful glance at the big man. He started forward to look for himself, then thought better of it. 'You shall have them at once,' he said. 'One of my friends will bring them.' He went out of the door, opening it just enough to slide through, and was followed by the others except for the thug, who remained on guard.

A few minutes later a tray with a bottle of Vin de Messe, a glass, a small basin of water and some lint were brought in, after which Craig was left alone. The moment the door was closed all sounds from the outside ceased, but Craig saw the door quiver, as some sort of locking device was operated. He wondered how it was done without being visible on the outside. Probably the back portion of the garage had been partitioned off to form the secret room. The door wall was of newer wood than the side and rear walls, but solid, and the door was quite immovable.

The construction was of thick boards nailed to studding—he could see the lines of the retaining nails, well punched into the wood. Near where the flex for the lamp was suspended from one of the ceiling joists a hole, six inches square, acted as a ventilator. He switched off the light for a moment and looked up through the little opening, but could see nothing but a pattern of evening sunlight on the leaves of a fleshy creeping plant.

They were amateurs, of course, even the thug. They hadn't checked the papers in his wallet and had left him his pipe, tobacco and lighter, and even his pocket knife. It looked as if they hadn't explored his pockets at all after he had been knocked out. They had a lot to learn.

He took off his coat, because the little room

8

was very warm, bathed his head, drank sparingly of the wine—because he wanted as much weight left in the bottle as possible—and lay down on the bed, his mind busy. There were various things he could do, such as sawing away at the side wall, where the marks would be hidden by the bed-head, but it'd take a very long time even if the knife blade didn't break. Or make a commotion and when the thug arrived lay him out with the bottle. Shouting would be no good, obviously, but if he pushed burning strips of Che Guevara through the ventilator someone would come running, and even if they'd gone away leaving a guard he'd burn himself an escape hole in the roof. Provided, of course, the whole roof, which would be tinder-dry, didn't catch fire. On second thoughts, *not* a very viable solution.

What else? He looked at the lamp. Switch off, disconnect the wires, attach one to the terminal in the switch and have a live wire handy to touch the muzzle of the thug's automatic when he pushed it through the doorway. An attractive idea, because he badly needed a gun, but it was wishful thinking. He'd probably electrocute himself, tampering with the switch in total darkness.

In any case, it was useless trying anything just yet. He must wait until the police hunt was on, and in the meantime be a model prisoner. After all, he thought, he was supposed to be Sir John Radcliffe, and must act like an

Ambassador. He went to sleep.

*   *   *

The crack of an automatic woke him up with a start. Craig looked at his watch. Eight o'clock. The sound had come from the ventilator in the roof. He pushed the table under the lamp and climbed on to it so that he could get his ear close to the opening. There was shouting outside, and then another shot, but from—of all things—a shotgun. A bellow of pain was cut short. Then silence. He jumped down, seized the wine bottle with one hand and the heavy lid of the bucket with the other and stood facing the door.

He saw it quiver as the bolt was thrown, and the door burst open. The leader of the gang was thrust forward into the room. Police, thought Craig, rejoicing, and lowered his weapons. The boy's face was white under the dark spectacles, and grimacing with pain from an arm-lock applied by the tall man who came in behind him. He was dressed in a loose dark jacket and slacks, with a black silk handkerchief knotted round his neck under the collar of the dark blue shirt. He held the young man easily with one hand, while with the other he pointed a shotgun at Craig, wordlessly inviting him to drop the bottle and the bucket-lid.

Craig looked up. The man's face was

10

concealed behind a nylon stocking which covered the whole of his head, outlining a jutting nose and broad cheekbones. '*Allons*, Monsieur Craig,' he said quietly. 'We are your friends.' Craig held on to his bottle but dropped the lid and stood aside while the newcomer pushed the young man forward and made him stand at the rear of the room. Another man in a stocking mask appeared in the doorway. Craig put the bottle back on the table.

Then he felt the boy's eyes on him. 'Are you not the British Ambassador?' It came in an anguished whisper.

'No,' said Craig.

'Come, monsieur,' said the man in the mask, 'we must get you back safely to your hotel.'

The boy who had kidnapped him sat down suddenly on the bed and covered his eyes with his hands. Craig felt oddly sorry for him.

'You see,' he said gently, 'the Ambassador *was* going to Le Kram as usual, and kindly offered to take me with him so that I could go on and visit the Punic excavations. But at the last moment an important telegram arrived and he couldn't go.'

'*Allons,* Monsieur Craig.'

But Craig was still looking at the young man's bowed head. '*C'est comme ça,*' he said. '*C'est la vie . . .*'

'*Merde alors,*' came in a muffled voice, with all the frustrated bitterness of youth.

11

*　　*　　*

Craig went through the door and found himself, as expected, in a garage.

The bonnet of the Citroën faced him. To one side the motorcyclist, the driver and another man, presumably the one who had held up the Ambassador's chauffeur, stood facing the wall. The moon had risen, and he could just see them in the reflected light, and the shadowy figures guarding them. No guns were visible. The tall man took him by on the other side and out into the open.

On the concrete apron of the garage the thug lay on his back, arms outstretched in a glinting pool of blood. The smashed spectacles were still over his eyes but there wasn't much left of the rest of his face. It was easy to see why his bellow of pain hadn't got very far.

'He attacked me,' explained the man with the shotgun, simply. He gently pushed Craig forward towards a car—it looked like a Mercedes 220—that was parked ten feet down the drive with a small cloud of condensing steam round its throbbing exhaust. 'We must leave quickly, before the police arrive.'

Craig didn't like the sound of this, or the idea of frying pan into fire. Nor did he like being pushed around. He took a step forward as if obeying his rescuer, then turned without warning and got both hands on the shotgun, which the man in the nylon mask still held comfortably cradled under his arm. Craig wrenched it away with a vicious twist that wrung a gasp of pain from the man, tripped him, pushed him over as he stumbled, and ran backwards to the other side of the drive. The tall man got to his feet as quickly as a cat, facing the shotgun in Craig's hands. He slowly raised his hands above his head, crying out something in guttural Arabic.

It was a position of stalemate for all of five seconds; the two men staring at each other across the width of the gravel drive. Then Craig heard the note of the car engine change, a small screech of gravel, and the grey Mercedes slid backwards between him and his *vis-à-vis*. He found himself staring into the eyes of a woman, who sat beside the driver. Ignoring the gun, which he lowered instinctively, she stepped out, a tall woman in a white sifsari, who held one of its folds across the lower part of her face. She faced him, shaking her head reprovingly.

'Really, Mr Craig,' she said in French, 'we are only trying to help you.'

'Then why don't you call the police? And why d'you hide your faces?'

'Good questions,' she said with a little laugh, completely at her ease, 'and there are equally good answers. But please get into the back seat. Just look around you.' He had done that already. There were two other men in

13

stocking masks standing silently, with their automatics pointing at his stomach.

'How do I know you're not trying to kidnap me, like your rival gang?'

That stung. 'We are not a gang,' she said sharply. 'We are a group of public-spirited citizens, trying to save our country from anarchy.'

'Isn't that the Government's job?'

'It's difficult for men in offices to understand the problems of the young. We do our best to help.'

'Very laudable. What are you planning to do with me?'

'Drop you off at the first place where you can pick up a taxi. We prefer not to get involved with the authorities; it is time-wasting. Besides, there is that unfortunate accident to be considered.' She nodded towards the body of the dead thug, which was being hauled to the side of the drive. There wasn't the slightest flicker of emotion in her voice. Craig stared at her.

She continued, 'I see that you still don't trust us,' and drew out of the folds of the robe a small Colt automatic, which she handed to him. 'You can keep me in the sights of this if you like.' She opened the rear door of the Mercedes and stepped in, with a swirl of draperies. Craig kept the shotgun under his arm, stolidly chocked the magazine of the little Colt, and handed the shotgun to the tall man, who now stood by, still massaging his arm. Craig had no intention of apologising to him; the sight of that gruesome heap of mortal remains was still in his mind. He got into the car and sat beside the woman, holding the gun in his lap.

She spoke to the driver in Arabic and the car moved off down the drive and turned into a road between suburban villas, separated by large gardens and groves of palm trees and eucalyptus.

As they passed into more densely inhabited areas the street lighting became more frequent, and he was able from time to time to catch glimpses of his companion as they talked.

The sifsari hid her figure completely, and her dark eyes and strongly marked eyebrows were all he could see. She gestured occasionally with the slender brown hand that lay on the armrest between them. It was her right hand; the other still held the fold of white silk across her face.

'How did you know my name?'

She laughed. 'Your Embassy issued a communiqué and I heard it on our car radio just before we arrived at the villa. It wasn't in the regular news bulletin, so that's why that young fool didn't know he'd got the wrong man.'

There was no need to ask what the communiqué had said; he would learn soon enough. It was she he was interested in. He wondered if he could get enough glimpses of her hand to be able to recognise it again.

'It was clever of you to know about the kidnapping and where they'd taken me,' he suggested. It was the hand of a young woman—twenty to thirty, perhaps, but difficult to be more exact when it was so obviously well cared for, with smooth, well-manicured fingers. No ring—yes, the marks were there, where she'd taken them off the second and third fingers. As the flashes from the street lamps lit up the hand for a few seconds at a time he studied it out of the corner of his eye, every contour, the knuckles, the set of the slim fingers, the way the wrist wrinkled.

'Yes,' she was saying, 'we keep track of what they're up to and when it's something very stupid, like today, we try and stop them.'

'By force, if necessary.'

'It's sometimes the only way.' She half turned, and he saw for a fleeting instant the dark eyes, intent on his face. 'You must realise, Mr Craig, that no one regrets more than we do what happened to that man. But he'd have killed my friend—he'd tried once already and had his pistol raised. The little finger of the hand tapped on the armrest. 'We'll have to help them get rid of the body,' she added thoughtfully, 'or they'll have trouble with the police.'

'Which you don't want?' That movement of

the little finger was interesting, perhaps characteristic. He must make her do it again.

'No. What'd be the use? And after all, we sympathise with their attitude towards the Government. It's just that we think the way is through constitutional channels.'

Craig saw that the car was about to pass a street-light. 'It sounds very proper and above-board,' he sneered, with his eyes on the white blur where her hand lay. 'Constitutional channels!'

He got the reaction he had worked for. Just as the flash of light illuminated the interior of the car he saw her hand bunch up, and the little finger, separated slightly from the others, tap nervously on the leather rest. 'I admit it's a cliché,' she said sharply, 'but some clichés have a meaning, and this is one of them. You can achieve reforms by constitutional means or violence. We prefer the former.'

The car had emerged from the suburban area and reached a highway he recognised. It approached the city from the direction of La Marsa and would soon pass the airport. The car began to gather speed.

'Violent revolution,' remarked Craig thoughtfully, waiting for another street-light. 'But of course it never gives the people what they want, does it?' The wayward finger was tapping again. 'It only produces anarchy or dictatorship.'

'Of course,' she said quickly. 'That's exactly

what I mean.'

I wonder, thought Craig, but aloud, 'I'm almost sorry for that other group, the ones who captured me. They're very young, you know. The police will get them.'

'I hope not. And if you want to make things easier for them,' she added, 'you can ask the Government to forget all about them.'

'And the man you killed?'

'Why not? It's no concern of yours, now that you're free.'

'With a little help from my friends,' said Craig lightly, in English.

She laughed suddenly. 'Ah, the Beatles. One of your better exports. I have the album with that song in it.'

The lights on the highway were frequent. 'A bit out of date, aren't you?'

The finger separated itself from its fellows, stiffly, outraged.

'Perhaps, Mr Craig,' she said coldly. Then tapped on the driver's shoulder. 'We'll let you out here. It's only a little distance to the airport entrance, and you'll find plenty of taxis arriving empty. Have you money?'

'They took nothing away from me. Unlike you and your—er—patriotic friends, they have no professional expertise. But thank you for offering, and also, I suppose, for rescuing me.'

She held out the slim brown hand. 'My pistol, please.'

18

CHAPTER TWO

The British Ambassador was standing at the window of his room in the Embassy building, which stands just inside the Medina of Tunis, opposite the ancient Bab el-Bahar. Sir John Radcliffe was a tall, well-built man of fifty-four, with grey eyes and dark hair tinged with grey. He was dressed in a dark blue tropical suit, with a college tie.

He looked down at the crowd milling around the gateway and entering the narrow Rue Jamaa Ez-Zitouna, which leads up to the network of soukhs inside the old walled city. Women in white sifsaris, men in western clothes, or fez and gondoura, or striped kashabias over bare brown legs. Hordes of children. They were a cheerful, friendly people and he liked them, although he had only been posted to Tunis a few months before and was still trying to master enough Arabic for casual conversation. Luckily, almost all the Tunisians he met spoke excellent French, which is taught in all schools as the second language.

A coachload of tourists arrived, spilling out a motley crowd of young and old, slung with expensive cameras, who pressed forward eagerly towards the narrow streets and soukhs of the Medina and all the exotic mass-produced tourist bait. To the watching, calculating Tunisian shopkeepers many were offensive, with their mini-skirts or long unkempt hair, or just funny, but all, they felt, were stinking rich and fair game. Small boy beggars were being coached in their opening gambit—a beaming smile, an appealing little face, and a carnation offered for free. *'Un petit cadeau madame!'* 'A present for you, pretty lady.' *'Fuer Sie, gnaedige Frau. Ein Geschenk.'*

Sir John frowned. That was the trouble. The explosive rise of tourism was doing wonders for the country's economy, but the sight of all that money going into too few hands caused resentment, and those who didn't benefit wanted more jobs, more consumer goods, better grants for the students. Especially the students.

He heard the door open, and turned. Michael Thorne entered the room in the established way, without knocking, and was standing just inside the door. He was a man of thirty-two, Head of Chancery and also Information Officer with the rank of First Secretary—a cheerful and engaging young man with a good command of Arabic after several postings in the Middle East.

'I've got Craig outside, sir, with Major Chaker, of the Surveillance du Territoire.'

'I'll see them now, Michael.'

Thorne opened the door again and ushered in Craig and a Tunisian with long-lashed dark eyes in a slightly sardonic brown face, clean-shaven, very much a professional soldier. He was in uniform.

The Ambassador spoke grammatically perfect French with a strong British accent. 'I'm delighted to make your acquaintance, *mon Commandant*. It seems we have a lot to talk about. Craig, I hope your head's better.'

'It's O.K., sir.' The Embassy doctor had cut away the hair, stitched the wound and applied a dressing. The pain had almost gone.

'Good. Michael, you stay. Let's sit down. Now, Major. I gather you met Mr Craig when you were representing your service at a seminar held at Oxford last Easter, and it was at your suggestion that he made this trip to Tunisia. Have I got it right?'

'*Parfaitement, Monsieur l'Ambassadeur.* There were some points in Mr Craig's excellent speech to the conference that I felt were of special interest to us, and General Farhat agreed we should ask your Ministry to let him come here for consultations.'

The Ambassador paused in the act of lighting his pipe and signalled to Thorne to pass cigarettes. He looked at Craig quizzically. 'Well, within a day of his arrival he's succeeded in making contact with someone's pistol butt, two groups of masked men and a veiled mysterious woman. Good going. Have your people any idea who they all are?'

'*No, Monsieur l'Ambassadeur.* There are a number of small groups of extremists in our country, as there are in most others, except police states. It is the price,' he added carefully, 'we pay for giving people the right to speak. In the message telephoned to the independent newspaper *Le Tunisien* yesterday afternoon the kidnappers asked, in exchange for *your* release, for twelve political prisoners to be set free, all students detained in connection with the violent demonstrations last March. By examining the antecedents of these men we hope to identify the kidnappers very soon, since they are likely to be personal friends of the men inside. But the others, the second group—' he spread his hands—'we have no idea.'

'I see.' Sir John puffed at his pipe thoughtfully. Then he pointed the stem at Chaker. 'But why *me*, monsieur. That's what I'm rather naturally interested to know. You'll remember that this isn't the first time action has been taken against this Mission. In 1967 a large crowd of students and other agitators set fire to the building and my predecessor had to take refuge on the upper floors while his staff fought a gallant rear-guard action on the stairs until the riot could be brought under control. Which is why,' he added, smiling, 'I am now safely housed, as you see, on the third floor, where I may be incinerated but where it is more difficult to attack me in person.'

'*Monsieur l'Ambassadeur,*' said Chaker hastily, 'that was after the Israeli Six Day War, and other attacks were made on the Americans and of course the Jews. The leaders were all given long sentences for plotting against the security of the State. But in recent years, and specifically in the March demonstrations, there has been no special animosity against the British. I feel certain that there is none in this case.'

'I see. Well, perhaps you're right, and I was just the easiest bird to get into the net. What do you think, Craig?'

'I agree, sir. And in any case, the group who kidnapped me were amateurs. I think they were only interested in getting their friends released.'

'*Amateurs?* They didn't make a bad job of putting you in the bag, surely?'

'With respect, sir, that's just what they did do. Having decided to kidnap you they discovered that you went by car every Thursday afternoon, using the causeway road, to your Arabic teacher who lives in Le Kram. Up to a point they planned quite well. Major Chaker thinks the traffic police uniform must have been hired from a theatrical costumier and adapted to look like the real thing, but it certainly deceived me. The police sirens on the motor-bike were probably home-made, and so was the registration number, which apparently doesn't exist. The attack was bold, but effective, and the hide-out made specially at the back of a garage—I assume the house and garage were taken on lease in a false name—was a good idea. They seemed to me bright young people, except for the man who was killed, and I expect he was a small-time thug hired for the job.'

'Then why d'you say they were amateurs?' interrupted the Ambassador impatiently.

'What would they have done if a real traffic cop had spotted the fake one, or if the driver of one of the passing cars had stopped to ask what was wrong? It was all too chancy. They even gave me a bottle when I asked for it.'

'A bottle?'

'Yes, sir. The handiest throwing weapon in the business.'

'Do remember, Craig, that I am not in what you call the business, and after all it was I they thought they had taken into custody.'

'All right, sir, I'll allow that. But the most glaring piece of amateurism was that they evidently hadn't made a dummy run.'

'You mean they should have followed me once or twice before D Day? But perhaps they did.'

'No, sir. If so, they'd have seen your security guard sitting beside the chauffeur in the front seat, with a gun ready to use, and your standard flying on the bonnet. When they collared me there was no guard and the standard was of course furled. Obviously wrong. What's more, they mistook me for you.'

'We're about the same height and colouring.

But after all, Craig, they did collar you, and as far as I can see they could have kept you there indefinitely. Now what about the second lot?'

'Utterly different, sir. As ruthless and well-disciplined as an Army coup-de-main party. Look at their modus operandi. They had good, up-to-the-minute intelligence, knew where to go and what to expect. The one man who resisted was shot dead. The leader of the kidnappers had his arm twisted until he showed how to get into the secret compartment. Then he and the others were kept quiet without fuss. The woman showed no sign of nerves in the presence of a horribly dead body. It was all very impressive, very quiet and very smoothly done. They are trained professionals, I haven't the slightest doubt.'

'It doesn't make sense. You say those who kidnapped you were mere amateurs, and the real professionals—by which I suppose you mean professional urban guerrillas—they were the ones who set you free.' He threw up his hands. '*Why*, for God's sake?'

'I don't know, sir. I think if it hadn't been for the shooting they'd have taken more trouble to appear as what the girl said they were, a group of dedicated Vigilantes acting in place of the law. But the dead body changed everything. It had to be disposed of. Some outraged householder—it was in a built-up area—might have heard the shots and called the police. So they had to get me away in a hurry and couldn't run any risk of making trouble before the body was dealt with. Hence all the guns pointing at me until I did as I was told.'

'You mean,' said Sir John reflectively, 'you saw no guns until you resisted?'

'Exactly. Only the shotgun, which is a respectable sort of weapon as long as its barrels aren't sawn off. In fact, this one was more than respectable.'

'What d'you mean?'

Craig hesitated. 'It was dark, or nearly dark, and I couldn't see the gun properly, but I would swear it was a hand-made gun, and very expensive. I have a pair of Purdeys, inherited from my father, and this gun had the same sort of feel and balance. I don't suppose for a moment it was a Purdey, but there's something unmistakable about the balance of a really good gun, and this one had it.'

'It's a pretty vague kind of clue,' said the Ambassador. 'Many of the Tunisians with landed property can afford to pay two thousand pounds or more for a gun. Haven't you any other clues? What about the villa? Could you recognise it again?'

'There's no need, *Monsieur l'Ambassadeur*,' said Chaker. 'We know which it is. Or was.'

'Was?'

'A villa on the road between Salammbo and Carthage caught fire early last night. The

26

garage had burnt out completely before the fire brigade could get there and the house itself was alight. Among the remains of the garage were several petrol cans and a body, almost completely consumed. There were shotgun pellets in what had been the face and the upper chest.'

The Ambassador shivered. 'I take your point about professionalism, Craig,' he said slowly. 'No bother about getting the body away from the scene, and no fingerprints or other indications left lying around. In this dry weather the place must have gone up within a few minutes.' He turned to Chaker. 'What do you think, Major?'

'I doubt whether they were Vigilantes, Your Excellency. We have never heard of such an organisation in Tunisia. I agree with Mr Craig. This is a group of revolutionaries who are not yet ready to begin their activities in the open.'

'And,' added Craig, 'who therefore don't want amateurs rocking the boat.'

'And there is no previous knowledge that such an organisation exists?'

Chaker hesitated. 'May I ask Your Excellency and Mr Thorne to treat what I will now tell you as completely confidential?'

'You may.'

'I haven't even told Mr Craig yet, but the fact is, we have for some time suspected that a small group of revolutionaries are plotting the overthrow of the State, and in great secrecy.

The evidence is fragmentary and inconclusive, and it is to help us to sift it and decide what preventive action must be taken that we asked Mr Craig to give us the benefit of his special knowledge. The subject of his celebrated lecture to the seminar at St Luke's College was a method of detecting a deep-rooted insurgency while it is still operating in clandestinity. It is a question of gathering what he called tell-tale indications of secret insurgent organisation. What happened yesterday, taken together with the other evidence, appears to show that our fears are justified.'

CHAPTER THREE

Note by Author

Several weeks before the events recorded in the previous chapters Peter Craig took part in an international seminar, held at St Luke's College, Oxford. He read a short paper on 'Indications of Clandestine Insurgency' which gave rise to animated discussion and, incidentally, led to his visit to Tunisia.

As Craig's ideas on this subject are of importance to my story, his paper follows.

K.B.

SUBJECT: Indications of Clandestine
              Insurgency

SPEAKER: P. V. Craig, Overseas Police
              Adviser, Foreign and
              Commonwealth Office, U.K.

Gentlemen, my talk concerns one particular kind of insurgency, and perhaps I had better clear the ground so that we can examine it in detail. Let us leave aside palace revolutions and military coups d'état on the Latin American, Middle East and African models, and also the wilder form of revolt whose leaders believe—as did the Baader Meinhof gang in Germany—that violence *per se* is a political act, and that if there is enough violence the whole of society will collapse and somehow recreate itself in a new and utopian form. Nor am I concerned with movements, like those of Palestinian origin, which use violence for its nuisance value, or as a means of giving their grievances maximum publicity and thus forcing a government, under pressure of international opinion, to resolve them.

I want to talk about small groups of people, each utterly dedicated to some cause, who believe that by working through the mass of the people, like a handful of yeast in a brewer's vat, they can make so much trouble for the government that it must fall because it can no longer rule. Some of these movements are essentially shallow and have no chance of success once they have alerted the authorities to the danger they represent. They are often riven by warring factions more concerned with publicity than with long-term planning; their ranks are open to penetration by government agents, and they tend to attract people who give support for reasons of private gain or revenge. The leaders of such movements can and do cause grievous and lasting damage if unchecked, but they have neither the training, the operational security nor even the patience to withstand sophisticated counter-action. Let us leave them out of our discussion.

Deep-rooted insurgency is a different matter altogether, and our problem is how to detect such a movement during its period of preparation, before the outbreak of open violence. This is when it is most vulnerable, and when, in some cases, every effort is being made by the insurgents to keep their very existence secret.

We have only to recall what has happened in many parts of the world during the past thirty years to see how effectively skilled revolutionaries can conceal their activities and the identities of their operatives. Even after crushing defeat at the hands of the government in power they were able to retain part of their cell system intact, to continue, like a half excised cancer, to divide and multiply. The re-emergence, after long quiescent periods, of insurgent activity in Malaya, the Philippines, Cyprus and Northern Ireland illustrates this remarkable capacity for self-regeneration.

Ideological orientations, incidentally, are immaterial to our discussion. The fact is that the technique of deep-rooted insurgency is available to anyone who cares to read the handbooks of Mao Tse-tung, George Grivas, Ernesto Guevara and many others, and it is being applied by men whose political ideas range from extreme right to extreme left. But let us be clear about one thing: in its most lethal form the technique requires harsh discipline, rigorous training and good intelligence in both senses of the word, and those who use it must be dedicated, ruthless men and women, indifferent to the shedding of innocent blood and ready at any time to betray those who have supported them if such action 'serves the cause'. As Mao Tse-tung said, in revolutionary warfare, there is no place for petty considerations of morality.

We may acknowledge the courage, self-sacrifice and idealism of these movements, but their capacity to harm a country's social and economic life and its image abroad is incalculable. Yet, strange though it may seem, they rarely attain even a part of their ends. General Grivas, who must be regarded as one of the most gifted insurgent strategists of this century, did not get what he most wanted, union with Greece. It is only in extreme conditions, when all men turn against intolerable oppression and are prepared to risk their lives and families, that a revolutionary movement has any chance of success, and even then, as a rule, it brings in a new dictatorship and a long period of hardship and poverty. In most cases, if the government is alerted, and reacts very quickly and wisely, the chance of success is nil.

To return to our problem. How can we verify the existence of such a movement before it bursts into open violence? For the answer, we must consider first, what the insurgents are trying to do, and second, how they go about it.

The aim is to promote a continuous campaign of harassment aimed at causing social and economic chaos, the spread of fear among the people, and the discrediting of the government. At the same time the security forces must be stretched to the point where they are unable to keep order or protect the citizen from aggression. The means used are terrorism, industrial sabotage, assassinations, intimidation, and urban guerrilla action; in addition—and most important of all—the sophisticated use of propaganda, disinformation, and psychological warfare of all kinds, with a view to influencing local opinion and winning support abroad. For this purpose, the use of 'popular front' organisations is common. The mainspring of an insurgent campaign—it cannot be said too often—is the struggle for minds and hearts, and the programme of psychological warfare feeds on the fear and unrest caused by bombings and intimidation, and on the strikes and violent demonstrations called by unions and front organisations whose leaders may have no idea that they are acting merely as the tools of revolutionaries.

Mao Tse-tung wrote that the strategy of guerilla warfare was to pit one man against ten; the tactics, ten against one. This principle underlies all insurgent operations. In the population as a whole they may represent a tiny minority, but when they act they apply overwhelming force, backed by the vital element of surprise. It is impossible to protect every provincial bank against a sudden attack by a team of armed man; a trade union leader, separated from his friends, is helpless against the group of insurgent bullies detailed to make him toe the line; an up-country police post cannot withstand an attack by a guerrilla commando using grenades or bazookas. In just the same way, the constant repetition of slogans and exhortations by a vociferous and determined group of agitators may in the end convince the average man that black is white.

With its morale crumbling, its popular support trickling away and the security forces stretched to breaking point by constant unpredictable attacks, a weak government will stoop to negotiate with the outlaws. If things reach this stage the insurgents are in a very strong position, because there is no reason why they should not continue their harassment until the government throws up the sponge. After all, the insurgents are self-supporting. They have already claimed 'martyrs' and can depend on gifts from well-wishers abroad. (There is truth in the Irish saying that when blood flows out, money flows in.) Arms can now be obtained quite openly by attacks on police posts and army depots. Bank raids, kidnapping for ransom and hi-jacking all help to keep the coffers full. It is said that some of the Tupamaros in South America have taken, for their own use, enough money to keep them in fast cars and fast girls.

In the end, so the insurgent theory runs, the government will give in. But note this. Even if it doesn't, and succeeds in containing the insurgency, this will be only at great cost to the country in terms of bloodshed, the partial wrecking of the economy and the tourist trade, and a legacy of bitterness, poverty and unemployment. It may take the nation a decade to recover, and during this time the insurgents will again begin to work underground, helped by the unfavourable image of their country abroad (which they have themselves produced), and exploiting to the full the suffering and hardship which follows any national crisis of this magnitude.

Gentlemen, you will have already taken the point I am making. If we once allow an insurgency to break out into violence it may profit even by defeat. It is vital to get at the leaders before this happens, and the key to one means of doing so lies in our knowledge of how they organise themselves. Let us look at a typical clandestine apparatus, and see what ideas we can get.

For security reasons, there is a cell system, so that if a rank-and-file member is arrested he can only reveal what happens in his own cell. Each cell has a meeting place where recruits can be indoctrinated and taught the techniques of insurgency. There is a whole network of secret communications, including couriers and both 'dead' and 'live' letter boxes. There is a psywar centre, with duplicating machines for producing leaflets, news broadsheets and stickers; there are field training grounds for teaching the use of automatic and sniping weapons and explosives; places where bombs and detonators can be made from raw materials, 'clean' hide-outs, not normally used, for men on the run; secret first-aid clinics for the wounded, with doctors and nurses available and stores of anaesthetics, antibiotics and other first-aid necessities, and these must be widely distributed, since a wounded insurgent cannot be left to fall into the hands of the law but must be treated within the area where he has been operating. There are stores of arms and ammunition and places where delicate explosives like gelignite can be housed in the proper conditions, to prevent spontaneous explosions.

Once the campaign breaks cover there will be no time for couriers, so there is a system of radio communication, which must be set up and tested in clandestinity.

Outside the secret apparatus the insurgent leaders are active, penetrating other dissident movements, trade unions, the mass media and the security and civil services. The men they select may at first be given a fairly innocuous description of the insurgent objectives, but as time goes on they will be persuaded or blackmailed into subservience and trained in the parts they have to play.

The universities provide the most fertile ground for recruiting revolutionaries and many teaching staffs include dedicated insurgents who are out to select the most promising of their pupils for the work of subversion. Students are often only too happy to cut lectures and tutorials and learn about tasks that require courage and all the romantic trappings of secret conspiracy and which, above all, offer the early prospect of violent action. The most promising may be sent abroad to one of the guerrilla schools in Cuba, North Korea, the USSR, Tanzania and other countries where, as we know, thousands of students are currently attending courses which last anything from six weeks to two years.

All these recruits, whether activists or fellow-travellers, must be trained, briefed and given their own secret means of contact with their controls. It is obvious that in a full-scale insurgency the amount of organisation and administration involved is formidable. There must be records to show, for each member, his progress and state of training, his security assessment, his contacts and the brief to which he is working. Other records are necessary for keeping track of operational planning, arms, stores, propaganda material and, most of all, how money is spent.

The quantities of money required may easily be so large that special bank accounts are kept in false names. During the clandestine period funds may have to be obtained through the diplomatic bag of a friendly country or through the sale of such things as smuggled-in gemstones. Sums raised locally are likely to be wholly inadequate. It may even be necessary to carry out bank raids, but at this stage they must be made to appear the work of professional thieves.

Once the insurgent campaign has erupted into violence the accumulation of money, men and materials will be much easier. This applies especially for recruitment, because when acts of intimidation have once been publicised a man will think twice before he rejects an approach, and in many cases will be too frightened to inform the police. But we are still discussing the clandestine phase when every recruit represents a calculated risk, and the first indication of the existence of a clandestine insurgency often comes from those who have rejected approaches by members of the movement.

There will be other evidence if we look for it. However secretly the insurgents make their preparations—and we have seen how complicated and wide-spread these must be if the campaign is to have any hope of success— there will be tell-tale indications which, taken singly, mean nothing; collated, they may form hard evidence.

You have in front of you copies of a list of such indications. Others may occur to you if you consider the nature of the infra-structure I have described.

If there is an increase, over a period, in the incidence of these indications, we can regard it as suggesting the existence of an insurgency in its preparatory phase. If a clear pattern emerges, of a general and simultaneous increase, we can regard it as proof. Let me take a couple of examples from the list, to show what I mean.

Explosives. Even if there is an assured supply of explosives from abroad, the stores have to be distributed so widely that there is always a use for the home-made product. Now the agricultural and other chemicals used for making bombs can be bought, or stolen. An unexplained increase in thefts or even purchases of these materials is therefore one possible indication. Gelignite and other sophisticated explosives must be manufactured professionally. They are not easy to buy, and thefts from mines, road construction companies and other commercial users are another indication. Detonators can be home-made, but are unreliable. These can also be stolen. In the training of saboteurs there will be some intentional, and probably some accidental, explosions. The occurrence of unexplained explosions is yet another pointer to insurgent activity.

Medical stores. Some can of course be bought, but antibiotics, anaesthetics and blood plasma are a different matter. We must look in the records of hospitals and medical supply stores for evidence of unexplained thefts and losses.

Flats, houses, farm buildings, leased but left normally unused; mysterious bank accounts; unidentified radio traffic; unexplained overflights by foreign aircraft and evidence of air drops; thefts of arms and even abnormal purchases from gunshops—all these are worth investigating.

Many of these indications, as you see, may reveal themselves in a careful study of statistics. Others on your list can only be discovered by the use of agents—and in some cases persons specially chosen and trained for their tasks. I am thinking in particular of the identification of students who have been approached and perhaps recruited by the movement. They are not likely to talk to anyone outside their own circles, so it will be wise to recruit informants among the university staff and students themselves. Theirs is a delicate task, and requires tact and understanding. Very often a young man will give himself away not by boasting of what he is about, but by his very silence, his demeanour, the outward signs of one who has acquired a new and secret purpose in life. The young lie easily about everyday things, not so well about those that really matter to them, and their friends and parents can often guess the truth if they know what to look for.

Then, with luck, the young man can be rescued before it is too late, and if so, he may identify his recruiter. Similar forms of investigation are appropriate for trade union circles, the mass media, the various branches of public life. Sometimes an analysis of trends in an opposition party's attitude may show clearly that new influences are at work, and people may be willing to indicate their origin.

While the insurgent movement is still underground the government has everything on its own side—secrecy of communications, the ability to use surveillance and wire-tapping, access to statistics and local government records, and the men to make the investigation. Best of all, they can carry out the work unobtrusively and in an atmosphere in which people are still not too frightened to talk. If the result is negative, no harm has been done. If positive, there will already be to hand some lines for offensive operations against the insurgent organisation.

I have mentioned just a few of the 'indications' you will find on the list in front of you. I think you will at once see that the method I have suggested for detecting the presence of a clandestine insurgency depends on its wholehearted application, which takes up much time and requires extensive use of manpower. Random checking on a few of the 'indications' can be misleading; it is only when we can cover the whole field, or at least a major part of it, that we are left with conclusions which prove whether the insurgency exists or not.

Gentlemen, before I invite questions may I say this? There is a danger of reacting too fast, and too superficially. Insurgencies are sensitive to probing and can withdraw their outward manifestations very rapidly. So it is like the situation of a man who sees his garden becoming choked with weeds. It's no good just slashing at the growths above the ground. He must trace back to the roots, and destroy them. The only sure way of rendering a secret revolutionary movement harmless is by eradicating the elements that gave it birth and continue to nourish it.

CHAPTER FOUR

It was a rather dark, foggy afternoon, and the runway lights at Gatwick airport were switched on, when Craig came into the forward cabin of the British Caledonian BAC 111, a month after his kidnapping. He was shown to a seat on the port side, next to a girl in a leather coat. He was mildly annoyed, because he'd hoped the first class would be sparsely occupied and that he could spread his papers over two seats. Major Chaker's long report, sent to Craig in London through the diplomatic bag, had several annexures containing the results of his investigations.

He tried to unhitch the steel chain that connected the leather attaché case to his wrist without the girl seeing it. But she did.

'My God!' she said. 'What are you then, a Queen's Messenger or something?' It was an attractive voice.

'Just something. If I were a Q.M.,' he added pointedly, 'I'd have both seats.'

'An absconding bank cashier?'

'That's it.' He turned to look at her. It was worth it. Rather small, with thick fair hair tumbling all over the place, a short nose, nicely shaped, wide mouth, and dark brown eyes. Large ones. And her shape looked good, too. What could be seen of it.

'Would you like me to take off my coat?'

'I'm sorry. I didn't meant to stare. But surely,' he added gallantly, 'you're used to it?'

'I suppose so.' She smiled at him, a nervous, worried smile, and went on as if she had a compulsive need to talk. 'You're *sure* you're a bank robber?' The wheels began to turn and the hostess leaned across Craig and said reprovingly, 'Miss Hamilton, your seat belt.'

'Yes, of course.' She began to fumble with the straps. Her fingers were trembling. That was it, of course. She was scared of flying, poor kid.

'Let me,' he said quickly. 'Sit back while I do you up.' He latched the belt and pulled the strap tight. 'Of course I'm a bank robber.' He patted the leather case on his knee and whispered hoarsely, 'It's full of the stuff.'

It made her laugh, and she glanced at him gratefully. 'How did you foil the cops?'

'Imitated the voice of Sergeant Lynch and sent all the Z cars to the wrong bank.' This time he got no laugh. She made a little gesture with her right hand and then dropped it to the armrest and held on tight. The engines roared as the plane wheeled off the apron on to the approach lane.

There was nothing he could do, and he sat back in his seat. A few minutes later he put down his *Times* and looked across at his companion. The jets were revving up prior to take-off, and the girl was leaning back in her

43

seat, eyes closed, white-faced.

Craig reached over and touched her hand. It jumped convulsively, then gripped his fingers. The brakes were released and the aircraft lurched forward. 'Don't worry,' he said. 'Nothing can happen to this kite with me and my loot on board. It'd be too bad, after all I've gone through.' It was rather feeble, he thought, and anyway, she wasn't amused. The fog-lights were flashing past, faster and faster. Her teeth were clenched and he saw a muscle twitching in her cheek. Eyes still closed. Then the bumping and rumbling ceased and the yellow lights fell away below, the ground tilted until the fields were standing on edge under the wisps of cloud. The grip on his fingers suddenly relaxed.

'Don't open your eyes yet,' warned Craig, solicitously.

But she opened them, looked out calmly at the crazy landscape and turned to Craig. 'Thank you,' she said composedly. 'That was very kind of you. It's only the take-off bit I don't like. Landing's O.K. You don't have to bother about me then.'

'It affects lots of people like that, you know.'

'Then lots of people,' she retorted, 'should feel thoroughly ashamed of themselves afterwards. As I do. That's why I blow the money and travel first, hoping no one will see.' She hesitated. 'I don't mean you. As I said, you were very kind. Thanks again.' She picked up a

44

leather satchel from near her feet and extracted a wad of newspaper cuttings. The conversation, Craig felt, was to be at an end. But he was curious.

'Why not when you land?'

She looked at him, then down at her knees. 'I suppose I owe you an explanation, why I'm only scared on take-off. You see, on a foggy day like this, some time ago in the Mekong Delta, I was in a plane that didn't.'

'Didn't?'

'It didn't take off. Instead it turned over, and we hung in our seat-belts for quite a time, with fuel from a ruptured tank trickling over us.' She shuddered suddenly, a movement of her whole small body. 'Luckily, no one thought of lighting a cigarette.'

'Oh hell!' muttered Craig. 'I'm sorry I reminded you.'

She laughed, edgily. 'The plane had done that already.' She began to read the cuttings, and this time Craig didn't interrupt. They were from Tunisian newspapers, in French and Arabic. Good Lord! thought Craig, horrified, she's a journalist. He opened the case and took out Chaker's report, sitting well back in his seat so that she couldn't see what he was reading, either by accident or design.

He was immersed in his work, sidelining the paragraphs to discuss with the Tunisian, when he heard the girl speak.

'I beg your pardon?' He saw her holding a

cutting in her hand and peering at it, then at his face, and back again.

'I said, why the scars?' She held out her hand. 'You're Peter Craig, and I'm Cleo Hamilton, *Daily News.* How d'you do?'

She was an extraordinary girl. Even her hand felt different, no longer trembling like a frightened little animal, but cool and firm—the hand of a professional woman, on the job. Christ! he thought, here it comes.

He took the cutting. It was headed *'Rapte d'un diplomate anglais'* and had appeared in *Nouvelles de Tunis* a month ago. There was a smudgy picture of Craig.

'I wonder where they got that from,' he muttered. 'I stopped the Embassy from handing one out.' Then he saw the scars, still unhealed, and remembered.

'They must have had it in records,' she said, 'or had it telephotoed. It says something about your having been through some horrid ordeal in Peru. And *that* rings a distant bell.' She started. 'Of course. You're the man we featured last year in the Sunday supplement, with precious little help from you, as I recall, but lots of pics of the mountain you rolled down, and all the Indians. Oh Lord! There was something about a plane, too, wasn't there? It hit a snow peak, and you opened the door and walked out.'

He laughed. 'Not exactly. In fact, that's my own particular nightmare. Still is.'

46

'I'm so sorry.' She examined his face searchingly. 'The scars have gone, as far as I can see. You can have a new picture taken for your next appearance in the press.'

'I don't really like appearing in the press.'

'So I gathered. I thought all policemen were avid for publicity.'

'Not when they're attached to the Diplomatic Service, they aren't.'

'Pity.' She continued to glance at his face after he had turned back to his papers. It wasn't handsome, no one could say that, but it had something—indeed, it had. Blue eyes deep-set in a dark, almost saturnine face, deeply lined. And that broken nose gave it a sort of humorous twist, engaging when he laughed, cynical in repose. She wondered whether he'd look like that when he was asleep . . . *Put it down, Cleo,* she told herself sharply. It's not your kind of bone. She began to read through the cuttings, making notes in shorthand.

When the hostess brought up her trolley of drinks, Craig pushed the report back into his case and looked at Cleo. The sunlight was flecking her hair with gold as it fell forward over her face. She seemed to be intent on her work, evidently not interested in him as a news objective. Which was as it should be. No need to talk to her at all, except—'Miss Hamilton.'

She pushed her hair back. 'Yes? Oh drink. I'd like—'

'What about a half bottle of Moët et Chandon? It's very cheering stuff during a plane journey.'

'Good idea.'

Cleo sipped her champagne. 'I've been reading about your kidnapping,' she said conversationally. 'Someone in the Embassy issued a detailed statement that played the whole thing down and managed to kill the story stone dead. Very clever, but bad for my line of business. Of course, if you'd like to answer a few questions . . .'

He'd practically asked for that. 'No, I'm afraid not. You'd probably know it all anyway, but the point is that I'm not allowed to make statements—er—without the permission of the Information Officer.' He explained, 'The Press Attaché, you know, in our Tunis Embassy.'

She smiled. 'I did know that,' she said gently. 'It's my job.'

'Of course. You see, in Tunisia I'm attached to the Embassy.'

'Yes. But it's not a statement I want—just some human interest bits.'

'But you've said the story's cold, so it isn't really that. What is it?'

'What are you doing, going back to Tunisia so soon?'

'Same as before, talks with the security authorities.'

'Not all this student trouble?'

'What trouble?'

'As if you didn't know!' She picked out an article in *Le Monde Diplomatique* and flourished it at him. 'Sit-ins, demonstrations, "Students for Democratic Rule" in the universities. Not to mention five more charges of incitement to riot.' She looked up at him, smiling. '*And* they've got inside the leader of the gang that kidnapped you. That's one thing you're to do, I suppose. Identify him.'

'That'd be a bit hard, when all I saw of his face was a pair of very large smoked glasses and a straggly little beard that's got another month's growth on it by now.'

'What about the other lot?'

'Vigilantes, I suppose. That's what they said they were. They treated me quite politely.'

'And the woman? She was wearing a sort of cloak-cum-shawl-cum-wrap, wasn't she? A sifsari. I thought they wore modern dress.'

'They do, all the educated women, I believe. But apparently, when they go out they often throw on a sifsari, to keep the dust out, or because they're in a hurry and don't want to dress, or maybe they don't want to be recognised. They can draw a fold over the lower face and it's a perfect disguise.'

'I like that idea,' said Cleo. 'It'd be useful in London.'

Craig smiled. 'I see what you mean. Put it on when you go out with a married man and your best friends can't tell on you.' He saw her frown. 'I didn't mean you, Miss Hamilton, *you*, impersonal.'

'That's better. For your information, I don't make dates with married men. There's no future in it.'

'You'd be safe with me,' remarked Craig. 'Not married.'

'It doesn't necessarily follow. But those Vigilantes, as you called them. Is it true they didn't stop you from seeing the street signs when they drove you away? That struck me as odd.'

No harm in answering that one. 'Why would they bother? The garage was burned down, probably within an hour of my leaving it. The kidnappers had disappeared, and the body was burnt. There was nothing for the police to discover about either gang.'

'I see. Thanks. So all you're going to do is to identify the poor chap they arrested?' she added casually, pouring out the remains of the Moët et Chandon.

'Look, Miss Hamilton, you know I can't say any more. Even if I had some secret knowledge of what's been happening it wouldn't be just my secret, to give away as I chose. I'm going to Tunis by invitation of the Tunisians, and that's all I can tell you.'

'You know what I think? There's something very important about to boil over in Tunisia, and I want to be there when it happens.' She looked at him over the rim of her glass. 'The country's ripe for revolution.' That ought to rouse him, she thought. It did.

'Don't talk nonsense,' said Craig irritably. 'What you mean is there are a few so-called revolutionaries and protest movements. But so there are in England and France and the States.'

'They're democracies; Tunisia has a one-party government dominated by the same man since independence. That hardly sounds democratic.'

'I didn't say it was. In a still developing country, with a long way to go, it's almost impossible to get anything done if you let everybody have a say, and of course every new reform throws up new grievances. So you've got to have control and disciplines or you get nowhere.'

The lunch trolley was beside them, and she said nothing until they had been served. Then: 'What was that you said—new reforms always throw up new grievances? Why?'

'Think it out. Take Tunisia. President Bourguiba achieved a spectacular rise in the standard of literacy, but what happens? Where are all the jobs for the literate, especially the graduates? Mention any kind of good, sound reform in a developing country and I'll tell you who won't like it.'

She was watching his face. How easy it was to get a man to talk about his subject. She tackled her smoked salmon, and suggested, 'Family Planning.'

51

'Too easy. The men who think four sons are proof of their virility and an insurance against old age.'

'All right. Co-operatives.'

'The farmer loses his ability to take his own decisions. And he can't go to market on his own, sell his goats and have a ball with the proceeds.' He caught sight of a fleeting smile on her face. 'You know all this perfectly well, so don't pretend you don't. But you started me off by talking about violent revolution. There's too much tedious adolescent rubbish talked about it anyway. It succeeds once in a hundred times, and only when it's directed against a regime that's so brutal and tyrannical that the people want it, even if it means sacrificing families and homes. They certainly don't in Tunisia.'

'No, sir,' she said with a hint of mockery.

'I'm sorry. I didn't mean to preach.'

She looked at him, interested. 'You feel deeply about this, don't you?'

'Yes, I do. I've seen so much of it, in Africa, in both Americas, in the Far East—worthwhile young people and older ones, liberal intellectuals, getting involved in something they don't understand. And getting killed too, or thrown into the nick. It's all such a God-damn waste.'

She was silent for a moment. 'I've been at the fronts is Vietnam and Mozambique, you know. I've seen it, and all the enthusiasm and courage. And I've met so many people of my own age, and younger, who genuinely believe that violent change is the only solution. I mean, a lot of them are my friends. It's hard to think they're all wrong.'

'Well, I'm afraid they are. If they realised that violence inevitably gives power to the wrong people they'd start to think up some other way of getting what they want.'

When the last luncheon trays had been collected Craig lit her cigarette and took out his cigar case. 'D'you mind?'

'No. Go ahead. You've made a study of organised violence and insurrections, haven't you?'

'I've read a lot of books by men who know,' said Craig cautiously. 'Tell me about your visit to Mozambique.'

She wouldn't be put off. 'You must know all about what's happening in Portuguese Africa. After all, the FCO is concerned with events both in foreign countries and the Commonwealth, isn't it?'

'Obviously.'

'Well then, FCO police advisors, like you, are there to give advice to any friendly government that wants it. I mean, a government that's in a spot of trouble from within, and needs help in dealing with it.'

'Like police problems.'

'And like revolutionary movements. After all, we've unrivalled experience of bloody

53

revolution and unrest all over the world. There must be a useful spin-off in terms of counter-revolutionary expertise.'

Craig said nothing. He was cornered.

'So,' she said, with an enigmatic smile, 'that's why the Tunisians have asked for your services, and they wouldn't do it unless they had reason to be very worried. So I was right. Q.E.D.'

He drew on his cigar and looked again at that intriguing half-smile.

'You're jumping to conclusions. This is just a police job.'

'You don't fool me.'

'Shall I tell you what I'm really going to do in Tunis? Just so that you get it right.'

'Try,' she said, guardedly, 'and see if I believe you.'

'But look here—er—this is off the record. Is that understood?'

'Oh, well . . . all right.' She was intrigued, in spite of herself.

'Actually, we've got a new invention for riot control, and I'm going to try and flog it to the Tunisians. D'you know how the bird preservation people capture whole flocks of birds and put little tabs on them to show where they've landed?'

'There's a sort of net.'

'That's it. We've adapted the idea, and it's an absolute winner,' he explained enthusiastically. 'This is the Mark Three Net (Anti Riot), and its great advantage is that it's invisible. You fire a fine nylon net from a sort of Verey pistol, and it spreads out in the air and envelops seventy-five square metres of screaming humanity.' He could read the suspension of disbelief in her face.

'What then?'

'Oh then, it's easy. They go quite mad, because they can't even see the thing, and start fighting each other. So that gives the police their justification, you see.'

'Go on,' she said grimly.

People, thought Craig, are always ready to believe the unbelievable of the police. 'Well, they jump in with their batons, club them into insensibility and haul them off to the nick. We're going,' he added casually, 'to send is some *agents provocateurs* to start a demonstration in the Place de la République, and try it out. Shall I let you know when?'

She burst out laughing. Then scowled at him. 'I didn't believe you for a moment. And I don't like people who try to take the micky out of me.'

'I can't stand attractive birds who try to wheedle the truth out of simple policemen.'

'I've got to get on with my homework.'

'So have I. And Miss Hamilton—'

'Yes, Mr Craig.'

'Please don't try to read over my shoulder.'

She gave him a withering glance and retreated into the corner by the window.

There was no further conversation until they landed at Tunis-Carthage. As the wheels came to rest they both bent down to pick up their hand luggage at the same time, and for a moment their faces were close together. They straightened up slowly, looking at each other. Automatically, Craig felt for the chain of his attaché-case and snapped the bracelet on his wrist.

She flushed scarlet. 'If that's meant to be symbolic,' she said bitingly, 'let me tell you that I'm not in the least interested in your precious papers.'

'I'm sorry,' he said quickly. 'I didn't mean that. I really am sorry, Miss Hamilton. But it's true that journalism and police work don't mix very well, do they?'

'You're darned right. Nor do journalists and policemen. May I get past, please?'

CHAPTER FIVE

Taieb Chaker was waiting on the tarmac as Craig came down the steps of the plane. Cleo was somewhere ahead. The Tunisian greeted him enthusiastically and took him rapidly through the immigration control and out of the airport building to a Citroën. He gave a note to a sergeant in Army uniform, who stood by a smaller car, and told him to clear Craig's

56

baggage through Customs and take it to the Tunisia Palace Hotel. He and Craig drove off in the Citroën.

'I've booked you a room, and we can go there first if you like, but there's a lot to tell you, so perhaps . . .'

'Of course, Taieb.' He showed Chaker the attaché-case tethered to his wrist. 'I've read your report. You've been busy.'

'Yes, but it's the final collation of the results I want to show you. We'll go to my office.'

The car turned into the Avenue Kheireddine Pacha near the spot where the veiled woman had dropped Craig a month before, and crossing the impressive Boulevard Mohammed V, by-passed the centre of the city and then worked its way round to the northern gate of the walled Medina, where there is an area of government buildings, ancient mosques and the great walls that used to defend the old Kasbah. The car stopped in the courtyard of the Ministry of Defence and they went up to Chaker's office.

It was a pleasant room, with tall windows shielded against the sun by wooden jalousies. There was efficient air-conditioning and a water-cooler with plastic cups handy. Chaker's big desk was covered with papers and files. He pulled up a chair for Craig and began to talk.

'As you saw from the report, we used your "indications" method to verify the existence of what you called a deep-rooted insurgency. The

57

General let me choose my own team of investigators. Some I borrowed from the political branch of the police, with permission to brief their agents for our purposes; others came from my own section and a few were recruited specially from outside.'

Craig smiled. 'Those'd be for the university side of the enquiry.' He saw the surprise on Chaker's face as he nodded assent. 'It's the same everywhere. Very difficult to find ready-made agents who can move around in university circles without being spotted. It's partly a question of age. To be any good they've got to *be* students.'

'Mine are.'

'Well done. I saw you'd got at the University records. How did you do that without it leaking out?'

Chaker's rather sombre face lit up in a smile. 'We managed to borrow keys and copy them, and carried out a series of raids at night. The records you talked about were all there, but needed some finding. Most of the other statistics we obtained from routine police and ministerial enquiries, and it wasn't too difficult.'

He unlocked a combination safe, drew out a folder and laid in front of Craig a series of charts on which graphs had been plotted, with explanations in Arabic and French. 'Look at the curves, Peter. If that isn't proof, what is?'

Each chart covered the period of the past

two years and the statistics relevant to one of the major Tunisian conurbations: Tunis, Sfax, Gabes, Sousse, Kairouan and Bizerte. Craig picked out the Tunis chart headed 'Thefts and unexplained losses of medical stores'. There were separate graphs for anaesthetics, antibiotics, dressings and other medical necessities, and these were combined in one master curve that began as a wavy line, varying from month to month and then, during the past six months, began to move upward, and the trend was still accelerating. The charts labelled 'Thefts from banks', 'Thefts and purchases from gunshops' and 'Thefts, purchases and unexplained losses of explosives and explosive-manufacturing material' showed broadly similar trends, but those covering radio and communications equipment, and motor vehicles were especially significant because the curves had only begun to rise during the previous two months. Craig's face was grim as he put down the papers.

'What about the provincial centres?'

'It's curious,' said Chaker, frowning. 'In Sfax, our second city, the trend is roughly the same, but much less marked. In the other main cities the patterns are irregular, with one or two peaks in the curves.' He rose from his chair and began to stride up and down, nervously, making ample gestures with his hands as he spoke. 'There's a small increase in general crime and one or two minor factors which have to be discounted, but there's no mistaking the upward trend. But there are so many questions still unanswered. Why does it seem to be concentrated in Tunis and Sfax? When will they be ready to start? Look at the total amount of money they've collected, even if we can attribute *all* the thefts to ono secret organisation. Six hundred thousand dinars, a little more than half a million pounds. Surely that isn't much for a full-scale revolution. What was it you told us about the Tupamaros? Didn't they amass something like ten million dollars, through bank robberies and kidnaping?'

'Something like that. But there may be sources of money across the frontiers,' pointed out Craig. 'Still, I agree it's a small amount. What about the other charts, absences of students, and so on?'

Chaker shook his head. 'The students are the most puzzling factor. There's been no unexplained increase in visits abroad. It looks as if they're being trained here, during vacations. Or in Algeria, where we know there's a flourishing guerrilla school. They could get across the border without attracting attention, if it was organised properly. Apart from the students, the other indication charts are very much the same, all twenty-three of them'—he grinned—'when you've got time to look at them.'

'For the moment I'll take your word for

them. But in general, the trend is the same? I mean, the upward curves begin during the past half-year?'

'Yes.'

Craig frowned. 'Of course, we're looking at what's been happening in the final preparation stage, and the movement itself could have been operating much longer. But all the same, it seems a short period of active preparation, if the communications and vehicle graphs mean what we think they do, that they're almost ready to break out into violence. The insurgents need a lot of things for training purposes, like bomb manufacturing, target practice and so on. How did you differentiate between the work of professional insurgents and what was done by other people?'

Chaker smiled. 'It was all in your lecture, Peter. Take the bank thefts. Some were the work of amateurs, extreme leftists. They scattered Maoist leaflets around and shouted slogans as they ran off. But the big raids, apart from a few that had all the hallmarks of known professional thieves, were very neatly and quietly executed, and well planned. In every case the attention of the local police had been diverted by some *canard*—a squabble in the street, telephone hoaxes, and so on. Again, some of the thefts of chemicals from agricultural supply stores were carried out clumsily, although the thieves got away with enough to make a few bombs and probably blow themselves up. But the disappearance of forty kilos of gelignite and three boxes of detonators from the iron mines at Tadjéronine was very professional. It wasn't even noticed until our man insisted on a complete check, because the ledger entries had been altered. They must have an inside contact, but we've made no investigation, of course. As for medical stores, I agree that you might get a hospital orderly fiddling antibiotics for what he could make on the side, but not five flasks of blood plasma. That was only last week. Nor a whole crate of antiseptic dressings. And look at the anaesthetics graph.' He pulled it out of the pile.

'They need a lot, Taieb, and spread all over the country, wherever they intend to take action, because when there's a casualty they've got to get the wounded man—or woman, for that matter—into a safe house, and quickly, before the shock wears off and he begins to scream. They can't risk his appearance in a State hospital.' He thought for a moment. 'I'm sure your conclusion is right. I also think that the gang who rescued me are members of the same conspiracy. What happened to the others, incidentally? I gather you've identified them.'

'The four students, yes. They're inside, and at first made a great show of bravery in not saying a word. But we've got them in solitary, and it's having effect. They're talking. The man who was killed we can't trace. As you know, there was little left of his face, so we can't use an identity kit. There's been a rash of violent demonstrations in support of the gang we captured, but it's small-scale stuff.'

'Why don't you release them on bail?' suggested Craig. 'Give them a stern lecture, take their fingerprints and tell them they may be called in for further questioning at any time. I'm pretty certain the Embassy don't want to prefer charges, and I certainly don't. I really think it's your best course. While they're inside they're a standing excuse for protest marches, which is just what the real insurgents want, to keep the police occupied. Would your General agree?'

'It's a good argument. I'll ask him. He'd have to get the Chief of Police to agree, too, but he's got to see him this evening to discuss what action is to be taken as a result of this enquiry. Incidentally, the General wants to see you.'

'Give me until tomorrow,' pleaded Craig. 'I'd like to study all the charts here, if I may, before I go to the hotel. There's a drinks party at the Residence tonight that I've been invited to. Perhaps we could have a final talk tomorrow before we see your chief.'

*　　*　　*

Craig had bathed, changed into a dark grey

mohair suit and was fastening his tie when the telephone in his bedroom rang. 'Mr Thorne's car is waiting for you, monsieur.'

While Thorne drove his Rover 2000 down the Avenue Bourguiba towards the La Marsa Road Craig talked to Phyllis Thorne, a pleasant girl who had been brought up in a setting of dogs, guns and horses. Tunisia, Craig gathered, had the advantage that she could ride every day, and watch races, without unduly neglecting her duties as the Head of Chancery's wife and hostess. For this party she had been carefully briefed by Michael.

She showed Craig the roneoed list of guests and explained who they were. 'It's really a reception given by Michael wearing his Information Officer hat, but H.E.'s agreed to be host because it's an important one. Which lets me out of the catering, thank God. Mostly press people, with some nice men from the Min. of Inf. The guest of honour is Ahmed Belcadi, who owns *Le Tunisien,* an independent newspaper. I mean, it's not controlled by the Party, as *L'Action* is. Belcadi, incidentally, is loaded—his stables make me green with envy—and a great power in the land. He's got a finger in several big companies and an ocean-going yacht. He's a widower, and his daughter Yasmin, who's quite an eyeful, does hostess for him. She's coming too. Then there's a girl called Cleo Hamilton—what's the matter? D'you know her?'

Craig groaned. 'Do I not! I sat next to her on the plane. She's like the Elephant's Child, full of satiable curiosity.'

'Well, what d'you expect? All journalists are, aren't they? Didn't you like her?'

'She's all right,' said Craig carefully, 'but I didn't expect to see her again so soon.' Yet he had to admit that the thought was—well, pleasurable. 'What other important guests, and what can I do?'

'We arrive five minutes early, of course, and if I find Lady Radcliffe is in a fizz about something I'll cope, and you hold her in play. Now about the other guests.'

By the time she had finished Thorne was turning into the drive of the Residence.

The building lies off the La Marsa Road, a very grand affair standing in an estate which includes orchards, a farm and formerly, as a result of an acute deal by an earlier Ambassador, its own private halt on the railway. At the top of the impressive double staircase that leads up from the forecourt is a great roofed terrace set into the façade. While Thorne parked the Rover, Craig and Phyllis went up the curved stairway to the terrace. Through the open doors in its inner wall, blue-tiled, they could see into the ballroom, brilliantly lit, with tables set out with drinks and silver dishes of party food. Phyllis disappeared through a side door in search of the Ambassadress.

As Thorne came up the steps the Ambassador emerged from another room flanking the terrace. He shook hands with Craig.

'Nice to see you again. The Tunisians seemed very anxious you should make this second trip. What's it all about? Have they confirmed what you seemed to suspect, that there's something sinister going on?'

Craig explained the position. Sir John looked thoughtful. 'I suppose it's a communist plot?'

'There's no saying what it is, sir, until the Tunisians make arrests of inside men, and I hope they won't do that too quickly. But it's almost certainly not an official Moscow job; they go in for bourgeois revolutions these days.'

'Why did you say that about acting too precipitately?'

'Because it's the leaders they've got to eliminate, and if they only nab fringe people the leaders will go to ground and start again. It's vital, sir,' added Craig putting it as tactfully as he could, 'that what I've just told you is treated as top secret for the time being. Even if you told one of your diplomatic colleagues in confidence it might—er—leak out, and that'd set the Tunisians back very seriously at this stage.'

'I'll keep my mouth shut then. That's what you mean? Tell nobody at all.'

'Yes, sir. I shall be making a report tomorrow to Sir William Dennistoun, if you agree. I'll show it to you before despatch.'

'All right. But let me know what develops, won't you? If there's going to be real trouble we'll have to think about the safety of British subjects here. You'd better draft a letter for me to Head of North African Department, and tell him to get in touch with Dennistoun. I mean, *suggest* that he should do so, and drop a broad hint why. Here come the first guests. We'd better get into line.'

He and Lady Radcliffe stood at the entrance to the ballroom, with Thorne and his wife behind them to take care of guests as soon as they had paid their respects. Craig hung around in the background, wondering when he could decently regard himself as off duty and have a drink.

The stream of people arriving thickened. Phyllis signalled and he went up to her. 'The Hamilton girl's coming up the steps,' she whispered hastily. 'Michael wants to get hold of her later to introduce Belcadi and some of the Tunisian journalists. Be a lamb and take charge of her, will you, Peter? Take her out on to the terrace, so that I know where she is, and I'll relieve you as soon as I can get away. O.K.?'

*   *   *

'You again,' said Cleo. 'I haven't forgiven you for that crack about reading over your shoulder.' She was wearing something smooth and white, with a necklace like chunks of butterscotch. Her hair was burnished, now, and drawn up into a cluster of curls. For a moment there seemed to be no other woman in the room.

'I'm anxious to make amends,' he said, taking her arm. 'Come out on to the terrace. I can't go down on my knees here, and what's more, there's a man there with a tray of whisky.'

They stood against the rail beneath one of the arches, looking out across the forecourt and the avenue of cypresses to the sea of orange groves beyond. The moon was rising, and the air warm, with the scent of flowers.

She stroked the wrought iron rail with her hand, thoughtfully. 'It's almost like being on a ship,' she said, and smiled at him. One of the white-robed waiters came up with a tray and offered them tall glasses of whisky, tinkling with ice. 'I gathered that Ahmed Belcadi is coming. Has he arrived yet? I want to talk to him.'

'I don't think so. Michael Thorne knows you want to meet him, though, and will lay it on.'

'Good. How are your consultations on the state of emergency going?'

'There isn't any. Pack it in, Miss Hamilton. It's no good.'

'Call me Cleo, since we're going to be such good friends.'

'We're not. You're dangerous, and I'm going to give you a wide berth.'

'A wide berth. It fits, doesn't it? All nautical. And sexy, too.' She wanted to tease him, and leaned forward, widening her eyes. 'They took one last look at the yellow moon and its glittering reflections in the ruffled sea, then he took her in his arms. Would there be a wide berth in her cabin, he wondered, in an agony of mounting desire.' She paused, looking at him provocatively. 'And then a row of asterisks, don't you think?'

'A narrow berth would be even sexier,' suggested Craig, 'and no asterisks. These days you have to spell it out.'

'Let's play it,' she said suddenly, laughing.

'What, the cabin scene?'

'No, idiot. The scene at the ship's rail. Here we are, moon, rail, everything. I'll start.' She put on an Elinor Glyn voice. 'Oh Mr Craig— or may I call you Peter? Alone at last. And to think that we've been together on this ship for so many days—and nights. And never knew we were meant for each other.'

Anything to keep her off insurgency, thought Craig. 'Cleo,' he muttered throatily, 'my dearest girl. It was the shuffleboard competition, sweetheart. It took my mind off the things that really matter.' He dried up. Then an inspiration. 'My desire is mounting,' he said hoarsely, contorting his face, in what be hoped was a rictus of lechery. 'Visibly.'

'Then quickly, dearest, while mama is still at the whist table. Our cabin—'

'Has it a wide berth?' He held his arms apart, as if measuring the width. They looked at each other and burst out laughing.

'What on *earth* are you two doing?' It was Phyllis Thorne's voice. They swung round; guiltily. She was standing behind them, with a tall dark girl in a scarlet caftan with a plummeting cleavage, who was looking on with amusement. 'Miss Hamilton, this is Mademoiselle Belcadi, who has heard all about you. She wants you to meet her father. Yasmin, dear, this is Mr Craig.' They shook hands, and she led Craig away.

'You're quick off the mark, Peter. I thought you didn't like the girl.' She cast a match-making eye at him.

'Oh, it was just nonsense. Quoting from a play.'

'What play?'

'Look,' said Craig, 'there's H.E. making signs. I'd better go.'

His Excellency turned to a short, very dignified man wearing a red fez, a white dinner jacket and dress trousers, who stood beside him. 'Ahmed, this is Mr Craig, one of our Police Advisors, who is here for talks with the Surveillance du Territoire. Monsieur Belcadi has been talking to me about these arrests of students, Craig.'

'You have the same problem in England, Monsieur Craig,' said Belcadi. 'I hope you can persuade our security services to show greater firmness.' He spoke excellent English, with a slight American accent.

Craig sipped his whisky, looking down at the dark, fleshy face of the Tunisian. 'It's hardly my job to give advice, Monsieur. I'm sure the Tunisian Government can form its own policies. But there are methods and techniques of which we've had experience, and I hope our talks may be of value to both countries.' Sir John concealed a smile. Not bad, for an amateur diplomatist, he thought.

And so did Belcadi. 'Very diplomatic, Mr Craig,' he said, smiling. 'But I'm not in the Government. How should we react to this senseless vogue of belief in revolutionary violence among some of the best of our young people? They seem to have lost their heads.'

'I don't think there's any simple solution, Monsieur Belcadi. You can't stop them from reading Mao Tse-tung or Che Guevara, still less Regis Debray, and it's heady stuff.'

'We can make them suffer if they're found doing it,' said the older man grimly.

'With respect, sir, I don't thing that helps at all. They'll get hold of the books anyway. And why not? They've got to work out the problem for themselves. The fault lies as much in the universities as anywhere. But I think better

71

communications between statesmen and people is one answer. And travel. The more the university students can see of other countries, and the faults in other systems of government, the sooner they come to realise that their own isn't so bad after all.'

'I hope you're right, Mr Craig. I have myself endowed twenty scholarships a year, so that selected students can travel during the summer to other countries. Under careful supervision, of course.'

And a fat lot of use that was, thought Craig. But he asked politely how the scholarships were allotted. Belcadi told him, in some detail.

The Ambassador broke in. 'It's an excellent scheme, Ahmed, and I know how highly the President thinks of your patriotism. But we must have a word about the visit of the Stratford company next month. I'm counting on your help to make the tour a success. Ah, here is your charming daughter. We'll talk later.'

Yasmin Belcadi came up with Cleo, who was introduced to Belcadi and quickly set out to charm him. Craig found himself left alone with Yasmin as Sir John moved off to talk to other acquaintances.

The Tunisian girl was looking at him with half-concealed laughter in her dark eyes. She evidently hadn't forgotten the scene she and Phyllis had interrupted. 'I'm afraid we cut you short in an interesting conversation,' she

72

suggested, in English. 'Miss Hamilton is a charming girl, don't you think?'

'Delightful, but I hardly know her. I'm looking forward to seeing something of your country, Mademoiselle.'

'Is this your first visit?'

'No, I was here for a few days last month, but this time I hope to have time to get around. I particularly want to see the new excavations at Carthage and Utica. I hear there've been some very interesting finds.'

She sighed. 'There's so much to be done, particularly at Utica. There's very little to see there at present. Why are you so interested in Utica?'

'It's where Cato made his last stand.' He saw her look of puzzlement. 'He held the town for two years, you remember, before his death.'

'But who is Cato?' The English pronunciation baffled her.

'Caton,' he said, *'le dernier chevalier de la république romaine.'*

'Ah, *celui-là!'* she exclaimed. *'Quel brute!'* She changed back into English, which she spoke equally well. 'He lent his devoted wife to a friend for a few years, just to oblige, and provide him with a son and heir.'

'Marcia wasn't as devoted as all that,' he said, laughing, 'and who could blame her, married to that strait-laced old Stoic?' But as he spoke a bell rang loudly in his mind. It was those few words she had spoken in French.

73

Could it be the same voice he had heard in the Mercedes, half muffled by the sifsari? There was a settee along the side wall, with a small table in front of it. 'Let's sit down for a moment, and try some of those canapés.'

He handed her the dish and signalled to a waiter for more drinks. Then he sat beside her, and turned, looking at the serene face—heavy dark eyes, ivory skin and broad intelligent forehead. 'I could swear,' he said slowly, 'that I've met you before.'

She didn't bat an eyelid. 'I'm afraid not, monsieur. And isn't that a rather out-dated—what's the word?—gambit?'

'Please forgive me—and it wasn't meant as a gambit. One does get these strange feelings occasionally, but I see I was mistaken. Her hand was very much like the one he had studied in the Mercedes a month ago. If only he could make her put down her glass, so that he could watch, and give that nervous little finger—if it *was* the same one—a chance to express itself. 'You're interested in the classics?'

'You mean *Caton*? But yes. After all, he's part of my country's history. Where did you learn about him?'

'The hard way, reading Latin at school. How did you acquire your really remarkable English?'

'Before I went to university I was sent to a place in London, called the Monkey Club.' She

74

sipped her drink, relaxed and completely assured.

'You're a credit to it.' He looked down. 'What a beautiful stone. I know a bit about gem-stones, and it looks—but it can't be. I suppose it's an amethyst.'

She put her glass on the table and raised her right hand so that the deep fibres in the ring sparkled. 'What d'you say now?'

'Good Lord! It *is* a diamond. I couldn't believe it—but what a beauty!' He took her hand, impersonally, professionally, and looked at the stone more closely. 'It's perfectly cut. Not here, surely?' He laid her hand back on the table, away from the glass.

'Well, no. But we have some very good jewellers, you know.' She began to talk about the shops in the Medina.

Craig had very little time. He could see Belcadi at the other end of the terrace, looking around, probably for his daughter. His dinner jacket meant that they were going out to dinner. It was Yasmin who gave Craig his chance.

'If you haven't many days here you must get someone from the Embassy to take you round the soukhs.'

'I usually get by,' he said casually, then raised his voice, 'with a little help from my friends.' His eyes were not on her face but on the little finger. It jerked sideways, nervously. 'You remember,' he added quietly, 'your favourite Beatles song.' The finger went stiff, sticking out at an angle, like a little pointer.

'I don't know what you mean,' she said coldly, and rose to her feet. Belcadi was weaving his way purposefully through the crowd. Cleo was talking to a man quite near, but looking past his shoulder at Craig. He stood up close to Yasmin, and lowered his voice. 'Of course you do. You don't think I'd forget someone who saved my life, do you? I owe you a debt, Mademoiselle, you and your friends, and I think I may be able to help you. Give me a ring at the Tunisia Palace, and we can talk about it.'

She turned blazing eyes on him. 'How could you know? It's impossible.' She hesitated. 'And we don't need your help.'

He took her hand, as if saying goodbye, but held it so that she couldn't break away. '*I* know, but no one else does—yet. Not the security people, nor even your father. Tunisia Palace, room 147.'

She snatched her hand away and turned to meet her father, who took her on his arm with an affectionate smile, nodded to Craig and went to take leave of his hosts.

Craig was staring after Yasmin's elegant figure when he heard Cleo's voice, with a tinkle of ice in it. 'Were you actually propositioning that girl, after half an hour's acquaintance? You really are a fast worker, Mr Craig.'

'Oh well,' he said easily, 'she's such a dish, isn't she? I mean, look at that figure.' He had to cover up, and it was the first excuse he could think of.

Cleo walked away, head up, very dignified, but in a flaming temper. She wasn't used to this kind of treatment. It was *her* figure that should be attracting the wolf whistles of men on the make, like Peter bloody Craig.

CHAPTER SIX

Craig left the party soon afterwards and got a lift back to his hotel. He rang Chaker.

'Listen, Taieb. I've discovered something quite important, and I'd like to tell you about it tonight, if possible.'

'I'm going to be at my desk for several hours yet,' said Chaker, in the voice of a very tired man. 'Come here, by all means.'

'You've got to eat sometime. I've booked a table at Chez Nous, Rue de Marseille, for nine o'clock. Could you join me?'

'*D'accord.* I'd be delighted. See you there.'

He arrived promptly, wearing civilian clothes, and they drank dry martinis in the narrow bar and ordered a *mechouia* salad, charcoal-grilled kebabs and a bottle of Vieux Thibar. A dozen tables were crowded into the small airless restaurant. People go to Chez

Nous for the food and not one penny of the considerable bill is wasted on decoration.

Craig let his guest relax, refusing to talk business until they were drinking coffee and *boukha*. Then he said, 'I've identified the veiled woman.'

The Tunisian raised startled eyes. 'You have? That's quick work. Have you got a crystal ball? I thought you saw nothing of her but a shapeless form in a sifsari and a pair of eyes. Who is she?'

'Yasmin Belcadi.'

This time Chaker fairly jumped. 'You're joking, Peter. It's quite impossible. How can you be sure?'

'It's her expressive little finger,' he explained.

'But *sacré bleu!* You can't depend on that. It could be anyone who happened to have that habit.'

'No, it's Mademoiselle Belcadi all right. She all but admitted it. And she's quite possibly telephoning me at the Tunisia Palace about now, or trying to.' He paused. 'I thought I'd better have a word with you first.'

'Good God, yes. If you're right—and of course if she telephones that proves it—we've got a big problem on our hands. Her father . . .' He stopped and took a much needed gulp of *boukha*.

'Tell me about him.'

'He's one of the richest and most powerful

78

men in Tunisia. He was with the *Suprême Combattant* in the early struggles of the Neo-Destour Party, before Independence, but refused an offer of a ministry and retired from politics into business, where he made his fortune. No one seems to know why he left politics; my own impression is that piling up money interested him more than anything else. But make no mistake about it, he's completely loyal to the *Suprême Combattant*—President Bourguiba—and his newspapers and glossy magazines support the Destour and all its activities.'

'And his daughter?'

'I've never met her. She moves in circles not frequented by Army officers with only their pay to live on. She's—what?—about twenty-six, I suppose, and has spent a lot of time abroad. I think she works for some women's organisation in the city.' He looked worried. 'The question is, what do I do? Tell the General, of course, but then what happens? He'd have to tell the President that Belcadi's daughter is—we *think*—mixed up in same revolutionary movement, and then the fat would really be in the fire. We'd have to interrogate her—'

'And she'd deny everything,' said Craig flatly.

Chaker stared at him, then said slowly, 'No witness, of course. You're right.'

'And what would my evidence count for if

her father complained to the President?'

'My career would end just like that.' He snapped his fingers. 'I told you it was a problem, Peter.' He finished his glass.

Craig ordered more *boukha*, a sort of eau-de-vie made from figs, and potent. 'Could you get me a very small and concealable radio transmitter—something that really doesn't show a bulge, even if I have to take off my jacket?'

'What are you planning to do, seduce the girl?'

'No, but it allays suspicion if you can take your coat off.'

'I see. Yes, I can. I bought some tiny Japanese ones for this investigation. They're self-contained, microphone, battery and transmitter, short-lived and short-range. I'll have a radio car with a recorder near. Is that what you want?'

'That's it, exactly. If she doesn't ring we'll have to think again.'

*   *   *

But she did ring. When Craig returned to his hotel there was a message saying that a lady had telephoned and would call again at eight o'clock the following morning. Craig took the precaution of locking his windows and propping a chair against the door handle. Then he went to bed.

Promptly at eight the telephone rang.

'Monsieur Craig?'

'A l'appareil.'

'I think it would be best if we talked here, in my house. It is Rue La Skhirra, number five, in Sidi Bou Said. Do you know where that is?'

'I can find out. Thank you, Mademoiselle. What time?'

'Is half-past ten all right?'

'D'accord.'

Craig rang Chaker. By nine o'clock a messenger from the Ministry of Defence arrived with a small parcel for him. When the man had gone he unwrapped a little box, containing a piece of plastic looking like an oversize coat-button, with a very thin piece of covered wire leading from it. There was also a length of adhesive tape.

He pulled up his string vest, strapped the disc well down on his chest and arranged the wire to run through the armhole of his shirt and down the sleeve. Then he walked to the Hertz agency in the Avenue Bourguiba to pick up the small Fiat he had hired, and drove out on the airport road.

The little town of Sidi Bou Said stands on a promontory high above the sea, between La Marsa and Carthage. Some of the white houses, their blue doors studded with embossed metal, have stood there, edging the cobbled streets, since the Corsairs chose the thirteenth-century sage Abu Said Khalafa Ben

Yahid el Temimi el Beji as their patron saint, the Master of the Seas. On the outskirts, built out over the terraces of olives, was the house of Ahmed Belcadi, white as a wedding cake, the domed roofs glimpsed above a high white wall garnished with spikes. A keyhole doorway was set into the wall, and the door itself, painted blue in the local tradition, was decorated in a pattern of brass fleur-de-lys. A heavy chain hung beside it, and as Craig pulled he heard a deep bell tolling somewhere in the background.

There was a scuffing of feet on gravel, and a boy of about fourteen in gondoura and embossed leather slippers opened the door. 'Monsieur Craig?'

'C'est moi.'

The boy led him down a gravelled path, between orange trees and mimosas standing in rectangular dishes of soil, all connected by an intricate irrigation system. The soil was still dark and damp from the first watering of the day, and the ridges of dry earth had been carefully raked over in curving patterns. There was no lack of gardeners in the Belcadi household.

The long white façade of the house, with its elaborately grilled windows, was broken by a shallow arcade, which covered the main entrance. Beyond a cool dark hall, in the sunlit patio, water splashed from a fountain into a circular basin. A Persian cat crouched watchfully on the marble rim, hoping one of the golden fish would stray near enough to be scooped out by an acquisitive paw. The boy led Craig through the patio, into the wide, airy room beyond, across the tiled floor shimmering blue and green, and out to a flight of steps leading down to a terraced garden.

The sunlight beat down on the crisply raked gravel surrounding a stone tank of clear water. Cypresses cast small pools of shadow amongst the lacy network of eucalyptus and oleander. Beyond the terrace wall was the sea, flat calm, stretching away to a misty horizon.

Sitting on a stone bench beside the tank was Yasmin Belcadi, with a large tin bath at her feet.

Craig had been ready for almost any kind of reception. She might have faced him with her father looming thunderously in the background; or alone, seductive and appealing; or with a gun in that memorable slim hand, with a gang of masked men in attendance. What he hadn't expected was that she would be engaged in bathing a small French poodle, who was covered with lather and struggling to get free. She had a pinafore tied over her jeans and there were flecks of foam on the silk, half-open blouse and her dark hair. An old manservant stood by, carrying towels and obviously scolding her for not allowing him to cope. She lifted the wretched animal out of the bath and the boy ran, giggling, to turn on a tap and bring a hose, spouting water.

It was only then that she appeared to notice Craig. Kneeling on the stone surround of the tank she held the dog with one hand under the stream of water and began, unhurriedly, to button up her blouse with the other. 'Oh, it's you,' she said in English. 'I'm afraid I'd forgotten . . .' Drops of perspiration ran down her face. '*Tais-toi,* Frimousse!' she shouted at the dog, who evidently understood French.

'I'll hold him if you like,' offered Craig, with a sigh.

'He'd bite you. I shan't be long.'

When Frimousse, yapping furiously, was completely soused she took the rough towel and began rubbing his coat vigorously and paying careful attention to his long ears and undercarriage. By this time her blouse was soaked. She put the collar with a medal round his neck. The poodle was at last free, and allowed to run around shaking himself and trying to find some dust to roll in. It was a very domestic scene. And meant to be, thought Craig.

She looked up at him. The wet silk clung to her breasts, and they were magnificent. The old servant, seeing Craig's glance, made a clucking sound, hurriedly produced a sifsari and enveloped her in it. She rose to her feet in one graceful movement, then drew a fold of the silk across her face. The dark eyes under the heavy brows looked at Craig mockingly.

'Just to remind you,' she said, laughing. 'Habib will show you where to go.'

She ran into the house. Craig thought, at least she isn't going to deny it.

He followed the old man across the sea-green tiled floor and through a cedar-wood door, to find himself in a room that looked out over the tree tops to the distant sea.

'If monsieur will be pleased to sit here,' said Habib, indicating a window alcove with an ivory-inlaid table and two cane armchairs, 'I will bring refreshments.'

The room was spacious, with a ceiling of carved cedarwood and what looked like—but could they be?—original French Impressionists on the walls. It was apparently her study, for there was a desk, a television set, a hi-fi counter with record and tape decks, two large mahogany loudspeakers set strategically apart opposite a sofa, and modern armchairs as well as the cane ones in the alcove. There was an open hearth, for winter use, and bookcases with texts mostly in Arabic and French; a few in English. It didn't look like a hotbed of insurrection. Perhaps, like the scene he had witnessed outside, that was the idea.

She came in, wearing a short dress the colour of ripe apricots. Her feet, in the gold sandals, were bare, the nails lacquered darkly, like garnets. Her face was still glowing from the exertion with the dog and her dark hair was caught back with a ribbon.

Habib followed her, carrying a tray with mint tea and plates of sticky-looking cakes. He served them, as they sat down in the alcove chairs, and offered a choice of Gauloises or English cigarettes.

Craig took a Benson and Hedges and lit her cigarette, then his own, looking at her thoughtfully as she leaned back in her chair and stretched out those long, silky brown legs. He wondered how she would start.

She looked at him through the smoke, 'I might,' she said, 'deny that I ever met you before last night. You couldn't possibly have recognised me or—to put it another way—your evidence to that effect would be useless. Unless you had some other reason. Who would believe that you knew me from my voice, when I had the sifsari in front of my mouth? In fact, I'm curious.' She looked at him expectantly.

'I'm not at liberty to explain, I'm afraid.'

'I thought so. When you said last night that no one else knew, you were of course lying. You knew before you saw me at the Residence.'

'No, Mademoiselle.'

'Oh yes, Mr Craig. Somebody talked, didn't they?'

'You can't expect me to reply, you know.'

'And if you knew, so did the clever Major Chaker.'

She was telling him a lot. 'Then why are you

86

still at liberty?'

She laughed. 'What for? What have I done? What did my friends do?' She stubbed out the half-smoked cigarette in the ashtray. 'I told you the idea that you could have recognised me was nonsense, and believe me, whoever the little traitor was who gave some story to the police, he'd be in real trouble if he tried to make it stick. My family has influence, Monsieur Craig, and it wouldn't be difficult to suggest that he'd been put up to make a false accusation. We have enemies.'

'I see. Then why did you agree to see me?'

She hesitated for a split second. 'Because you said you were grateful to me and my friends —and so you ought to be—and something about wanting to help me.'

'I meant what I said. To tell you the truth, I had an impression that you might be involved in some activity against your will and that I could—believe me, as a friend—find some way of helping you to disentangle yourself.' He was rather pleased with that fly, but would she rise to it?

Yasmin turned, and looked at him closely— those honest deepset blue eyes and the serious, dependable face. Like many others before her, she found it difficult to believe that Peter Craig was lying.

'The fact is,' he added, 'that you're right. It would be impossible to *prove* you took part in that rescue operation.' He could feel the slight pull of the adhesive tape as he leaned back in his chair. 'And even if it were, what would that show? Only that you and your friends took, for whatever reasons, a highly commendable action.' He extinguished his cigarette. 'Although,' he added, 'at the cost of a life.'

'What man is dead?' she snapped. 'Have the police identified the body? And after all, it was in self-defence.'

'Exactly. So what have you to worry about if there were an enquiry? Unless it's because you don't want your father to know you're involved with some political activity he doesn't approve of.'

It was a shot in the dark, but its effect was dramatic. She looked away from him, her face expressionless. Then jumped to her feet, leaning over the table, with her eyes on his face. 'Can you prevent it?'

'It's not for me to say, but I don't see why not, if you'll tell the authorities what you know. You mentioned Major Chaker. You could trust him to keep your secret, if you co-operate with him.' He saw her looking at him speculatively, and added gently, 'But please, Mademoiselle Belcadi, *don't* pretend you're part of a movement of Vigilantes. It would ruin your chances of keeping your involvement from being disclosed. You see—I shouldn't be telling you this—but Chaker knows perfectly well that your group is something quite, quite different.'

She started involuntarily, then turned to the window and reached out absently for another cigarette. He held out his lighter, but she ignored it, watching the far away sea and the sails of the fishing boats. Her face was beautiful, rather than pretty, with those strong imperious features.

'And if I did,' she murmured, still without turning to meet his eyes, 'how could I be sure that the movement wouldn't learn about my— betrayal? And take its revenge.'

'There are ways by which that could be prevented. Am I right in thinking that the movement has so far done nothing illegal? Assuming we can regard the shooting of that man as an act of self-defence?'

'Yes. That's correct.'

'But it is preparing for violent action, isn't it? That's why they intervened when I was kidnapped. My life, or my kidnapping, meant nothing to them. What mattered was that a gang of young hotheads was taking the kind of action that should have come much later, and putting the police on the alert.'

She looked round at him, eyebrows raised. Then smiled and sat down again. He lit her Gauloise. 'You've worked it out correctly,' she said.

'Then why,' asked Craig, 'why, for God's sake, did you join them? What could you hope to get out of a violent revolution?'

'I had no choice,' she said. 'I was forced to

join.'

'Tell me.'

'I had been—very indiscreet, and they threatened to send some letters I had written, to my father. It would have broken his heart.' She smiled bitterly. 'And he would have robbed me of my liberty. He's old-fashioned.'

'And you got the letters back?'

'Oh yes, I got them back, but I'm not so naïve as to think they haven't kept copies. It's a very common story.' She looked at him appealingly. 'As I said, so far we've kept within the law.'

Craig remembered the graphs he had seen in Chaker's office. Was it possible she didn't know about all those thefts?

'It's what happens later,' she was saying, 'when the violence starts.' She shuddered. 'I'll do anything not to get involved in that.'

'Bank robberies to get money, attacks on police posts, arms depots, assassinations, intimidation?'

Her eyes rounded. 'Is that what it'd mean?'

'Good God, don't you read the foreign press?'

'They said it would only be violence on a limited scale, in support of the propaganda campaign.'

'The idea is to provoke the police into over-action, isn't it? And then weaken them by attacks all over the country, without warning. And cause such chaos and demoralisation that in the end the government can't govern, and has to give in. Wasn't that the plan?'

She covered her face with her hands. 'I *don't know*,' she sobbed. 'They don't tell me. I'm just a member of a cell, and we never see the other people in the movement.'

'What sort of cell?'

'It's for internal security, as they call it. If some other cell, here in Tunis and the suburbs—I don't know what happens in the other parts of the country—steps out of line I drive the leader and two or three other cell members to the place and they lecture them and punish whoever is responsible. I don't *see* anything, because they won't let me leave the car.'

'So they don't trust you entirely?'

'Of course not. How could they?'

'And how does your cell get its orders?'

'Oh, I do that too. I go and pick up a letter from a hiding-place. It's called a D.L.B., I don't know why.'

'A dead letter box. International spy's jargon. What then?'

'I leave it somewhere different each time. It's really my car they need, rather than me. I don't know what's in the letters because they're always sealed.' She leaned on the table with her head in her hands, and her shoulders shook convulsively.

'It's all right, Mademoiselle, don't worry about this. I'll have to tell my Tunisian friends, but I'm sure they'll find ways of protecting you and getting you free of the movement before the real trouble starts. When will that be?'

'Not for a long time,' she said, raising her head. 'They say these things take years to prepare.'

'Of course they do. So that gives us plenty of time. When can we see you again?'

'We? Who else?'

'Possibly the Tunisian officer you mentioned. Could we come here?'

'No. My father's in Tunis today, but he's usually here. He mustn't see you or Chaker. In your hotel room?'

Craig smiled. 'It wouldn't do your reputation much good, would it? No, probably in a car somewhere. You can use yours without anyone worrying?'

'I told you,' she said, half smiling, 'that's my contribution to their *sacré* cause. The police know my Mercedes, as long as it's wearing its own number plate.'

*　　　*　　　*

Craig's hired car was like an oven when he opened the door and got in. He drove down the hill to join the La Marsa Road.

Two hundred yards away from the Belcadi house a man in mechanic's overalls, pretending to work under the bonnet of a battered old Renault, saw a small red light extinguish itself. He closed the bonnet, wiped his sweating head and face and got into the car. To make sure, he looked into the glove compartment but, as the little light had signalled, the tape recorder connected to the radio receiver had stopped working. He drove back to his garage, removed the cassette, put it into an envelope and handed it to the man who stood waiting. Fifteen minutes later the cassette was inserted into the machine on Chaker's desk. Craig was with him.

The first sounds that emerged were so odd that the Tunisian switched off and looked at Craig.

'That's Frimousse, a poodle,' he explained, and added, 'I think she wanted me to feel from the start that she wasn't in the least worried by what I had told her last night, and that she was a thoroughly ordinary girl, except for her looks, and not in the least like a desperate revolutionary. But listen carefully, Taieb. Half-way through there's a subtle change of stance.' Chaker pressed the 'Start' button.

The recording stopped with the slamming of the Hertz car door, the first point at which Craig had felt safe to reach under his shirt, find the transmitter and move over the switch on its edge. Chaker's face was smiling broadly. He got up, went round his desk and patted Craig's shoulder. 'You've given me a real break, *cher collègue*. The General must hear this.'

'But what do you think of it?'

Chaker ticked off the points on his fingers. 'First, she couldn't believe you had simply recognised her, and was sure that someone had talked. Second, she didn't know who had talked or what had been said. It might have been one of the kidnapping gang, who had told the police under interrogation. If so, she might still have got away with the original story. Then you bluffed her, very neatly, into thinking we knew her movement was a revolutionary one. So she changed her line. What happened?'

'She started, and turned away to the window, thinking. That's when she decided to tell the truth. If it was the truth,' he added, thoughtfully. 'I must say it was very convincing. She had her head in her hands and was sobbing. You heard her. I felt rather a brute.'

'Tears?' asked Chaker cynically.

'No tears. She pressed a handkerchief to her eyes and smudged the mascara, so that she looked very woebegone, but there was no trace of tears. So she was acting. But perhaps only to get my sympathy. That's when I stopped feeling too sorry for her. But all the same I thought it best to leave. If I'd bullied her I doubt whether she'd have said any more at this stage. She has a lot of character, Taieb.'

'Our women are known far it. My wife is a good example. She has a nasty habit of being right and not pretending to hide the fact, as a

94

good wife should.'

'Nonsense. You're a very lucky man, and you know it. But listen. There are two things that make me think she knows more than she says she does. One is that if the movement's leaders have such a strong hold over her, why don't they use her more than just as a chauffeur to an action group and a courier. She's got a position in society, and that's where they want to recruit fellow-travellers, who can influence public opinion when the time comes. She must see all kinds of journalists and publicists and broadcasting people in her father's house. In fact she must act as hostess to them frequently. It's the mass media men who promote the flattering image of the insurgency that is so important, and when the balloon goes up that's what the insurgents want more than anything. And of course, there are the foreigners—press, broadcasting and diplomats. Surely she'd have been asked to select or even approach those who could be most useful?'

'But she said they didn't trust her. Would they give such vitally important tasks to someone whose heart wasn't in the job?'

'No. I suppose you're right.'

'And your second point?'

'How did she know your name?'

Chaker frowned. 'I admit that worries me a lot. There was never any publicity about my appointment. But her father might know what

I'm doing. At that level I can't be sure somebody mightn't have told him I was working on the student problem, and after meeting and talking to you last night about it he *might* have said to Yasmin that you were here for talks with me.'

'Yes, I suppose that fits,' said Craig reluctantly. 'What are you going to do now?'

'Will you come in with me to see the General?'

'Of course, if I can help.'

'You certainly can.' He picked up the intercom.

* * *

The ADC met them at the door of the General's ante-room and exchanged a few words with Chaker while they waited. Then a light came on above the door of the inner room, and the ADC straightened his uniform and went in, saluting. He came out and signalled to the two men.

General Farhat came across to greet Craig, while Chaker placed the tape recorder on a corner of the big desk. They sat down. Chaker spoke first, in French, so that Craig could understand, and the General listened, frowning.

'I asked Monsieur Craig to accept your friendly offer to see Mademoiselle Belcadi, at her request. But this is getting serious. I don't feel we can ask you to become further involved. Let me hear the recording.' Chaker switched it on, first explaining about the dog. The General smiled enigmatically.

But as he listened he began to tap with a pencil on his blotting pad, and when the tape had finished he thought for a moment.

'I know Ahmed Belcadi and his daughter fairly well,' he said finally. 'It's true he's of the old school and a disciplinarian. But on the other hand he has lost his wife and has this only daughter, to whom—as everybody knows—he is devoted. But what was that she said, that it would break his heart?' He smiled. 'I doubt it. His heart is as tough as they come. For all his affection, his reaction would be to beat her black and blue, and then cut off her allowance unless she married, at once, the man of his choice, not hers.' He saw the expression on Craig's face. 'Such things can happen in the privacy of a man's house, *mon cher* Monsieur Craig. Believe me, she has plenty to worry about. But then, of course, so has he, if this story gets out to some of his press rivals. He wouldn't be able to face their ridicule, after all he's said and written about the so-called revolutionaries. What is your plan of action, Major?'

'I should like, *mon Général*, with your permission, to see the woman myself and interrogate her, so that at least we know all she can tell us.'

'If she will tell it. She's a clever woman. And then?'

'Continue to run her as an *agent-double, mon Général.* She said the next stage in the insurgency was far ahead—that is, the outbreak into open violence. But we think she's wrong—perhaps deliberately kept in the dark by her superiors in the movement. The evidence of the charts I showed you indicated that plans for action were well advanced. Stores of money, weapons and explosives have been formed, and the necessary medical supplies collected. All points to an early outbreak.'

'Well?'

'If we can keep in touch with Mademoiselle Belcadi she will be able, even in her limited capacity, to show us when to expect the attack to start.'

'And if she gives you names of other members of the movement?'

'Take no direct action, but keep them under very discreet supervision and find out as much as we can about their contacts and meeting places. But that would be all. We must preserve her from the suspicion of her colleagues at all costs.'

'Who knows about this matter?'

'Only Monsieur Craig and myself. All notes dealing with Mademoiselle Belcadi, and this recording, will be kept in my own safe.'

'And who else has the combination?'

'It is in the sealed envelope in the drawer of your safe, *mon Général.*'

'Monsieur Craig, have you told anyone else? Sir John Radcliffe, for instance?'

'No, *mon Général.* Not so far.'

'Do you feel you must inform him or any other British authority?'

'This is a Tunisian matter, sir, and no concern of my Government unless there is a likelihood of danger to British persons or property. That is Sir John's attitude, I know.'

'Thank you. All right, Chaker. You may proceed with your plan, informing me in person at each stage of your enquiry. I don't like this business of using Belcadi's daughter, but agree that our paramount need is to find out who the insurgent leaders are and when they plan to begin overt action. There is one thing I want you to understand.'

'*Mon Général.*'

'If the connection between Ahmed Belcadi's daughter and a revolutionary movement becomes public knowledge it will not only cause a major scandal, it will be a source of considerable embarrassment to the Government and to the *Suprême Combattant* himself. You must take no risk whatever of this happening. If it does, I shall hold you responsible.'

'*Entendu, mon Général.*'

'And Monsieur Craig should be kept out of the action. As he said, it is a Tunisian matter.

You will understand this, Monsieur Craig, I'm sure. I have already told the President how useful your advice has been, and I hope you'll still continue to help us while you're here. But advice is one thing, action—particularly action which might bring you into personal danger—quite another. We must handle this investigation and take counteraction ourselves.'

Back in Chaker's room, the two men looked at each other.

'It's up to you now, Taieb. She'll be expecting you to call her and arrange a rendezvous.'

'Yes. But you don't have to go back to London until the end of the week?'

'No. The Office told me to stay as long as the General wanted me, inside of a fortnight.'

'I'd be very glad of your advice about the programme of counter-measures I have to submit to the General and the Chief of Police. I have roughed the scheme out in French, but it's pretty long and detailed. Could you come in during the mornings, perhaps?'

'Of course.' He added, encouragingly, 'Your General is a very impressive man, Taieb, and he's obviously got confidence in you.'

Chaker smiled grimly. 'I think you're right, but that won't help me in the least if I make one mistake.'

CHAPTER SEVEN

When he went into the hotel dining-room he found Thorne and Cleo sitting at a table in the window, consulting the menu. Craig realised, without much surprise, that he was delighted to see her again, and indeed she was something to look at, in her tawny silk shirt and cool linen suit. She was obviously out to enslave Thorne, and making progress.

How odd it was, thought Craig, that all his instincts as a policeman should be urging him not to get involved with the girl, when in fact . . . He walked towards their table.

'Peter,' cried Thorne. 'Just the man I wanted. Come and have lunch with us.'

'If Miss Hamilton doesn't mind.'

'Charmed,' she said coldly. He sat down. His final remark to her the night before still rankled, evidently.

Over the lobster bisque Thorne said, pointing to Cleo, 'She's plaguing the life out of me, and as she came with half a dozen letters of introduction I've got to do something. The trouble is my usual contacts won't play.' He ignored Craig's black look at this broad hint of what was to come. 'Peter's the man you want, Cleo. He knows what the police are doing.'

'If he does,' she said tartly, 'he won't say.'

'What is it you want to know?'

'Inside stories about student aims and aspirations, and what's behind the sit-in at the shipyard and the trouble in the co-operatives up and down the country.'

'And you're surprised,' said Craig, amused, 'that the Ministry of Information doesn't at once arrange interviews for you?'

'It looks as if they've got something to hide.'

'Oh no it doesn't. They just don't want you to get a hopelessly one-sided view. Haven't they told you what they think about the student troubles?'

'Have they not? *Ad nauseam*. But it's all sweet talk, washed down with the coffee and mint tea they ply you with so assiduously.'

'It's so typical of you journalists,' said Craig, judiciously. 'What the cock-eyed revolutionaries tell you is news. But when the Government explains what it's doing, and what the Destour Party is doing, to create more jobs and improve the standard of living—that's just sweet talk.' He waited while the waiter cleared the soup plates away. 'If someone rang you and invited you to come to a clandestine meeting of insurgents, all terribly secret, with passwords and masks and a lot of hot air about what the Thirteenth Commando is going to do with its home-made bombs, would you go?'

It was an obvious trap, but Cleo was honest. 'At the drop of a hat. It's my job.'

'Of course it is, Peter,' said Thorne, rushing in to her defence. 'It's news, after all.'

'And what she wants. Not the truth, just the news. All she'd be doing is to give the revolutionaries, or whatever they call themselves, the publicity they need. It influences public opinion. People begin to think there must be at least thirteen commandos, when there probably isn't one. She wouldn't stop to ask the Government side what they thought of the story, would you Cleo?'

'Oh yes I would, but,' she added with a mischievous smile, 'I'd get the story in first. Then I'd go and listen to more sweet talk.'

Craig threw up his hands. 'And your editor would spike *that* report, wouldn't he?'

She looked at him coldly. 'My stories don't get spiked. And the *News* is a responsible paper.'

'Are there any responsible newspapers, these days?'

'Oh have a heart, Peter,' cried Thorne. 'Don't take him seriously, Cleo.'

'I don't,' she said, and added impishly, 'I think he's just hungry. Eat your nice blanquette de veau, Master Peter. You'll feel better, dear.'

For the rest of the meal they argued quite amicably. Craig watched the girl's face as she was telling Thorne about her last visit to Vietnam. There was so much vitality in it, as if every moment was something to be savoured and enjoyed. He wondered if she'd let him take her out to dinner.

Thorne ordered coffee, and Cleo looked at him, smiling. 'It's all right about the introductions to your contacts, Michael. I won't bother you any more. I got on to a story this morning that will do very nicely, for today.'

'I thought you were going to the University, to talk to some of the students who were let out of jug last night.' So they had let them go, thought Craig. That was sensible.

'I did. Including the boy who kidnapped Peter.'

'I'm glad they let him out on bail,' said Craig. 'To tell you the truth, I was sorry for him when the other bunch of thugs broke up his little plan.'

'He realised that,' said Cleo, 'from something you said, and it made him furious. So I said I knew how pompous and patronising you could be—'

Thorne interrupted. 'I thought you two had only just met.'

Cleo ignored the remark. 'So I chatted him up and—well, in the end he told me something really important.'

Craig smiled. Her face was slightly flushed with the secret she was longing to tell him. 'The story of his failed *coup*,' he suggested, lighting a cigar.

'The story of the successful *coup*,' she said triumphantly. 'Hached told me the name of the man who led the rescue gang.'

Craig started. 'Now that *is* interesting. What are you going to do? Tell the police?'

'Of course not. Nor you either. He told me in strict confidence.'

'But why did he tell you?'

'Because I was sympathetic, talking about his ideals and so on, and because he hates this other man, who humiliated him in front of his friends. He wants to show him he's not as clever as he thinks he is.'

'But how did he know who it was?'

'Apparently, as soon as you had been taken away, Hached and his friends were pushed into another car—the Citroën—and dropped several miles away, in the country. There was no bus until the morning and they had to sleep at a farm. They knew nothing about the fire, or the disposal of the body, until the next day. But they knew someone had betrayed them, and guessed who. They got hold of him and held his head in a basin of water in the Faculty cloakroom until he talked, and then they learned he'd been in touch with the leader of the Vigilantes group for some time. And who it is.' She finished her coffee, enjoying the riveted attention of the two men. 'They were going to take their revenge on him, but the police collared them and put them inside. Now they're watched all the time, pending the trial, so Hached—after I'd convinced him I wouldn't bring his name into it—thought it would be a good idea if I saw the Vigilante leader and exposed him in the foreign press, and everyone in the University would avoid him like the plague in future.'

'But why,' asked Thorne, 'didn't he just tell the police?'

'Oh, get with it, Michael. None of the young will tell the police anything unless they're tortured.'

'They don't torture prisoners here,' said Craig, primly. 'But listen, Cleo. I'm very serious about this. If you're thinking of seeing this man, please don't. He's dangerous.'

'But he's on the Government side, isn't he? He only killed in self-defence. He's got nothing to fear if his name comes out.'

'I think he has,' said Craig. 'Please, Cleo. *Don't* go and see him. You might get hurt.'

'He can't do much at four in the afternoon at his place of work, can he?'

'So that's when you're going to try and see him, this afternoon?'

'I didn't say that. It'll be all right. If absolutely necessary I'll keep his name secret. All I want to know, after all, is how he and his Vigilantes work, what they're planning to do. It's a good story.'

'They may not be Vigilantes,' said Craig angrily. 'Have you thought of that? They may have another reason for stopping that amateur kidnapping.'

'Such as?'

'They may want the balloon to go up on D-

Day, not D minus fifty.'

Her eyes rounded in surprise. 'Is that possible, Peter?'

'Of course it's possible. I shouldn't tell you this, but if it'll stop you going to see this man—'

'But of course it won't. Quite the opposite. Don't you see, if he's a proper revolutionary. making plans for some time in the future, he'll want to get sympathy abroad for his motivations.'

Craig slapped the table with his hand. 'I might have known you'd say that,' he said roughly. 'It's typical. And it's wrong. You don't understand the first thing about real revolutionary movements. If it is one—and of course it's just speculation on my part—that man's first and biggest task is to hide both his plans and his real motivations at this stage. He'd tell you damn-all. He and his friends might be at the back of all the troubles you've been nosing into, but you wouldn't find a trace of their hand anywhere. And most of all, they want to keep themselves unknown. It's the classic pattern. I don't say it's happening here, but it might be. If the men I saw were Vigilantes, I'm a Dutchman.' He avoided looking at Thorne.

'Peter,' she said, looking at him with amused eyes, 'you've actually *said* something, and it's intriguing. You mean, there might be one serious, long-term conspiracy, that uses all kinds of small causes like the students and the shipyard workers and so on—just to keep the Government on edge, while they themselves got ready for the big bang?'

'They'd use them for a lot of other things, like making Government and people draw further and further apart, and wrecking the economy by random terrorism and industrial sabotage. You've seen it all in Northern Ireland.'

'But surely there's a lot of genuine anti-Government feeling here, there are so many spontaneous demonstrations, and all the agro.'

'Demonstrations are never spontaneous—or so rarely that if you see a riot in the streets you can safely say that someone triggered it off deliberately. Sometimes you get a genuinely peaceful and spontaneous demonstration, and then a different group converts it into a bloody riot.'

'I suppose you're right—'

'He is right, Cleo,' said Thorne. 'It could be just like that. So that man, whoever it is, *could* be dangerous. Just don't go and see him alone.'

'It's the only way I can possibly get a story out of him. If I've got a witness there's no way of bargaining about what to reveal and what to keep quiet. But I'll be O.K.' She bent down to pick up her bag.

Craig put his hand over hers. It was as he remembered, warm and struggling like a little animal. He held on to it. 'Listen. Can't you get another journalist to go with you?'

They were staring at each other, faces close together, oblivious to their surroundings. There's something between those two, thought Thorne, that neither seems to be aware of.

Cleo looked down at her bag, and said quietly, 'And share the story? What d'you take me for?'

'A very stupid girl,' said Craig angrily. He dropped her hand and walked away from the table, with a word of thanks to Thorne, who stood up, looking down at Cleo with a worried expression on his face.

Suddenly, she jumped to her feet, ran after Craig and seized his arm. He turned round, and found her small face looking up at him, furious. 'If you put the snoopers on to me,' she said between her teeth, 'I'll never fogive you. D'you understand, Peter? *Never.*'

'But that's just what I'm going to do,' he said calmly, hoping she wouldn't realise that if she slipped away now there would be no chance of following her. She had her own car, and his was back with Hertz.

'You brute!' she cried explosively. 'What does it matter to you?' People were staring, and Thorne was coming across the room with the head waiter in pursuit, holding the bill. 'You're only prying into my affairs for the sake of your precious Tunisian cops.'

Craig took her by the arm and walked her, protesting, into the foyer. 'It matters a lot,' he said quietly. 'To me as a man. I like your face as it is—er—very much. I don't want someone whom I—oh hell!—whom I like to get involved with a thug who blows people's heads off with a twelve-bore.'

That shook her. She was silent for a moment, then, 'Did you really mean that? About putting a tail on me?'

'Of course. No problem. But if I came with you I could keep out of sight and you could give me a shout if you felt worried. I wouldn't even have to know the man's name.' With any luck Yasmin would be telling Chaker all about her cell leader, any time now.

They were both aware that Thorne was standing near, watching them curiously. She turned. 'I suppose you're both right,' she said. 'You'll keep in the background, Peter?'

'I'll do just what you ask, so long as I'm not too far away.'

'All right.' She smiled suddenly. 'I'm just going to my room.' She looked at her watch. 'We'll have to start in about ten minutes, the traffic being what it is.' She took her key from her handbag. 'I'll be down here then.'

'Promise?'

'Promise.'

The two men watched her trim legs as she ran quickly up the stairs. 'Attractive girl, isn't she?' remarked Thorne, tentatively.

'Very. D'you think she'll keep it?'

'What?'

110

'That promise.'

'You've got a suspicious mind, Peter. Of course she will.'

'That's what I think, but—what was the number on her key? One-five-seven, same floor as mine. Thanks again for the lunch, Michael. I'll just slip up to my room.'

'You *are* a suspicious bastard.'

*   *   *

Craig quickly unlocked his suitcase and took out his stubby little Colt Commander, a loaded magazine and a canvas shoulder holster. It was a lightweight automatic, and fitted well under his coat. He strapped it on and ran back into the corridor. He knew there was a staff staircase at the other end, but he gave Cleo the benefit of the doubt. As he passed her room he could faintly hear the sound of running water. He waited at the top of the staircase until he heard her door open and her footsteps approaching. Then ran downstairs and was waiting when she appeared. He felt guilty for thinking she might have tried to give him the slip, but it had been right to run no risk.

He offered to drive her in his car and she nodded. Silently, they went out and into the Avenue Habib Bourguiba. The Hertz car was parked nearby. He got into the driving seat and headed east down the avenue and out on to the lake road, following her instructions.

Cleo glanced sideways at him, the odd profile, the lean long hands on the steering wheel. 'If only,' she said lightly, 'your kidnapping itself wasn't as dead as cold mutton. A month ago I could have made a story out of this drive which'd have been some justification.'

'What would you write?' he asked, amused.

'With Peter Craig, the kidnapped policeman-diplomat, by my side, I drove out of the busy city of Tunis, baking in the sultry heat, and took the lonely stretch of highway that crosses the lake. We passed the spot where a young revolutionary, posing as a traffic cop, thrust the muzzle of his gun through the window of the Ambassador's Rolls-Royce, and cried—'

'Everybody out!' put in Craig.

'What did you do? I asked him. Your turn.'

'Cowered back into my corner, watching the nicotine-stained finger trembling on the trigger. But he missed. The soft purr of the engine changed to a shattering roar. He'd shot through the exhaust.'

'He didn't?'

'No. That's journalist's licence. Even quite dishy ones use it, didn't you know?'

She said nothing for a moment, then, 'Don't you want to know where we're going?'

'All right. Where are we going after this?'

'Past Carthage and the Punic Ports and apparently there's a large area of ruins on the

112

right, first the baths of Antoninus and then a great jumble of Carthaginian, Roman and Byzantine remains. They discovered last year an underground temple of Tanit, still full of the ashes and bones of sacrificed children, and it's been cordoned off and is being excavated by a young lecturer in archaeology called Mahmoud. Doctor Mahmoud. He's the chap.'

'I thought you weren't going to tell me his name?' He turned to look at her. She was frowning.

'Well, I don't see how you can skulk around an archaelogical site without being seen. And I've an idea.' She paused, still doubtful if it was a good one.

'Go on.'

'Couldn't we go in and find him together? Then you could say you wanted to thank him?'

'That's an excellent plan. Of course.' Whether Mahmoud would buy that explanation of his presence was another matter.

*　　*　　*

There was a track leading off to the right between the fallen stelae and tombs, and a notice *'Temple de Tanit No. 7. Excavations, aux soins de Docteur Mahmoud, Faculté de l'Archéologie, Université de Tunis.'* And underneath, in big letters, Arabic and French, ENTREE DEFENDUE AU PUBLIC.

They drove a little farther on, to park the

113

car under the shade of a tree, and walked back and down the track until they came to a gate. On either side a high barbed-wire fence separated the excavation area from the rest of the ruins. An old man in a striped jellaba emerged from a small hut on the other side and came to the gate, which was locked.

'Monsieur le docteur Mahmoud est là?' asked Cleo, showing her press card, and added mendaciously, *'Il m'attend.'*

'He's not here,' said the old man gruffly, in broken French. 'He's gone into the city, with the bones.'

Cleo swore under her breath and turned away. Craig touched her arm. He said to the guardian, 'It's a pity. We've come so far to see the excavations. May we go in?'

'It is forbidden. They aren't yet ready to be seen by the public.' He saw the dinar note in Craig's hand. 'Did he say he would be here?'

'Perhaps I made a mistake about the day. But it would be kind of you to let us just have a quick look round, Monsieur.' The note crackled attractively.

'There's no one here. They aren't excavating today. But if you just want to see the caves, I suppose you can come in.' He pocketed the note, unlocked the gate, let them through and locked it again. 'Only for a few minutes, you understand?'

'Of course.'

'What's the point of this?' whispered Cleo.

'We don't want to see a lot of crummy ruins.'

'It'd look odd if we didn't, wouldn't it?' But there was an idea at the back of his mind.

The track, rutted by the passage of heavy vehicles, wound its way round what looked like a quarry, but there was a shorter way down a flight of steps. The old man descended them, creakily, and they followed.

It was an extraordinary sight. In one face of the 'quarry', opposite where the track came out on to level ground, were three great arches of cut stone, two of them filled almost to the top with piles of dark ashes and small charred bones, the remains of the babies thrown into the red-hot womb of the Goddess Tanit, two and a half thousand years ago. The centre arch had been cleared, and the bones piled up outside. An excavator stood at one side, and a small trailer, filled with its grisly cargo. At the rear of the level area was a pre-fabricated office building and a wash-house.

The old man went into the cleared archway and switched on an electric light. They saw an immense chamber lined with marble tombs, the roof held up by columns, some original and others rough temporary supports, made of brick. The air was bitter with acrid dust. The gate-keeper took a torch from his pocket and beckoned to them to follow him across the ancient paving to the nearest tomb. He shone the light on the thick slab of stone that covered it, and they saw an inscription. *'Sarcophage*

115

punique,' he explained. Craig took the torch and inspected one of the other tombs, while the gate-keeper wandered uneasily back to the archway.

There was the sudden, strident sound of a car's horn, which seemed to terrify the old man. 'He's come back,' he whispered, wringing his hands. 'Stay here, Monsieur, he mustn't see you. He'll be gone again soon. Stay at the back. He won't go in there.' He was running towards the steps as he spoke, calling out something in Arabic.

Craig took Cleo's arm and ran towards the dark recesses of the chamber, using the torch. 'Keep quiet,' he whispered.

She struggled to get free. 'But if he's here I want to see him.'

'He'll be back again, when he's delivered another load somewhere in the town. Then we can walk in from the road, all proper. You don't want to get the old man into trouble, do you?'

'I suppose not.' They saw in front of them, in the rear wall of huge building blocks, a gap, covered roughly by a hurdle.

'We'll be safer in there,' said Craig. 'Hold the torch.' He lifted the wooden hurdle to one side and they squeezed through. Then he shone the torch round the inner chamber.

It was smaller than the outer one, and seemed to be a repository for excavation tools—iron crowbars, spades, picks and

116

shovels, and sieves with meshes of varying size. In the stone walls ware deep niches, in which ancient coffins were laid. A great heap of charred bones lay at one side and along the back wall was a pile of empty crates, stencilled with the letters FAC. ARCH., UNIV. TUNIS and words in Arabic.

'Put the light out,' whispered Cleo fiercely. 'They're coming.' They stood behind the hurdle and watched through the outer chamber as a jeep slowly came into view at the bottom of the ramp, with an empty trailer bumping behind it. The man at the wheel was tall, long-haired, with a narrow, acquiline nose and sunburnt face. He and the two young men with him wore jeans and open shirts. They jumped out when the jeep came to rest on the level ground and quickly disconnected the trailer, which was hauled to one side. Then the leader reversed the jeep and manoeuvred it so that the laden trailer could be attached. Once this was done he wasted no time, but began to drive slowly up the track, with his two companions pushing the trailer from behind. Its wheels sank into the soft earth.

'*Heavy,*' said Craig, under his breath. 'Why should a load of dry bones and ashes be so heavy?'

'Oh come on, Peter,' she whispered. 'Let's get out of here. It smells of death.' It was true. Even after two thousand years and more the reek lingered in the confined air and caught at their throats. She shivered, and pulled his arm. 'The old man'll be back any moment.'

'Hold the torch for me.' He picked up the longest crowbar he could find, ran to the pile of bones and thrust it in. Then again, a foot further away. There was a sharp chink of metal on metal. 'Hold the torch higher, girl. I can't see.'

'What are you trying to do?'

He said nothing, but seized a spade and began to throw the bones aside. Then he dropped it and scrabbled with his hands. 'Bring it near, for God's sake.' She shone the light downwards.

They were staring at the uncovered end of a long steel box. There were markings in Cyrillic characters. 'It's Russian,' she whispered.

'Or Bulgarian or Serbo-Croat, I think. I'm not sure. But they're arms.' She bent down, but he stopped her. 'It's enough for one of us to get filthy.' He hastily pushed back the bones until the box was completely covered, spaded more on top, and had just returned the tools to their places when he heard the gate-keeper calling. They scrambled through the hurdle, put it back in position and ran out into the fresh clean air. The old man was coming across the level ground, in great distress. He could scarcely bring out a few words of French, but it was clear what he wanted. That they should go away, and quickly. When he saw the state of Craig's light suit he was visibly

118

distressed.

'It's all right,' said Craig soothingly. 'I tripped and fell into that heap of rubbish. In there,' he added casually, jerking his thumb towards the shadows.

'We didn't want to get you into trouble, *mon vieux.* The lady's dress would have shown up if we'd stayed where you told us to go. I couldn't make the torch work, and fell into something. Just look at me,' He was dusting down as he spoke. 'What have you got in there, more bones?'

'*Les ossements, oui. Il y en a partout.*' He was still scared, but Craig's manner was reassuring. Even more so when he took out his wallet. 'The doctor stopped the excavations today and tomorrow so that he could clear some of it away.'

As they walked towards the road Cleo quickened her pace until she was half running. He took her arm. 'You've got your story, Cleo darling,' he said. 'But I hope you won't use it just yet.'

'Why did you *tell* him we'd been in that awful room?'

'Because if he goes in there with his torch he'll see at once that the heap of bones has been disturbed. If so, he'll probably accept my story and put things right.' He grinned. 'The poor old boy isn't likely to admit that he let strangers in there.'

'But does he know? I mean, about those—

what are they, rifles?'

'I don't know, but I can get the markings checked, if I can remember them well enough. Probably machine-guns. That was about the size.' He turned her round so that he could see her white face. 'Are you all right?'

'Of course I'm all right. But I feel— contaminated. I can't get the smell of that place out of my nose.'

He opened the car door for her.

'Don't bother about me,' she said irritably. 'Just get moving. I'm sorry, Peter. But just— could you please take me somewhere I can see a lot of sky, and sea, and no sour dust or bones?'

'Yes, that's what we'll do. Look at the sea, and smoke a quiet cigarette. And then, d'you know what?'

'No.'

'We'll drive slowly home, by the other road, back to the hotel, hot bath, cold shower—and then I suppose you'll have to get your hair washed.'

'How did you know that's what I wanted more than anything?'

'But so do I. We'll both have a long bath—I mean, you have a bath and I'll have a bath—' At last he'd got her to laugh. 'Then the shower, and change all clothes down to your skin, mind you, and I suppose I'll have to wait for an hour or so, moping, until you're ready for a cold drink at the bar and we go out to dinner.'

'Stop the car here.' Ahead, the sun was shining gold on the white houses and domes of Sidi Bou Said perched above a sea that rippled peacefully under a brilliant sky.

He stopped the car, and felt her arms round his neck. 'Look at me.' He turned his head. Her face was very close.

'I think you have the most wonderful ideas.' She kissed him. Her mouth was soft. And sweet. 'Your face is filthy, but it tastes of you, not charred bones.' She was still trembling a little. He kissed her mouth, firmly, almost formally, as if some pact was being sealed. But what it was he didn't exactly know.

She held his head in her hands, looking into his eyes. 'You know what's worrying me a lot?'

'No, darling. What can I do about it?'

'You're such an accomplished liar. You must admit it's rather worrying for a girl.'

'I'll never tell a lie to you.'

'That's what I wanted you to say.' She disengaged herself. 'What exactly has happened to us, do you suppose? I mean I'm not—I wouldn't have thought this possible, I do assure you. Even a few hours ago. Honestly.'

'Nor would I. So don't let's worry about it. D'you want a cigarette, or shall I drive on?'

'Let's go straight back to that bath. Two baths.'

He drove on.

'D'you know something?' she said. 'It's only

when you're excited that I can tell you're a Scot.' She snuggled up to him. 'Peter,' she said, 'what's that hard thing you've got?'

'What exactly do you mean?'

'Under your arm, idiot.'

'Oh, that. It's a gun. I told you I didn't like Doctor Habib Mahmoud. But I'd have hated having to use it.'

'I suppose you're going to get the Tunisians to arrest them all,' she said resignedly. 'And bang goes half my story.'

'Good Lord, no. If the Tunisians know their business—and they do—what they'll want to find out is where those cargoes of bones and et-ceteras end up. They'll keep their knowledge of the dump strictly under their hats for the time being. My God!' he exclaimed. 'What a cover!'

'What d'you mean?'

'The last hiding-place anyone would think of, with plenty of room and a perfect camouflage for distribution. Who would want to ask what's inside a load of charred bones? And so-called volunteers from the University to help with the dig and be trained as revolutionaries on the side. I told you, they're dangerous people, and very, very bright.'

'Let's talk about something else, for God's sake. Did you wear a kilt when you were a little boy?'

*   *   *

He stopped the car at a café in La Marsa and telephoned. When they arrived at the Tunisia Palace Chaker was idly turning over the pages of a magazine at the news-stand and ignored him. He took Cleo to her room, went on to his own, and gave a message to the telephone operator. A minute later Chaker was with him, followed by a waiter with drinks.

Craig took a deep swallow of the whisky, set down his glass, lit a cigar, and told the whole story. Chaker's eyes glistened. Then he frowned.

'I can imagine what the General will say when I tell him. You weren't to be involved.'

'It was just an accident, you saw that.'

The Tunisian laughed. 'D'you think he'll believe that? He'd say you seemed to be curiously accident-prone. However, that's my headache. Let me tell you about Yasmin Belcadi.'

'You've seen her already?'

'Yes. She seemed quite willing to tell what she knows, but it isn't much.'

'What?'

'She says she only knows her fellow cell-members by their noms-de-guerre. She described Mahmoud accurately, according to what you've just told me, but doesn't know his name or what he does. But she's told me about the other cells her action squad has visited, at least the approximate addresses, and we can

123

follow up. She's also given me the description of the dead-letter drop she has to clear tomorrow, and I've arranged to meet her afterwards so that we can unseal the envelope and copy the contents before she passes it on to Mahmoud.'

'But how can she do that if she doesn't know his name?'

'She meets him in a café in the town, muffled in her sifsari, and he takes the message and gives her instructions for the next contact, or the next job, if there is one. Incidentally, we've given her a pseudonym—Janus.'

'I see,' said Craig thoughtfully. 'So she's simply a security cut-out, and occasional chauffeuse. All the same, she'll see some action now. It looks as if they're going to start something.'

'Seems so. I've got a transcript of the talk I had with her, but it's in Arabic.' He finished his drink. 'We'll translate it for you.'

'Never mind about that. I'd better get a shower.'

'Are you coming to the office?'

'Er, no. Listen, Taieb. I've got to take Miss Hamilton out to dinner.'

'Oh have you?' said Chaker, smiling.

'Yes. You see, she's had a traumatic experience. She's not quite as tough as she thinks she is. So as she's still rather shaken, I said I'd give her dinner. Calm her down, you know.'

'Is that what you call it?' said the Tunisian, laughing. 'All right, Peter. And I can see you need a bath, badly. Attractive girl, is she?'

'Yes.'

'Good. I'll see you in the morning in my office. At eight if you can manage it. There's a lot to do. And Peter—'

'Yes.'

'Be sure it isn't you who needs calming down.'

CHAPTER EIGHT

At eight o'clock the following morning Craig was shown into Chaker's office. The atmosphere was stale with smoke and the ashtrays full of cigarette butts. The Tunisian was giving rapid orders into one of his telephones. He put the receiver down and looked up. There were dark circles under his eyes, and he was unshaven.

'It's good to see someone looking relaxed and cheerful. Your concern for Miss Hamilton's state of mind was—er—fruitful, I hope.'

'She seemed to think so. And what's more important, from your point of view, she agreed, reluctantly, to hold up her story for the moment. But on one condition.'

125

'No conditions. If she prints it in the middle of a police operation we'll ask her to leave the country and not come back. But what was it?'

'That you or someone else in the know gives her an interview.'

Chaker passed a hand over his bristly chin. 'O.K. A bit later. We owe her that.'

'What's happening?'

'I've been up all night, arguing with the General and the Chief of Police, making arrangements for action.'

'You're surely not going to raid the Tanit site, are you?'

'If the decision were mine, no. And I've talked them round, I think. Arguing that we shouldn't show our hand until we know where these arms are being cached. But the action has to be taken by the police, not the Army, at this stage, and the C. of P. at first wanted to raid the place in the middle of the night. It was only when I told him you might be mistaken—'

'You said what?'

'I'm sorry, Peter, but it was the only way. I said our evidence was based solely on what you saw—or thought you saw, because after all you hadn't time to open the steel box—during a few seconds, in that inner chamber. And the apparent weight of the trailer, too. I said I was afraid that the police might look very silly if they found nothing.' He saw the look on Craig's face, and hurried on. 'So in the end the C. of P. agreed that I should maintain close

126

surveillance and see what happens. But if those cargoes of bones are taken to some place where they've no right to be, the police will raid it.'

'Probably more than one. Surely you want to discover all the locations, and then clean the lot up in simultaneous operations? Or better still, keep them under observation until you can arrest the people who go to pick up the arms.'

'Ideally, yes. But the Chief of Police maintains he hasn't got enough men skilled in really unobtrusive surveillance.'

'I can appreciate that. It'd need a lot of men, and one slip would warn off the whole gang. Has anything happened yet at the site?'

'The transfers of bones are going to take place, as you expected. Mahmoud arrived very early, by jeep. The watchers can't see into the excavation, so they can't tell what he's doing. But there are eight men on the job now, all young. The other seven arrived in a second jeep . . .'

'They may be going to use the two trailers together.' Craig put his hand on Chaker's arm. 'You can't do anything yet. Let Captain Tibaoui take over the surveillance reports, and come out and have breakfast.'

'I've had it, thanks. But I need a shower and a chance to shave and put on clean clothes. Stay here, if you like.'

Ten minutes later Captain Tibaoui came

into the room with a sheaf of notes in his hand. 'They're moving, Monsieur Craig,' he said excitedly. 'Both jeeps together, going towards Tunis. I've sent the trail cars after them, and we'll be getting their reports any moment now.' He darted back into his room.

*　　　*　　　*

Two hours later Chaker took Craig to see the General. The Chief of Police, a tall, dignified man in uniform, was sitting with him. Chaker saluted them both, punctiliously. He looked more cheerful and a good deal smarter, with his face shaven and a clean shirt under his lightweight tan suit. The Tunisians, with their customary politeness, switched to French, effortlessly, as Craig was introduced to the police Chief. General Farhat asked Chaker to report.

'The two trips taken so far by the jeeps had the same destination, *mon Général*, a farmhouse to the west of the Bizerte road.' He produced a large scale map from under his arm and spread it out. 'As you will see, the approach is along a side road and then across an open field, not much more than a cart-track. The vehicles passed into a barn at the left of the farm and when they emerged the trailers were empty.'

'How do you know they carried arms?' asked the Chief, gruffly.

'When the trailers left the Tanit temple site, *Monsieur le Directeur*, they had notices painted on the back, *"Université de Tunis, Faculté d'Archéologie."* While they were being towed past the Bardo Museum boards were hoisted over the back of each jeep by men sitting on top of the *ossements*, and secured in place. On the return journey the boards, which bear the name of an agricultural supply firm, were removed.'

The General turned to the Chief. 'Are you satisfied, *mon cher collègue?*' he asked, smiling.

The Chief of Police said thoughtfully, 'Yes, I'll accept that as proof that the consignments ought to be examined. H'm. All four cargoes went to the same place, did they?' He looked at Chaker. 'That doesn't seem to tie in with the ideas you were airing last night, Major, does it? Or were they Mr Craig's ideas?' Chaker flushed.

'With respect, *Monsieur le Directeur*,' said Craig, 'it seemed obvious that if the arms were being sent out to units, in preparation for their use in action, they would go to a number of distribution points. What is actually happening is interesting. It looks as if action is not planned for the moment, but that for some reason the farmhouse is a better entrepot than the temple of Tanit. It could also mean that the temple is the first storage place after the arms are smuggled into the country. It is very near the coast.'

'You may be right, Monsieur,' said the Chief in quite a friendly tone, 'but this is all theorising. What we have in concrete terms is quantities of arms now held in two different places, and eight men engaged in handling them. To my mind, that is enough. If we wait, the men may scatter when they have completed their transfer operations, and we shall have difficulty in tracing them. If we strike now, that is, when the next loads are being delivered—if indeed they also are to be sent to the farmhouse—we shall at least capture the arms and the men, and from the latter we may learn enough to destroy this abominable conspiracy once and for all. Where are the jeeps now?'

'On their way back to the temple site,' said Chaker. 'I should have added that two men were left at the farmhouse, without transport, so far as can be seen. So it looks as if there will be another trip.'

'Good. I have three troop carriers standing by, with armed police in full readiness for action. Two will be sent to a place on the Bizerte road beyond the turning that leads to the farm, so that they won't be seen by the drivers of the jeeps. While the next two loads are being delivered they will launch their attack. In the meantime the remaining carrier will take up its station near the temple site, and the police will move in as soon as they are informed by radio that the attack on the farmhouse has begun.' He turned to the General. 'Have you any objections, *mon cher collègue?*'

'Of course not, *mon cher Directeur.* It is your responsibility and your plan seems admirable to me.'

'Thank you. How long would you expect the rebels to take before they arrive back at the farmhouse, Major?'

Chaker looked at his watch. 'About an hour, I should think, if not more. It took them twenty minutes to load last time. More likely an hour and a quarter.'

'More than enough. You would oblige me, Major Chaker, if the General agrees, by briefing Commissaire Filali who is waiting in the courtyard on the exact position of the farmhouse and any other background information he may require.' He rose and straightened his uniform. 'I am most grateful to you, Mr Craig, and you, too, Major, for your careful investigation.' He turned to Craig. 'This Miss Hamilton. She appears to be a responsible journalist?'

'Indeed yes, *Monsieur le Directeur.*' Provided, he added to himself, I vet everything she writes.

'I think, General, a little objective publicity for this operation might have a useful deterrent effect.' He picked up his gloves, and missed the fleeting glint of amusement in the General's dark eyes. 'I shall be informing the news editor of *Le Tunisien* in strict confidence and suggesting he sends a reliable reporter to be attached to Commissaire Filali. It would do no harm if a foreign correspondent were also on the scene so that there is no misrepresentation abroad. I should have preferred a man, but she seems to have deserved, by her discretion, to get this—er—story. She must of course be kept right out of the way.'

'I will accompany her myself, Monsieur, if you wish, and do my best to see that her reportage is objective and complete.'

'Excellent. *Au revoir*, Monsieur Craig. Major Chaker.' He returned the younger man's salute. 'I think you'll find that my officers also can play a distinguished role in matters of this kind.'

* * *

Craig and Cleo Hamilton were sitting in the back of a grey Renault as it worked its way round the Place Bab Saadoun and entered the Avenue du 20 mars. In front was a police driver and a smartly uniformed inspector, who held a personal radio in one hand, close to his ear. The tiny loudspeaker bleeped, and spoke briefly in Arabic. The inspector turned round.

'They have left the Ouled Haffouz and are on the Boulevard Belhassen Ben Chabane, opposite the gas-works, moving at forty kilometres, approximately.' He laughed. 'They're running no risk of being pulled up by the Traffic Police. We'll go ahead of them to the Bardo turning and remain there till they pass, and still not move until the Commissaire signals that ht is about to attack.'

'We're going to miss the whole bloody thing,' whispered Cleo, mutinously. Craig pressed her arm.

Five minutes later the Renault turned into the Museum approach and stopped, facing back towards the main road. They waited, tensely.

'Les voilà!' Across the entrance to the approach road two jeeps passed along the highway, towing trailers with high loads covered with black plastic sheets.

'I will explain,' said the inspector, 'what the Commissaire plans to do.' He turned in his seat and spread out a map so that they could see. 'This is the Bardo, where we are. Three hundred metres further up the road this little side-road leads off through olive groves. Now at this point where I have put a cross, there's a cart-track that goes off to the right of the side-road, first through trees, then across flat open ground for about five hundred metres until it reaches the farm gate. During those last five hundred metres there is no cover, but it will be too late for the rebels to escape. There is a way out at the back of the farm—here—to another road, but we have armed men hidden

there, and if anyone tries to escape—b-r-r-r—'
He imitated the noise of a machine-pistol.

Cleo shivered, then rallied. 'Can we go to the edge of the trees, Monsieur?'

'Yes. But you must stay in this car, please. You will find the reporter from *Le Tunisien* there, Monsieur Badra. The Commissaire will drop him off before he leads the attack.'

'Not if I know Jacques Badra,' grumbled Cleo, restively, in English. 'He'll stay in that troop carrier if he has to shackle himself to the seat.'

'You'll see quite enough,' said Craig, 'so pack it in. You stick with me, and I'm going to keep well out of the way of the firing.'

The receiver bleeped again, and the inspector listened. 'Get moving,' he said to the driver. 'Fast.'

The Renault charged out of the approach road, swung into the highway and accelerated. When they came to the side-road they could see the back of the second troop carrier disappearing round a corner, among the olive trees. The Renault followed. A quarter of a mile further on there was a track leading away to the right, and the car turned into it. Some way down it, where only a thin belt of trees screened the open country, the carriers had halted and the officers were speaking to their men. The inspector stopped the Renault at a discreet distance. They could see the policemen putting on steel helmets and

134

holding their machine-pistols unslung. The man from *Le Tunisien,* in civilian clothes, was busy with a ciné camera. Then there was a wave of the Commissaire's hand, as he stood in the first carrier, and both vehicles moved forward.

'*En avant!*' ordered the inspector, and the Renault moved forward to the edge of the open ground, and stopped. There was no sign of the other reporter. He had got his way, and was by the side of the Commissaire.

They could see across a sandy field of coarse grass to where the two jeeps, with their trailers, were still bumping slowly down the last stretch of rutted track, between the gate and the barn. It all looked so far away, and peaceful. The windows of the farmhouse beside the barn were unshuttered, but blank. A man was standing in the open door. He ran into the house when he saw the troop carriers break cover. The jeeps disappeared into the darkness of the open barn.

The carriers were roaring down the narrow track between the drainage ditches, the men swaying from side to side. The helmets and gun barrels glittered in the bright sunlight.

They were only sixty yards from the gate when it happened. There were two deep orange flashes, almost simultaneously, and two dense clouds of red dust and smoke which formed even before the double crack of the explosions reached the ears of the watchers in the Renault. The command carrier skidded and overturned, and the other, thirty yards behind, was blown to one side and crashed in the ditch. As the police tried frantically to pull their wounded comrades out of the wrecked vehicles there was a sudden, methodical rattle of gunfire from the windows of the farmhouse. The muzzle flashes of the automatic weapons could be seen clearly. Four, counted Craig. Jesus! he thought. At that range it's massacre. He opened the car door and jumped out.

He was right. Men in the open field were dying. Then the petrol leaking from a punctured tank caught fire, and a sheet of yellow flame claimed what was left of one carrier and the men who could not escape. Cleo screamed, then sat rigid with horror, staring at the great fountain of black smoke that rose slowly in the still air, billowing into masses of changing colour.

The inspector was running forward with Craig when he recalled his duty. He stopped, took out his transmitter and pressed the call button. As he began to speak he stopped suddenly and called Craig back. His face was white and grim. 'What was it?' he shouted. 'Was it rockets? I couldn't see.'

'Mines,' said Craig. 'The second one fixed to trigger only on the second pressure.'

'It couldn't have been, man. The jeep had just passed—'

'Electrically controlled from the house.

There may be someone waiting to blow you up if you try to drive down that track, so don't. They'll try and escape by the back way. Tell your control.'

The inspector swore luridly, and turned to his radio, speaking rapidly. Craig ran forward beside the truck, trying to see past the drifting smoke. He could only catch glimpses of the farmhouse, but beyond it there were flashes, and he heard the sound of distant gunfire. The front of the farmhouse was now silent, and he thought for a moment that the rebels could see no one to fire at because of the smoke. But then he saw steel helmets, five of them, advancing to meet the two jeeps that were crawling out behind the farm on an unseen track. It was a brave act, but suicidal, to show themselves. The jeep men were standing and firing continuously. The second of their two vehicles swerved and turned over, pitching the men and the cargo on to the ground. But that was the last the police unit could do. They were all wounded or dead.

The leading jeep stopped. Its trailer was disconnected and two men, one limping badly, joined it from the crashed car and were hauled on board. The lone jeep drove off, further and further away, until the trees hid it.

Craig, panting, had nearly reached the scene of disaster by the cloud of smoke when he heard the Renault behind him, bumping across the open field behind the track. It stopped beside him and Cleo jumped out, holding a box with a red crescent painted on its lid. They ran to the forlorn group of survivors.

The Commissaire and one of his officers were dead. Jacques Badra had a broken arm. Of the twenty-one men who had taken part in the frontal attack thirteen were still alive, three of them badly wounded. Someone had gone to examine the overturned jeep, and later reported that the driver had been shot and another rebel crushed to death by one of the metal crates, which had fallen on top of him. Two of the police who had tried to stop them were dead, the others wounded.

A helicopter came over the scene, and the inspector spoke to the pilot by radio. The machine rose and sped off towards the copse where the jeep had disappeared.

'Can't we get some sticks from the farmhouse, to make splints with?' cried Cleo. Her face was black with smoke and there was blood on her blouse and slacks. She held the head of a groaning man while one of his comrades tried to straighten his broken leg.

'Not till the engineers have checked for booby-traps,' said Craig laconically. 'If they had the mines all rigged up ready for emergency, they've probably left some device for blowing up any intruder.'

'They're—they're devils,' she said, uncertainly.

'Yes. That's just what they are.' He finished

tying a bandage and smiled at her. 'There'll be help soon.'

'But have those men got clean away?'

'It's very possible. They had a good start, before the chopper arrived.' He looked up at the sound of a car. 'Thank God. They've got an ambulance.'

The police officer who seemed to be in charge walked slowly to where the white van and two Land Rovers had stopped at the edge of the trees. Men with stretchers rushed past him.

*   *   *

An hour later the Renault, with a broken spring from its rugged trip across the field, dropped Craig and Cleo at the Tunisia Palace. She had sat silent throughout the slow journey, utterly exhausted, her head against Craig's shoulder. He took her up to her room, ignoring the concerned exclamations of the hotel servants, and ordered brandy. 'Drink it when it comes and have a shower. Then lie down.' He held her in his arms and stroked her dusty hair. 'You're a very brave girl. And you need yet another hair-do.'

'I've got to file the story,' she said, dully, clinging to him.

'Damn the story.'

'It's no good saying that. If I can't keep my head and do my job when I've actually seen—

all that, what good am I?'

'Remind me to tell you the answer another time. Get your clothes off. I'm going.'

'Where? Peter, you're not going to—?'

'Chase them with a gun? No, darling, you forget I'm just another observer, like you. But Chaker may need my help. See you later.'

He went to his own room, showered, changed his clothes, and ran downstairs. A car was waiting to drive him to the Ministry.

CHAPTER NINE

Chaker said, 'The General's out, seeing the President.' His eyes burned as he looked at Craig. 'Those dogs of rebels won't stop now, Peter. It's true they've lost two men killed and twenty-two cases of machine-pistols, eight of ammunition—except for the few weapons they took away with them—but they'll act again—speed everything up—while their student friends are chortling with delight at the thought of what the police have suffered.' He swore. 'I ought to have thought of mines.'

'I didn't either, and yet it should have been obvious. That's why they chose the farmhouse. Clear view all round and a single, narrow approach road, just made for land-mines. But the idea of activating them electrically was bloody clever. They waited till their own vehicles had passed over them, and then threw a switch.' He started. 'Have the police raided the temple site?'

'No. It's cordoned off, of course, but the Chief—if he still is Chief after his interview with the *Suprême Combattant*—won't risk losing more men. He says how can he know they haven't mined the track at the site as well.'

'He's right; that's what I was afraid of. It's a job for experts.'

'It's up to the Army, now. The General's got a platoon of paras standing by.'

'But are there any insurgents there at all?'

'I didn't think so. All the men who arrived this morning in the two jeeps are accounted for. We thought it'd be empty, except for your old gate-keeper.' He paused, and passed a weary hand over his eyes. 'But it's not empty. The other police troop-carrier moved in as soon as the inspector in charge heard that the raid on the farm had started. All according to plan. They were met by automatic fire before they even got to the gate. Two men were killed.' He looked down at the floor. 'That makes twelve dead, Peter. Not wounded, *dead.*'

'It wasn't your responsibility, Taieb.'

'No. But they were comrades.' He swore again. 'I'd give a month's pay to lead the paras in.'

'But the General won't allow it?'

'No. My job is to get the intelligence. In Allah's name, what intelligence is going to help now?'

A buzzer sounded, and he snatched up the receiver of the intercom. When he put it down, 'The paras are closing in. They'll use mine detectors on the track down to the site, but if the rebels keep up their fire it'll be a slow business. If the paras can get to the edge of the excavation they'll throw in gas-bombs and smoke them out.'

The buzzer again. Chaker listened, making a note of an address on the pad near the telephone. He murmured something in Arabic and hung up, with a more cheerful expression on his face. 'Intelligence, did I say? Well, here's our chance. Something we can do, for a change.' He looked down at the pad. 'Rue du Divan. Right under our noses.'

'Are we going out?'

'We are. No police necessary for this bit of investigation. Are you carrying a gun?'

'Yes.'

'Good. I'll get mine.' He went to a cupboard and strapped on a shoulder holster, with the butt of a Police Special projecting. 'I'll explain as we go.'

On the way down the stairs and out into the baking heat of the streets Chaker said, 'You remember the Belcadi woman said she had to pick up a letter from a dead-letter box, late this morning? Well, about two hours ago, after

142

the attack on the farmhouse had so signally failed, she got a message at her home. A boy brought a note addressed to her and ran away. It told her to ring a certain number, but from a public telephone. When she did so she spoke to a man—she didn't know his voice—who told her on no account to go to the D.L.B., and that all standing instructions were cancelled. But—and this is the interesting bit—there was, he said, to be a student demonstration at nine o'clock tomorrow morning on the waste ground opposite the Place du Gouvernement, and she was to park her Mercedes in the Boulevard Bab-Benat at that time and wait. If anyone came up and gave the password "Death to tyrants"—in Arabic, of course—she was to accept his orders.'

'Interesting,' said Craig thoughtfully. 'A getaway car for agitators who stir up the mob and run away when the trouble starts. It's typical. But of course the important thing is the telephone number.'

Chaker laughed out loud and slapped Craig's back. 'I like working with you, *cher ami*. I was afraid it would be a call-box, but not so. It was used by the curator of the Museum of Arabic Inscriptions, who had a flat over the museum. The flat is now used by a couple who act as caretaker and cleaners. That's where we're going.'

They were walking down the length of the Place du Gouvernement, flanked by the ministries of finance, foreign affairs and other departments. At the bottom of the cobbled square they entered the Medina, turned left from the Rue de la Kasbah, then into the Rue du Divan and finally, at the end of a short sidestreet, to an old palace, which backed on to the soukhs. The house was in disrepair, but the façade was still imposing, with an elaborate double doorway sculpted out of sandstone, and ochre-painted doors. The great knocker was in the form of a woman's hand clasped round an iron ball, and at the side were slender Corinthian columns holding up an Islamic arch of black and white slabs. There was a brass plaque, 'MUSEE DES INSCRIPTIONS ISLAMIQUES', and underneath a notice, tacked to the wooden door. For the sake of foreigners it was repeated: *'Fermé—Closed—Geschlossen—Chiuso'.*

Chaker lifted the knocker and let it resound against the black iron boss. 'I wonder how long it's been closed,' he said, 'and why.'

The door at length opened a few inches, and the sallow face of a youth appeared in the crack. Chaker thrust his way inside, and Craig followed. Between the carved stone columns of a cloister they could see into the patio, and row upon row of marble and sandstone slabs, covered with the strange and beautiful characters of Arabic. The red roof sloped down on all sides to cover a gallery on the second floor.

Chaker held the caretaker firmly by the arm while he showed an official pass. Then he questioned him in Arabic. The man protested and shook his head.

'He says he hasn't got a telephone,' said the Tunisian officer grimly, 'but he has, and he's going to show us where it is.' He pushed the caretaker forward towards a small door. 'That's where the staircase is likely to be. Guard my rear. There may be some of those thugs around.'

They went up two flights and came out on to the gallery they had seen from below. Doors and windows opened on to it. The young man pointed to one of the doors and muttered, *'Chez nous, maman et moi.'* He seemed to be asking Craig to prevent any invasion of the privacy of his home.

'And the telephone?' asked Chaker, also in French.

He shook his head. As Chaker brought out his gun there was a shriek from the doorway, and an old woman appeared, screaming to the youth to do what the men wanted. He gave in and indicated a door at the end of the gallery.

'I've never used the telephone,' he protested. 'It belonged to the curator, when he lived here.'

'What was his name?' asked Craig. But he thought he knew the answer.

'Le docteur Mahmoud.'

'And he was here today?'

145

'No, monsieur, not he—'

'Then who was here?' asked Chaker.

'One of his friends. I don't know who they are, monsieur. They use the little room but won't let me go in. Not even to clean. They say the inscriptions they've got there are too valuable.'

Chaker held out his hand. 'The key.'

'I haven't got it, monsieur, I swear by Allah. They changed the lock.'

'Is there anyone there now?'

'No. He left at mid-day. He had the key. You won't . . . .?'

It needed the weight of their two bodies, hurled at the stout door simultaneously, to break the lock. They staggered forward into the room, followed by the caretaker, protesting vociferously.

It was long and narrow. Opposite the door was a loosely shuttered window and beneath it a small table, pushed against the sill. The only light came from the open door until Chaker found the switch. The naked bulb shone palely on some chairs, an iron bed, and cupboards, but otherwise the room was bare, except for the strange collection of objects on the table. There were no inscriptions to be seen. The youth had come through the door and was staring around as if mesmerised.

The telephone handset appeared to be normal, but from under it two wires ran to a metal box, connected to a dry battery, and thence to a home-made piece of electronic equipment, which included a tape-deck, with a recording cassette in position. There seemed to be no controls but a simple on-off switch, and no loudspeaker. At the other end of the table was a small Philips tape-recorder and a stack of cassettes.

Suddenly, as they watched, they heard a loud click, and the spools of the tape deck began to revolve silently. The caretaker cowered back against the wall, staring at the little machine, fascinated.

Chaker snatched up one of the spare cassettes and waited, holding it poised above the tape deck. After about ten seconds the metal box clicked again, and the spools stopped turning. Chaker quickly replaced the used cassette with a fresh one and took it over to the Philips at the other end of the table. He ran the tape backwards until it came to the beginning of the recorded messages, then pressed the 'Start' button forward.

When the little loudspeaker in the Philips began to speak it reproduced a series of telephone messages, mostly in Arabic but three in French. Each began with the name of a revolutionary hero.

'Ici Ben Barka. Zero-six-thirty-two hours. Message received. I have contacted all members of my student group and armed them as instructed. I shall be at home from twenty-two hundred hours for further orders.' *'Ici*

Che. Zero-eight-zero-five hours. Arms distributed. My group will activate the Science Faculty students. We hope for four hundred. I am prepared for contact tonight as usual.' *'Ici Giap.* Eleven-thirty-five hours. The Arts Faculty groups have been activated and arms distributed. I propose to initiate action against the pigs on the south side and draw the crowd into the Place du Gouvernement as soon as its state of feeling allows. If you agree, tell other leaders to rally around my groups. I shall be available at home between nineteen and twenty-two hundred hours. *Victoire!'*

The caretaker tried to run away, but Craig caught and held him. The metal box had again switched on the apparatus, and the new cassette was recording a message. 'What did the Arabic ones say?' he asked. 'Same sort of thing? All preparations for turning the demonstration tomorrow into a riot?'

'Les salauds!' Chaker ground his teeth. 'Yes. It's fiendishly clever, because you can imagine what mood the police are going to be in, after what happened this morning.' He frowned. 'Why didn't the man who left here at mid-day take the cassette with him? All the messages we've heard were timed earlier than that, except the last two. And this one, of course,' he added, as the machine clicked off.

'I suppose he played it through and took notes,' suggested Craig. 'What are you going to do now?'

148

Chaker picked up the telephone. 'Get a squad of men here, to keep this man and his mother incommunicado and seize the person who comes to collect the cassette. And make him talk,' he added grimly.

While he dialled Craig listened for a click from the metal box, but it was silent. It only operated on incoming calls. He reached across the table to open the shutters wider, but saw something outside and dropped his hand, signalling to Chaker to ring off. He pointed to the window. Silently, they flattened themselves against the walls, one on either side of the table, Craig holding his hand over the caretaker's mouth.

There was a slight scuffling noise from outside. Then the shutters were pushed inwards, so that they swung round at right angles, blocking the men's view of the window. But they could see a thin bare arm stretch out and lift the cassette from its place on the tape-deck, replacing it with a fresh one from the pile. At this moment Chaker pounced.

He jumped out from behind the shutter and grabbed the bare arm, but the table was in his way, and something more. The window was unglazed, but securely barred. The thin arm squirmed out of his grasp and was withdrawn. For a moment the scared face of a child stared at them through the bars, then it disappeared, and when the table was pushed aside they could see nothing but a small gondoura and a pair of legs scampering away across the flattened dome of a roof-top a few feet below the window. The cassette lay on the table where the boy had dropped it. Chaker swore long and fluently.

As in many parts of the Medina, the domed roof-tops were continuous and the boy was thirty yards away, darting from one to another, before he disappeared behind a water tank. He did not re-appear.

Craig said, 'Even if you'd caught him—and what could you do, with the bars in the way— you wouldn't have found out much. He probably comes to change the cassettes, every few hours, and takes them to a man he doesn't know, sitting in a café that's different every time. They know their technique these people, and I must hand it to them. The trick was well worked out. That boy couldn't even know who was here earlier. In any case, they've been warned. I suppose they'll call off the demonstration. What is it exactly? You said—' He realised that the caretaker was listening.

'We know the students have planned to hold one tomorrow, but all our information is that it'll be peaceful. Otherwise it wouldn't be allowed. But it is on a piece of waste ground in front of the University, and they won't interfere with the traffic. Or that's what we thought.' He frowned. 'These messages tell a different tale. The police'll have to be prepared for trouble, although as you say the

150

insurgents may call off their activists, after that little devil tells his story.'

'If he does.'

'What? You mean, he may be too scared to report? It's possible. We shall see if the messages coming in here are cut off. If not, then the police will be ready. Or ban the demonstration, of course. I'll get all calls to this number traced, but they'll probably be from public telephones. Oh well, I've an appointment to see the General and the C. of P. Not one I'm looking forward to.' He rang his office.

Craig watched his friend's face change as he listened to a long message from Captain Tibaoui at the other end. He put down the receiver and scratched his head.

'That's odd,' he said slowly, picking up the two used cassettes, putting a new one in place.

'What's odd? Doesn't the General want to see you?'

'He certainly does, and I'd better go and get it over. But after that he wants me to drive to the temple site and find out why the paras could discover nothing.'

'But you said they met gunfire. At least, the police did, earlier.'

'So they did. But when the paras went in with their mine detectors, although nobody had been seen to leave the place, they were unopposed, except for a couple of mines, which they spotted and dug up. They walked straight into the caverns. No booby-traps. No insurgents.'

'And no arms either?'

'No. The paras think it's a great bore. Will you come? I'll get some sandwiches made for you while I see my boss.'

'Try and stop me.'

*   *   *

An hour later, shortly after four o'clock, they stood under the open archways of the temple, listening to the paratroop major who had led the attack. He was contemptuous. 'The flics must have let them get away,' he concluded. 'There wasn't even a shot when we went in.'

'Did you search the inner chamber?'

'Of course we did—threw a grenade in first, just in case they were hiding—but nothing, except a bad smell. See for yourselves.'

The hurdle that had been in front of the inner chamber was lying on the stone floor. The major gave them a powerful torch and stayed outside, understandably. The blast of the grenade had blown scraps of bone and ash everywhere, and the mixed stench of explosive and charred bone was daunting.

Craig exclaimed. The shape of the pile of empty crates against the rear wall was somehow different from when he'd last seen it. He took the torch and ran forward, holding his handkerchief over his nose. At one side of the

152

pile a crate stood upright. Behind it was a narrow space through which a man could have crawled. Chaker helped him to drag away the crates and expose the wide dark orifice behind, leading into the massive foundations of the temple. They called.

The major swore. He ordered them back and summoned a corporal and another of his men, with automatic rifles at the ready, to go into the tunnel, and went ahead of them, a torch in one hand and a revolver in the other. 'I'm sorry,' he shouted back to Chaker, 'but it's my job and I don't want you to come unless it's clear.'

Craig took his cigarette lighter and bent down to look at the floor where the crates had stood. He pointed to the marks of heavy wheels. Then they both ran outside and breathed in lungfuls of fresh air.

'If they hadn't used that grenade,' said Chaker, 'they'd have seen the tracks, but the blast covered them up effectively. Just like the paras.' He looked at Craig. 'Wherever the rebels have gone, through that tunnel, they've got more than a hour's start. I suppose it connects with another ruin, and they popped up to the surface and got away.'

'But the trolleys? For that's what I suppose they were.'

'Yes, you're right. Why take them, too?'

The paratroop corporal came out of the entrance, saluted Chaker, and said, 'The major

153

suggests you might like to go in now, *mon Commandant.* I've got to get two more men.' He handed over his torch.

They went down on hands and knees and crawled in. It was evident that the last insurgent to go had roughly stacked the crates to hide the entrance, and as he squeezed through the gap he had drawn one crate after him and lodged it upright in the opening.

After passing through the thickness of the wall they found a short descent, earth-floored, to a place where building blocks had been set aside to make a further opening. On the other side they could stand at full height. It was a passage with stone walls and wide enough for two men to walk abreast. It stretched in both directions, but a few yards to the right was completely blocked. Leftwards, it sloped gently downwards, with a smooth stone floor. A long way ahead they could see a flickering light. Then came the flash of torches behind them, and the three paras passed by and ran forward. Craig and Chaker followed.

It was nearly ten minutes before they joined the silent group of men creeping along on both sides of the smooth passage towards the wooden door that closed it from floor to ceiling.

The major played his torch on the door. It was made of cedar boards and set in a concrete frame. Hardly Carthaginian. He turned the handle, and threw his weight at the wood, but to no effect. He unslung his carbine, waved his men back and fired a burst at the join between two boards near the lock. Then again and again, with smoke swirling round the waiting men, until he had cut out a square of wood. Daylight shone through the gap, but the smoke concealed all detail.

Craig touched his arm. 'It could be booby-trapped.'

'We've got to risk something,' he growled, thrust his arm through the gap and wrenched away the lock. The door swung open, and the paras ran out, disciplined, each man ready to fire.

It was a peaceful scene that met their eyes. The beach sloped down to the ripples of a placid sea. The heavy marks of the trolley wheels showed in the shingle, leading straight down to the water. They were in a little cove, hedged in by low cliffs. Nobody to see, and no boat. There were a few fishing vessels far out towards the horizon, but that was all. Even the trolleys had disappeared.

Craig turned to look at the broken door. On it appeared, in old, flaking paint, *'Fac . . . d'archéo . . . Université de . . .'*, and a date, 1961.

* * *

As they drove back to the city Chaker said, 'There've been literally hundreds of excavations

155

around Carthage, and it's impossible to keep track of them all. Most schemes run out of money at some time or other, simply because there's so much to be done. I suppose Mahmoud knew about the old Punic passage that ran from the beach to the temples, and found he could cut his way down into it. Then, of course, it was as you said just now. The store under the temple of Tanit was stocked from the sea, and they used the cargoes of bones and ashes to transfer the crates to the farmhouse, which was isolated and easy of access. I'd be glad to know where the arms came from originally, from down the coast—or somewhere abroad. *Sacré bleu!* What's that?'

The car was passing through a busy street, with high apartment buildings on one side. A little cloud of white papers was drifting downwards on to the throng below. He stopped the car and told the driver to collect some of the leaflets. He translated one for Craig's benefit: STUDENTS UNITE! GREAT PEACEFUL DEMONSTRATION TOMORROW AT NINE O'CLOCK. PLACE DE LA KASBAH. CLOSE YOUR RANKS. LONG LIVE THE RIGHTS OF ALL STUDENTS. LONG LIVE OUR COUNTRY. They were all the same.

'Peaceful demonstration!' mutttered Chaker bitterly. 'With guns under their shirts.'

'But ninety per cent will turn up with nothing but their bare hands,' said Craig. 'And it's they who'll suffer, while the real instigators run for refuge in Yasmin Belcadi's Mercedes. It makes me sick.'

'It'll make the Chief of Police more than sick. After what's happened today he won't be in a mood to treat them with kid gloves.'

'And that's just what the insurgents want, Taieb. They *want* the police to over-react. That's what the whole thing's planned for. It's an essential part of the campaign, to make the people hate the forces of order. And to get a bad image abroad for your Government.'

'But do you imagine,' said Chaker soberly, 'that after hearing what's on those tapes he's going to order his men to stand still and be fired at? Those messages said the students are going to be armed, and if they've got guns they'll use them.'

'But can we believe the messages?'

Chaker turned sharply in his seat. 'What d'you mean?'

'It could all have been a plant, to make the police think there's going to be an armed riot—and react accordingly.'

'You mean Janus is double-crossing us?'

'She hasn't given you much, has she?'

'Nonsense, Peter. She gave us that telephone number. It led us to an insurgent communications centre. That isn't a bluff.'

'I suppose not. But I find it hard to believe what she told us is all she knows.'

'In the name of Allah, why?'

'Look at what she said. She didn't know

157

Mahmoud by name—it was Cleo who got that from the young man she interviewed. Janus said he was just the leader of her cell, and that their job was to watch internal security and so on. But it was Mahmoud who used that room, received the messages and gave the instructions. And he's more than that, even. He is, or was, the organiser for the importation and distribution of arms. It doesn't sound like a humble cell-leader. And *why* did she tell you that telephone number? She's intelligent. She must have known you'd trace it, and then, as soon as the insurgents found out that you'd been investigating that room in the museum, it'd blow her involvement with you sky high. Didn't she point that out?'

'You're getting too theoretical, Peter. No, she didn't, but she presumably depended on me to protect her.' He stopped, frowning. 'But you're right in one thing. I must warn her to stay at home. If she goes to that rendezvous tomorrow in her car she'll be a sitting duck for anyone in the movement who concludes she's been a traitor to their precious cause.'

'What are you going to do now?'

'Wait. See whether more messages have gone to that patent recording machine. If they've stopped it'll mean the boy has talked and that line of communication is blown. Then I'll try and trace the boat that presumably took off the men and arms from the beach. We know the approximate time, and someone may

158

have seen it. And you?'

'I'm going to see Miss Hamilton and try and keep her out of mischief. I won't have her going to that demonstration tomorrow.'

'Becoming a bit dictatorial, aren't you?' said Chaker, smiling.

'It's all in the interests of law and order. Where she goes, there's trouble.'

'That,' said Chaker, 'is the oldest reason I've ever heard for following the heels of an attractive woman. And anyway, it's a bit unfair. It isn't she who causes the trouble—except in your vulnerable old heart.' He met Craig's glare with a friendly laugh. 'I'm just guessing, Peter. But I'm a good guesser as a rule. Go and enjoy yourself, while I embark on another sleepless night.'

*   *   *

Cleo's spirits were rising. She had filed two eye-catching stories during the afternoon and evening, and after an excellent dinner at the Colombo the horror of the scenes she had witnessed at the farmhouse was comfortably dimmed. She felt Craig's eyes on her, and knew that her clinging dress gave them something interesting to look at.

But, as usual, they were bickering.

'Of course I must see it,' she said scornfully. 'From what you say it's going to be front-page stuff.'

159

'It may well turn out to be a shambles,' said Craig seriously, and put his hand over hers—carefully placed on the table so that he would do just that. 'I can't tell you how I know this, but it's true. The insurgents are arming some of the students, and they're going to provoke the police to over-reaction.'

'And what does "over-reaction" mean, in copper's speak?'

'Overstep permitted limits in riot control.'

'What that means, presumably, is that they'll try to make the police clobber them?'

'Yes. And if it's done cleverly they'll succeed. Look, darling, I gave you a lot of background stuff for that second story, didn't I? In fact I had to get Chaker's permission specially. But I wanted you to understand, and bring out in your piece, the seriousness of the whole conspiracy. And you did, very neatly. Now listen. I'll do the same tomorrow—give you a factual account of just what happens when the demonstration goes out of hand. So you'll have your story. But just keep out of the way, right off the streets in the centre of the city. That's all I ask.'

'But Peter, dear, that isn't what our public wants, just a factual account. They want to know what it was like to be there, in the middle of the action, and the sounds and smells and individual stories, and everything. And if you're going to see it, why shouldn't I?'

'Oh for Christ's sake! Because I can look

after myself in a scrap, and you can't. You're only pint size, anyway.'

'Then come and look after me.' She saw the hesitation in his face. 'I suppose you think I'd be just an encumbrance?'

'No. Not if you do exactly as I tell you.'

'Oh all right.' She glanced at her watch. 'Look at the time. I've got to go.'

He called the waiter. 'We're both going. We'll have a look at the belly-dancers at that joint behind the hotel, and then—'

'Peter, I can't. I meant to tell you, but you see, Jacques is giving a drinks party at the Press Club at ten o'clock—it must have started—and he won't forgive me if I'm not there. We're the only two who saw the fight, and he's very proud of being blown up, and his broken arm. If I don't back him up, no one will believe us.'

'Oh hell! I was thinking . . . Meet me later somewhere.'

She leaned forward and kissed him swiftly. '*No*, darling. Not tonight, when I'll be full of the Press Club's drinks. They're knock-outs. We—we shouldn't be in too much of a hurry, you know.'

'When you say that, just try not to look so adorable will you? You put a man under strain.'

CHAPTER TEN

They were breakfasting together in the dining-room of the Tunisia Palace. 'Look at us,' said Cleo brightly, 'sharing coffee and brioches like two old married people.'

'Very old,' commented Craig, sourly, 'the kind that sleep in separate beds. What was your party like, anyway—a drunken orgy?'

'It was quite good fun, actually—but a bit childish, as these things always are. There were a lot of foreign press people, who flew in yesterday evening after the news of the farmhouse affair broke, and I met some friends. They're all going to the demo.' She glanced at her wrist. 'Balloon goes up in half an hour.'

'What was the childish part?'

'Oh—well, it was very silly, but you'll probably hear all about it. One of the Tunisian cartoonists had made an enormous charcoal drawing that was hung in the bar. It showed Jacques being blown into the air, clutching his typewriter.'

'And you?'

She bit her lip. 'If you must know, it showed me—very sexy peering out from behind a cow.' She saw Craig's lips twitching, and changed the subject. 'Have you seen the bit about *you* in *Le Tunisien*?'

'About me? Hell's bells! No, I have not. Where is it?'

She produced the newspaper, with a short paragraph outlined in ink.

'UNWANTED ADVICE FROM THE FOREIGN OFFICE:

'Monsieur Pierre Craig, one of the experts who advise Her Britannic Majesty's Foreign Office in police matters, was also present—in a safe position at the rear of the action—when our own police failed so signally to take proper precautions and were defeated, with grave loss of life, at the Farmhouse of Death.

'Monsieur Craig is staying in Tunis at the invitation of our Government, who have at last realised that they are in need of advice in the enforcement of law and order.

'If it was Monsieur Craig's wise counsel that led to the failure of a simple police operation, then we say "Go home, Mister, before you waste the lives of more of our young men."

'See our leading article.'

Cleo watched anxiously as he read it through, his face colouring slightly. He said nothing, but turned to the leader, signed by Ahmed Belcadi. The last paragraph again referred briefly to Craig and added:

'Tunisians, we do not require outside help to solve our problems of law and order. We need a firm stand by the Minister of Home Affairs, and stern but just action by the forces of security. Let us at least see that the

163

demonstration which the authorities—unwisely, in our view—are allowing to take place today at nine o'clock in the Place de la Kasha is carried out peacefully.

'For that is what the faceless men who are the organisers have said it will be—*peaceful*. If there is violence, let those secret revolutionaries and wild-talking, pot-smoking hippies who disgrace our universities learn that the hand of the law can be heavy.'

Craig put down the paper and sipped his coffee, thoughtfully. 'If Belcadi thinks this stuff is going to make the average student stay at home, to keep out of trouble, he's wrong. And of course, there'll be hundreds of tourists out to see the fun.' He looked across at Cleo. 'I'd give a lot for a pair of handcuffs,' he said ruefully, 'but I suppose I can always pull you back by your hair.'

* * *

The area where the Kasbah, the ancient citadel of Tunis, stood until the French authorities razed it to the ground twenty years ago, is mostly waste land, with a large parking space opposite the great mosque and the modern Ministry of Information and Cultural Affairs, which skirts the southern side of the area. Eastwards lies the Place du Gouvernement, through which Craig and Chaker had passed the previous day on their way to the Medina and the museum.

The organisers of the demonstration had chosen their ground well. There was plenty of room on the waste land, and the parking space, cleared of cars by the police, provided more. The University behind the Kasbahh site was very close, and so was the Place du Gouvernement, lined with ministries. There was no danger that what happened would be unobserved by the country's leaders.

Cleo had shown some sense, admitted Craig. She had persuaded a contact in the Ministry of Information to allow her to stand at one of the windows overlooking the parking place, at least for the first part of the demonstration. Then she planned to go down into the streets and interview some of those who had taken part. She had a small tape recorder in the pocket of her dust coat.

They looked down, across the road, past a line of mounted police, at a large group of students carrying an Arts Faculty banner who were assembling on the near side of the parking lot. The south side. Craig started. If the telephone message from 'Giap' could be believed this was where the action against 'the pigs' would be initiated.

A loudspeaker van had been manoeuvred on to the raised ground beyond, which covered some of the ruins of the Kasbah, and beside it was a platform surrounded by Tunisian flags and slogans painted on boards carried by students. In all parts of the area groups of young men and women were collecting, shouting at the police who hemmed them in. But it was good-humoured chaff, and when the first of the speakers took his place on the platform they quietened down.

The speeches were in Arabic, but the official who was with them gave Cleo and Craig the gist. It was mostly about student grievances, and one dealt with canteen meals, illustrated by brandishing giant sausages that burst and spewed out sawdust. Others demanded participation in the election of professors, and student rule. Some speakers pointed scornfully at the ministries across the road, and one stamped his feet, reminding his hearers that the place where he stood had been the centre of resistance against the French.

Then a young man stepped on to the platform. He had long hair and a beard, and seemed to be well known. He held up, one after the other, caricatures of the Rector and some of the professors and made remarks which must have been both lewd and funny, from the crowd's reactions. As he finished with each cartoon he spat on it and skimmed it towards the watchful ranks of police. A squad of police, batons in their hands, advanced towards the platform. He had obviously gone too far.

He snatched up one of the national flags

and draped it round his body, calling on his friends for help. The mounted police on the south side of the parking lot surged forward through the running men and women. Behind him, among the Arts students, Craig saw the sudden flare of a paper torch. He thought it was to be used against the rumps of the horses, but instead it was passed rapidly from hand to hand. The next moment there was a series of loud cracks, and the horses began to rear and buck.

'What is it?' cried Cleo. 'I can't see.'

'Fire-crackers. And the next thing will be glass marbles. There they go.' They could see the marbles shining in the air as they were thrown to fall in front of the horses' feet. Two fell down, and the crowd roared with laughter. The cracking increased as more fire-works were ignited, and the horses broke ranks, struggling against the bit and turning away from the devilish noises coming from under their bellies. The Arts Faculty students broke through the cordon behind them and tried to lead a rush towards the Place du Gouvernement, but the police drove them back.

In the middle of the open space, fast being reduced by wildly excited groups of students, the police squad had captured the man who had last spoken. As they led him away, there was the sound of a shot and one of the escorting policemen fell, with blood streaming

167

from his face. The sergeant drew his revolver, aimed at the man he thought had fired, and shot him through the arm. It was a tourist.

A tall man with a great red beard pulled a gun from his pocket, and fired deliberately at the back of a policeman who was struggling to control his horse. From the corner of his eye Craig saw him drop from the saddle, but he was watching red-beard, who was already elbowing his way back through the crowd. On the way, the beard vanished, and the man who issued from the crowd was clean-shaven.

From the courtyard of the police building in the Boulevard Bab Benat, where they had been held in reserve, the troop carriers of armed police and riot control vehicles came swinging out into the street, their sirens wailing, followed by a line of Black Marias. The police deployed, running, with their rifles held diagonally across their chests, and, forming a long line, pushed the demonstrators back across the parking space. The students resisted, jostling around them and trying to snatch their guns away. Shots were fired into the air and they gave way, some with blood flowing down their faces from contact with swinging gun butts. The carriers and prison vans formed a hollow square in the centre of the parking space, from which the riot squads issued forth to identify the activists and bring them back to be bundled into the vans.

There was a loud *crack* of a grenade, and a

burst of smoke and flame rose from one of the troop carriers. From parts of the crowd there were more explosions, and the demonstrators became desperate to get away. The noise was indescribable, and orders shouted by police officers, using their megaphones, only reached the men nearest. There were more bangs in different parts of the crowd, and smoke drifted over the heads of the students.

The first of the police vans, full of shouting prisoners, pushed its way out through the crowd, led by a squad of armed men who used their gun butts to hack their way.

'The brutes!' cried Cleo passionately. 'Look at the way they're bashing those boys.'

Craig was coldly furious. 'For God's sake, what d'you expect? They've seen their own comrades shot down and blown up and savaged by ten times their number. They're behaving much better than those boys have any right to expect. They haven't even used tear gas.' He seized her arm. 'Look there.'

The police in the street beneath them had opened a gap in their ranks, through which the crowd was streaming, knocking each other down and stumbling over the bodies. They were screaming and shouting defiance—but escaping from the menace and chaos of the interior of the mêlée. Some were shouting '*Le Tunisien*', and Craig saw a police officer pull out his radio and speak into it urgently.

'This is all over,' he said soberly. 'If you

must see action at ground level we'll go and look at what's happening at the newspaper office.'

They found his car and had to make a long detour to reach the Belcadi building on the other side of the Medina. They were passing down a one-way street near the Square Habib Thameur when Craig swore and braked to a stop. Two men in police uniform stood in the street, signalling to the traffic to halt. They had machine-pistols slung over their shoulders. Cars behind Craig formed a queue, hooting angrily.

One of the armed men came up to the car. *'Deux minutes, monsieur, s'il vous plaît.'* He pointed to a building twenty yards ahead, which bore a swing-sign reading 'Banque de Crédit.' There was a van parked in front of it.

There was a sudden rattle of shots from the bank and three men ran out, two of them carrying canvas bags, the third backwards, with his machine-pistol firing. Then he turned and scrambled into the van behind the other two.

The men in police uniform were also backing towards the van. Suddenly, their guns were pointing menacingly at the line of parked cars.

'Do something,' urged Cleo.

'Not me,' said Craig grimly. 'They've got fifty rounds in their magazines. They'd riddle us.' The men jumped into the open back of the van, which swung into the middle of the empty

170

street and roared off.

Craig gunned the engine and let in the clutch, racing after the van, whose rear doors were still open. He saw men moving inside it, pulling something forward, a roll of wire. Barbed wire.

It fell on to the roadway, bouncing and loosening out into a writhing coil that covered half the width of the street and was still lengthening. Craig slammed on his brakes and skidded to a halt with the front tyres almost touching the wire. He leapt out and dragged it out of the way, while the cars from behind drove past, horns blasting at him as if he were responsible.

He got back into the car, swearing, and followed. 'It's the classic pattern,' he told Cleo bitterly. 'They've done their homework. Lured away half the police force to deal with that demo, and meanwhile they've probably done half a dozen raids to get money and arms.'

'But how many insurgents are there? There must have been hundreds on the Kasbah site, so how many more have they got?'

'There weren't more than about a dozen in the demo, I should think.'

'Nonsense. I *saw* that man shoot the policeman in the back, and it must have happened in lots of other places.'

'We'll see, but I'd be surprised if more than three or four police were actually injured by gunfire. Just enough to make them get tough—and as I told you they kept their heads admirably on the whole. In many countries they'd have fired at the crowd, especially after the bomb thrown into the troop carrier.'

'It wasn't just one bomb. There were bangs and smoke everywhere.'

'Most of them were fire-crackers. They did the real damage. Besides scaring the horses they got the police edgy and threw the demonstrators into panic. With all that row going on it was impossible to tell which bang came from a bomb.' He glanced at Cleo. 'This is off-record. The cleverest thing the insurgents did was to warn the police that some of the demonstrators would be armed.'

'But how?'

'By a neat bit of what the Russians call *disinformytsiya*.' He was turning into the Avenue Bourguiba as he spoke. Ahead, they could see a line of steel-helmeted police, rifles across their chests, standing across the entrance to the side-street in which was the towering Belcadi building. Facing them was a big crowd of jeering students. He stopped the car thirty yards away and turned to Cleo.

'Now just watch, and see how a crowd can be provoked into action. Those students will do nothing but taunt, unless they've thought of bringing something to throw. But ten to one they haven't, because they know what to expect—I'll give them that much sense—if they're arrested with brickbats in their pockets.

Now, if I'm right *someone*—or perhaps two or three people, you don't need more—will start the action. And then run away.' He peered forward through the windscreen. 'If one comes this way I'm going to jump him, so try and spot one.'

She pulled his arm. 'Not if he's got a gun.'

'This is small stuff. They don't need guns.'

More students were streaming down the avenue from the gate of the Medina, into which they had escaped from the demonstration half a mile away, on the other side. They were assembling under the trees in the middle of the avenue, opposite the line of armed men. The morning traffic was passing by Craig's car and on between the line of police and the waiting throng of students.

The rush of cars stopped as the signal lights behind went red. A bunch of demonstrators took the opportunity and ran out into the empty traffic lanes, displaying a banner with the words *'A bas Belcadi, ami des agents-cochons!'* The Arabic inscription was underneath.

Two foreign journalists with cameras ran to kneel in the road and take photographs. The lights changed behind Craig's car and the students ran back to the shelter of the trees. But they left on the tarmac what looked like a dozen milk bottles coloured green, that rolled slowly, heavily, and burst open under the wheels of the advancing cars before the drivers

173

could stop them.

What happened then was spectacular. The plastic bottles squirted out jets of motor oil, that spread over the road surface. Cars swung sideways and crashed into the trees or mounted the pavement, forcing the police to jump for safety. Others skidded to a stop and more cars crashed into them, smashing in sides and puncturing petrol tanks. Within seconds there was a solid jam of vehicles unable to move and blocking the roadway from side to side. A man ran out from under the trees, threw something into the middle of the obstruction, then ran off towards the Bad el Bahar. There was a loud *phut-t*, and flame shot into the air.

The demonstrators fled, dodging between the cars moving on the other side of the boulevard. Some had evidently hoped the police barring the entrance to the side-road would break ranks, and tried to get through. The line held, and they were thrust back. One of the vehicles was now burning fiercely, and the leaves of the trees above were shrivelling and catching fire. By the time the people in the other crashed cars had run for safety a petrol tank exploded.

A troop carrier of armed police bumped its way between the trees in the middle of the avenue, and Craig heard the wailing siren of a fire engine. A smell of burning rubber was carried into the car.

'I've had enough,' said Cleo shakily. 'Let's get out of here. I've got to get to the Press Club.'

'And file your story, I suppose.'

She turned to look at Craig, startled by the white-hot fury in his voice. 'Don't take it out on me, Peter. I've seen what you brought me to see, and I'll give the police their due.'

'I know you will. I'm sorry. I can't stand being in a situation like this and able to do nothing but talk, talk. We'll have to go on foot.' Other cars had blocked the roadway behind them, those nearest the signal lights trying to back out. A traffic policeman was trying to restore order. 'It isn't far for you. I'll take the keys to the Hertz agency and ask them to send someone to drive the car away, when they can. I'll pick you up at the Press Club at one, O.K.?'

'Thanks. But if I can't get a stint on the London teleprinter I'll have to wait till I can. We can lunch there. Where are you going?'

'To see Chaker.'

*   *   *

It was half-past eleven when Craig reached the Ministry, and he had only been with Chaker a few minutes when a message came from the General. He would like to see them both, at once.

'Before I hear your accounts of what has

175

been happening this morning,' said General Farhat, 'I must tell you that there has been a new development, and one with wide repercussions. Yasmin Belcadi—your agent Janus, Chaker—is in the hands of the insurgents, who say they will only set her free on payment of a quarter of a million dinars and the release of those arrested at the Kasbah site. Otherwise they threaten her life. When was your last contact with her, Major?'

'At five o'clock yesterday afternoon, *mon Général*, by telephone. I warned her that she might be compromised, because we had followed up the lead she had given us and discovered the communications room. She took it very calmly and in fact insisted, against my advice, on obeying her orders and driving to the rendezvous this morning. She said if anyone accused her of treachery she'd bluff her way out. But she didn't turn up there. We had a man patrolling the Bab-Benat from half-past eight onwards, and there was no sign of her.'

'H'm. That's about the time she left home. They must have picked her up on the way somehow. Belcadi is of course hurling thunderbolts in all directions, not least at me.' He smiled, then turned to Craig with concern on his handsome face. 'That reminds me, Mr Craig. That article in his newspaper was inspired by Belcadi himself. I hope I needn't tell you that I found it quite as offensive and unjust as you must have done.'

'Thank you, sir.'

'Right. Now let me hear what you've both been doing.'

When they had finished he sat silent for a while. Then he said slowly, 'I'm going to sum up what we know, and ask some questions.' He lit a cigarette, and began briskly.

'First, the insurgents have gone over to the offensive. It may be that the farmhouse incident forced them to bring their plans forward, or perhaps it is just a coincidence that they should come out into the open today. It doesn't matter. The point is that we are faced with a war of harassment, and we still don't know why. The note from Yasmin Belcadi's captors is signed "The People's Democratic Army", but that means nothing.'

'Che Guevara wrote,' put in Craig, 'that it wasn't necessary to wait for a revolutionary situation before starting an insurrection. The insurrection itself could produce it.'

'So he did. Perhaps that's what they're hoping for. They're certainly going about it cunningly and efficiently, with a very small deployment of activists. You said just now, Mr Craig, that a handful of professionals could have instigated the riot. You meant that? It could have been just a few men?'

'Yes, *mon Général*. With two dogs you can direct a flock of sheep. With two thousand sheep you can stop a squadron of cavalry.'

'Exactly. You see, while it was going on there were several attacks on banks and arms depots carried out here and in Sfax. They were all, I'm afraid, successful. Nevertheless, where the police have been engaged they have stood up well to provocation. They didn't fire at the demonstrators, as I suppose the insurgents hoped, and they didn't allow the rioters to get through to the Belcadi building, which they had presumably intended to set on fire. But if this kind of thing happens frequently we shall have to use troops. Belcadi is pressing the President to declare a state of emergency and introduce martial law.' He looked a question at Chaker.

'It's much too early, *mon Général*. At this stage it'd be playing into the hands of the insurgents. How could you convince people here and abroad that the situation already requires military tribunals and detention without trial?'

'I agree. You can't, and it's a good argument against declaring an emergency. We cannot afford to lose the support of the people.

'Next thing. What kind of offensive can we expect? I said a war of harassment, and I would judge that the main thrust will be psychological, through sympathisers and fellow-travellers in the mass media, the trade unions and the opposition parties. And also, of course, in liberal intellectual circles abroad. But to get the sympathisers active on their side they'll work hard to "stretch" the security forces and throw a bad light on the Government by actions such as those of yesterday and today, and by producing a state of general chaos. There will be random bombing and industrial sabotage, and intimidation to get the people edgy and frightened of taking the Government side. This means more urban guerrilla action. But what about the provinces?'

'I think,' said Chaker, 'that there's too little cover for open action in the countryside. They know we've got helicopters, paratroopers and armoured cars ready to snuff out any flame of open insurrection in the provinces. I feel they'll stick to Tunis and the bigger towns like Sfax and Kairouan.'

'Mr Craig?'

'I agree.'

'Right. Third question. Mr Craig, you were with Major Chaker when those messages were telephoned in to the communications centre. They gave the impression—did they not?—that there would be large numbers of student agitators supplied with arms for use in the demonstration?'

'Yes, *mon Général.*'

'Then why,' said the General, 'have the police found no arms at all on the two hundred or more students they have detained? Two automatics were found lying on the ground, as if thrown away. But on the persons of the prisoners *nothing,* except for these.' With a look of strong dislike he pulled out of a drawer half a dozen glass marbles and some firecrackers. (He had been a cavalry officer before joining the General Staff.)

There was a pause. Chaker said, 'I don't know, *mon Général.* Mr Craig has a theory . . .' The General turned to Craig.

'It may be, sir, that we were deliberately misled. In other words, we were given that telephone number on purpose, so that we should find the room in the museum and read the messages.'

'You mean, so that the police would be forewarned to expect armed violence and would therefore be more likely to suppress the demonstration harshly as soon as it showed signs of getting out of hand.' He leaned back in his chair, stroking his grey hair. 'It's not as far-fetched as it sounds,' he admitted. 'Luckily, as I said, the police kept their heads admirably. That communications room, I suppose, had become expendable. From now on the rebels will be in communication with their agents by radio. They can't wait while little boys run across rooftops. I think, Major, Mr Craig is right. It fits. It was a move to provoke the police into violent reprisals. They wanted something like the Kent State affair, or your Bloody Sunday in Northern Ireland. Something to develop in anti-Government propaganda everywhere. They'll still do it, of course, making the most of the wounded and blaming all the firing on the police. But where does that leave us with Mademoiselle Belcadi, or Janus as you call her, and her curious motivations? Major Chaker?'

'She may have double-crossed us, *mon Général,* but I don't think so. It's more likely that they already knew yesterday that she was in touch with us, and fed her the telephone number, knowing she would pass it on to us. They made her into an unconscious triple agent.'

'How very complicated. But it may well be true. Now, my final point. What are our counter-measures? You have already worked out a programme, Chaker, covering what can be done to protect what we may expect to be insurgent targets. But you drafted it when we thought the insurgency would remain clandestine for a bit longer. I shall be discussing further measures with the Chief of Police and the Defence Chief of Staff, but something Mr Craig said in that paper you showed me sticks in my mind. Troops and armed policy won't prevent surprise attacks if they are intelligently planned and ruthlessly carried out. The only effective way of stopping this insurrection, before it causes great damage to our country, is to root out the insurgent nucleus, the faceless men, as Belcadi called them. We know one of them, Mahmoud, and an intensive search is being made for him.

His jeep was found this morning, hidden in a wood only two kilometres from the farmhouse. There was a man in it who had died of his wounds. So Mahmoud is on the run, with two others.

'Major Chaker, that will be your job, to find Mahmoud and any other leaders you can identify, and bring them in alive. That is your sole task, and I will relieve you of all other duties. You may have what men and funds you need. You have the intelligence network you set up to investigate whether the insurgency existed, and you will have to convert those agents for offensive operations. The police political branch and Army G.Z will have instructions to give you what other help you need. Mr Craig, any further advice you can give Major Chaker will be very welcome.'

He stood up, and shook hands with both men. 'I wish you good luck, Chaker. You'll need it. You're up against very clever young people. D'you notice how neatly, by this last action, they knock down three birds with one stone?'

'Three, *mon Général*?' Chaker was puzzled. 'They defy the Government, they strike a blow at their main enemy, Ahmed Belcadi, but—'

'They also eliminate his daughter, the traitor in their ranks.'

*　　*　　*

When they returned to Chaker's room Captain Tibaoui was waiting for them, with a sheaf of papers in his hand.

'I've gone through the reports filed by the foreign correspondents,' he said, 'and most of them are reasonably objective, with the exception of the Tass man and some of the other communists, and they're not too bad. In fact, Tass is obviously going to sit on the fence for the time being. But there's a really bad one from Benoit, of all people.'

Chaker explained. 'He's a reporter for a Paris daily, and usually goes out of his way to show goodwill towards our Government. I asked Captain Tibaoui to get hold of the transcripts because you said the insurgents would try to influence world opinion through the press. But Benoit? I don't believe it.' He took the paper from Tibaoui's hand, and read it, with Craig looking over his shoulder.

It was a clever piece of bright reportage, covering the events of the morning and harking back to the failure of the police to arrest the insurgents at the farmhouse. They were ridiculed for their 'ineptitude' and condemned for reckless use of fire-arms and general brutality. By implication the demonstrators, anxious to hold a peaceful meeting, had been set on by the police and grossly mishandled. The grounds for the student protests were given in some detail, all very unflattering for the Government.

'What about the British correspondents?' asked Craig.

'Some criticism of the police, but not bad,' said Tibaoui. 'Let me see—Reynolds, Troubridge, Hamilton —'

'What was her report like?'

'Very objective. One of the best.'

'Well done, Peter,' remarked Chaker, smiling, and then added, more soberly, 'I don't like this Benoit story. I wonder if they've got at him. They might, because—*il a des goûts spéciaux*, and if they have found the right little boy—'

'I'll ask Cleo about him.' Craig looked at his watch. 'She's at the Press Club, so I'll see if I can have a word with Benoit.'

'Do that,' said Chaker. 'But don't let him or anyone else know you've seen the texts of their stories, or I'll have a ton of bricks fall on my head.'

CHAPTER ELEVEN

Cleo was standing at the bar of the Club with Robert Troubridge, the *Sunday Times* correspondent, who had flown in from London the previous day. She slipped her arm through Craig's and introduced him.

'Who else d'you want to talk to?' she said, looking around. 'Heh, there's Jacques.' She

184

waved to the Tunisian, and Badra, seeing Craig, made an elaborate pretence of being frightened and trying to run away. Then he came up, smiling, his arm still in a sling. 'Don't blame me, Craig. I'm really sorry about that bit of nonsense in my paper.' He pointed upwards. 'Belcadi's order, I'm afraid.'

'It doesn't matter. I don't think anyone who saw what happened at the Kasbah site could think that your police needed advice from the outside. They behaved very well, in all the circumstances.'

'Maurice Benoit doesn't think so. Where's he got to? Maurice, come over here. Meet an Englishman who thinks our police are wonderful.'

A fleshy figure in a white sharkskin suit joined them. He had a broad, intelligent face with a tiny petulant mouth, and his heavy jowls overhung the black *matelot*. He was introduced, and said mockingly, 'All policemen hang together, don't they? If you think so highly of your Tunisian colleagues, Mr Craig, how do you explain all the student casualties?'

'I'm afraid they were egged on by professional agitators, Monsieur. I saw it happen. Were you there?'

'Of course. It would have been a perfectly peaceful meeting, if those *sacré* policemen hadn't interfered.'

'Didn't you see the fire-crackers?'

'I did not. But I heard a lot of shooting from

police carbines.'

Craig put his hand in his pocket and drew out two glass marbles and an unused fire-cracker. 'Those were taken from a student arrested during the demonstration. If you set those off behind a police horse and scatter the marbles in front of him, you must expect trouble.' The others craned forward to look.

Benoit turned away, and spoke quietly to one of his friends. 'We have only his word that those things were taken from a student.'

But Craig had heard. He reached quickly forward and swung the man round. 'What exactly did you say, Monsieur?'

Benoit saw the look on his face and blanched. 'I didn't see the fire-crackers or the marbles.'

'Then perhaps you weren't there.' Craig saw the sudden fear in the man's eyes. 'Did anyone see you there, Monsieur Benoit?'

'Peter,' cried Cleo, thoroughly alarmed, 'you can't say things like that. Of course he was there.'

'Did you see him? Did anyone see him?'

There was a tense silence. Benoit finished his drink and put the glass on the bar. 'I didn't come here to be insulted,' he muttered, and walked rather unsteadily out of the room.

'I don't know what's got into him,' said Troubridge. 'Of course the students let off the crackers. I saw them being thrown myself. Let me get you a drink, Craig. What'll you have?'

During the afternoon they went to the Embassy, Cleo and Troubridge to ask Thorne to arrange an interview with Ahmed Belcadi, and Craig to report to the Ambassador on the events of the past two days, and add his gloomy forecast of future developments.

'Do they want you to stay on for a bit?' asked His Excellency.

'Yes, sir. Just till the end of the week. After that, I think Chaker's plans will have been worked out, and there'll be nothing I can do.'

'I see. I'm glad they haven't asked for your services in a more concrete form—I mean as official advisor. I didn't like that Belcadi article at all.'

'Neither did I. But there's never been any question of that, sir. I'm just here to be consulted, if they wish to.'

'Yes. But you've seen quite a slice of the action, haven't you? There've been some signs of restiveness by the Americans and the French, who both regard themselves as having special relationships with Tunisia—the States because of all the aid they've pumped in and the French because of the cultural link. And because they're French, I suppose. I rather think the CIA and the SDECE have working liaisons with the Tunisians, and they want to know what you are doing, muscling in.'

Craig smiled. 'I'll be gone in a couple of days, and they'll just have to swallow my presence until then. But the Americans, at least, would agree with every word I've said to Chaker and his boss.'

'Do you think there'll be attacks on foreign embassies?'

'I should doubt it, but they might try to get hold of a senior diplomat for barter purposes. If you like, I'll have a word with Michael. You ought to have some protective device in the Rolls.'

'What does that dreadful bit of jargon mean?'

'Well, something like an ammonia bomb, say, fixed to the underneath of the car, with wires running to places inside where either you or your chauffeur can reach them easily. If ether of you can pull one of the wires it quietly bursts the bomb, which sends a great whoosh of ammonia in all directions. All Lucien has to do is wind up his window fast, and get away.'

'Hm. I somehow don't see old Lucien doing that. He'd be thinking what the gas would do to his precious paintwork. If you decide to fit such a thing, have the trigger where I can get at it, and no one else. Under the armrest, for instance.'

When Craig went downstairs he found Cleo waiting for him. 'How about a nice drive in the country?' she asked. 'In your car. Mine's laid up.'

'Nothing better. Where d'you want to go?'

'To Sidi Bou. Mean old Ahmed Belcadi won't give an interview.'

'I'm not surprised. So—?'

'I've got a Minox in my bag. I thought I'd try to get a picture of his house and write it up for the supplement.'

'O.K. Let's take bathing things, just in case we see a likely beach. I can describe the villa for you.'

*　　　*　　　*

Cleo got her photograph, but only of the splendid doorway in the high wall of the Belcadi villa. They went back to the car and Craig drove on slowly into Sidi Bou Said and they drank iced mint tea, sitting on the steps of the Café des Nattes, looking out over the white roofs at the sea, which, though they didn't know it, was to play such a dominant part in their lives during the next few days.

Those calm, contented moments together were the turning point. The tensions and thrills of the discovery of an insurrection, the plots and counter-plots, the personalities, were all behind them, and so too their role as observers. From now on they would be completely involved, and with other kinds of tension.

And all, as Craig saw the events afterwards, because of one disastrous coincidence, and one outrageous piece of luck. The coincidence came first.

* * *

They had driven on through La Marsa to Gamarth Plage. On the right of the road were villas, half-hidden behind trees and garden walls, and beyond, the sea lay quite near, sparkling under the afternoon sun, and very inviting.

'If we go beyond Gamarth,' said Cleo, who was studying the map, 'there's a secondary road that seems to run close to the beach. We might bathe.'

'Or we might just sit in the back of the car, and—'

'We'll bathe.'

But it wasn't to be, because of one of those coincidences that never ought to happen, but often do.

They were about a mile beyond Gamarth, on a still un-made-up road with isolated houses on the right, between the car and the sea, but still no access to a beach. Suddenly the engine coughed, spluttered, fired again, and stopped.

'Damn,' said Craig. 'I ought to have got petrol earlier but look at the gauge. It must have stuck. Still, it's all right. I told the man at the hotel garage to put a two-gallon can in the boot.' He got out, opened the boot and seized the can. It was empty. He found Cleo watching his face with amusement.

'This is the kind of thing,' she remarked, 'that doesn't happen when I'm in charge of a car. What are you going to do?'

He looked up and down the road, but there wasn't a car in sight. He picked up the can. 'Walk back to Gamarth.'

'I'll go with you. We might ask at that last villa.'

They soon came to the wall of the garden and walked along in the scanty shade of the trees growing on the other side. They came to a closed gate, and looked through. A dog barked challengingly.

He was standing inside the gate, a small French poodle, trailing a steel chain attached to a collar round his neck. He had the look of a dog who is bored and feels it is time someone took notice of him, even if it is only to scold him for breaking loose.

Craig stared at him, unable to believe his eyes. Then he called softly, 'Frimousse'. The poodle came up, wagging his tail, and Craig opened the gate—it wasn't locked—and bent down to fondle him. He detached the chain and put it in his pocket.

'Is he a friend of yours?' asked Cleo.

'He's Yashmin Belcadi's dog. I didn't tell you, because it was an official thing, but I went to see her the other day, and she was bathing this dog.'

'Official!' snorted Cleo. 'It sounds like it.'

'Well it was. I'll explain later. What interests me is what he's doing here. I think I'll go and ask them to lend me some petrol. You stay here.'

'Not on your life. If you're going to have another cosy quote official unquote chat with that girl I want—' She stopped. 'But you can't. Yasmin Belcadi's supposed to be—'

'Kidnapped by the insurgents. Exactly. And they were kind enough to kidnap the dog too, for company. Very considerate of them. And very odd. Stay here.'

'Oh no, I'm coming. Look. Frimousse is waiting to show the way.'

Hearing his name the dog barked briefly, then turned and led them down the drive. They followed while he trotted ahead, importantly, a dog with a mission. They didn't know where his mistress was, but he did.

They could see the tiled roof of a house above the trees in front of them but the dog turned off to the left, along a narrow path between flowering oleanders which hid them from the house. Craig kept one hand on the butt of his Colt, and held the petrol can with the other.

The trees opened out in front of them, and they could see a wooden building beyond a lawn of springy grass. It had shuttered windows facing them and a flat roof, surrounded by a wooden rail. From behind it they could hear the sound of waves breaking on the rocks below.

The dog turned round to satisfy himself that they were still with him, then bounced across the lawn, yapping.

From the roof of the house came a voice, 'Tais-toi, Frimousse.' Craig ran forward, his steps silent on the thick grass. Then he stopped.

She stood up behind the white railing of the roof. It was Yasmin Belcadi, no doubt about that, her naked brown body and arms gleaming with sun lotion.

'I think,' said Cleo, in a very clear, cold voice, 'you had better put something on.'

Yasmin turned her magnificent back, picked up a bathing robe from a place hidden by the railing, then faced them again, taking her time while she put her arms through the sleeves and tied the towelling belt. Her eyes did not leave Craig, and the gun he held loosely in his right hand. Then she walked to a stair at the side of the building and came down on to the lawn, her feet with their brightly lacquered nails treading the grass delicately.

Craig looked around quickly as she did so. He saw a broad path leading straight through the trees to the main house, from which anyone could see them. But there was no sign of movement. Beyond the wooden building, which seemed to be a grandiose beach house, there was nothing but the sea, twenty feet

193

below the cliff on which it stood.

'What exactly do you want?' asked Yasmin, and her voice was as cold as Cleo's.

Craig smiled at her. 'Some petrol. We ran out, on the road just near here.'

She looked down at the can. 'Just that?'

'Just that. Can you help?'

'I think my host may have some full cans in the boathouse.'

'Oh let's stop playing games,' cried Cleo impatiently. 'Why aren't you locked up somewhere, in the hands of the insurgents?'

Yasmin looked her up and down, contemptuously. She turned to Craig. 'Should I be?'

'For God's sake,' said Cleo, 'that's what they've told the Government, that you're in their power. They want a ransom.'

'But what nonsense!' She looked genuinely astonished. 'I've been here since yesterday afternoon. It must be some irresponsible—'

'You're hiding?' asked Cleo sharply.

'If you must know, yes.'

'Why?'

'I'm afraid, Miss Hamilton, that is something I can't tell you. After all, you're a journalist, and you might spread it on the front of the *Daily News*. But if you'll kindly stand aside, I will explain to Peter Craig. I think he's a man of honour and will respect my confidence.'

If her words had been carefully chosen to

annoy Cleo—and they had—she succeeded. Cleo pulled Craig by the arm. 'Come on, Peter. You don't want to listen to a lot of lies. She's just trying to chat you up. Let's go.'

'You won't get far, will you?' pointed out Yasmin. 'Without petrol. As I said, I think I can get some for you, but first I want to explain my actions to Peter, so that he'll stop waving that gun about.'

'It's all right, Cleo,' said Craig soothingly. 'I think I know what she's talking about, and it really is a secret. Be an angel and just let me talk to her alone for a moment.'

Cleo stamped her foot. 'Oh all *right!*' she said furiously, and walked away stiffly to the other end of the lawn.

Yasmin looked at Craig. 'I expect you know that I was working with Major Chaker?' He could smell the scent of the sun lotion on her body.

'Yes. And also that he wanted you to lie low after you told him a certain telephone number. Is that it?'

'Yes. I was frightened, because I hadn't understood the significance of what I'd told him. So I went to a friend, who owns this house, and asked him to let me hide here for a few days.'

'And you didn't even tell your father?'

'No. Is it true what the girl said, that the insurgents claim to have captured me?'

'Yes. It is.'

'I will go with you now, if you wish, and prove the insurgents wrong.' She smiled at him. 'I'm glad you believe me, Mr. Craig.'

'I don't. Not a word you say.'

Her face darkened. 'What d'you mean?' she spat out.

'You're a good liar, but your story doesn't hold together. Your friends the insurgents would never have made a statement which they knew could be disproved so easily. And *why* didn't you tell your father? I think, Miss Belcadi, because you didn't want him to know where you had gone. It was a neat idea to have yourself notionally kidnapped, so that you could concentrate on your insurrection, for that's the truth, isn't it. You never ceased to work for the insurgents, and when you gave Chaker that telephone number you did it deliberately, so that your friends could feed the police with false information.' He turned away from her and called to Cleo.

She stared at him across the lawn, by no means mollified.

'It's all right,' said Craig. 'Miss Belcadi was just trying to pull the wool over my eyes. And also, I think, to gain time.' He looked up sharply. There was the sound of a car turning into the distant drive. He knew that he and Cleo could run through the shrubbery, using the narrow path they had come by, but it would be useless. They wouldn't get far. Even if there had been petrol in the car, it was several hundred yards away. He backed towards the wooden building, pointing the Colt at Yasmin.

She turned on her heel and began to walk towards the main house.

He shouted, 'If you don't stop, I'll fire.'

'Fire at a woman, Mr. Craig?' she said over her shoulder, mockingly, and continued on her way. A car had stopped by the house.

'Give me the gun,' said Cleo between her teeth. 'I'll use it.'

Yasmin stopped, and turned back. 'Lady Macbeth in person,' she said laughingly. Behind her, men with machine-pistols in their hands were running up. Then, without taking her eyes from Craig's face, Yasmin suddenly cried out some words in Arabic.

Craig heard a slight noise above his head. Cleo looked up and screamed. The tall swarthy man, naked except for a loin cloth, who had silently climbed over the railing of the low roof, sprang outwards, aiming at Craig's shoulders. He was all of thirteen stone of rippling muscle and although Craig tried to dodge the impact, the man's arms caught him around the waist and he fell headlong, with the man on top of him. The gun flew wide.

The thick grass had resilience, and Craig had twisted to face his opponent before hands began to tighten around his throat. He found the black man's eyes with his thumbs and pressed viciously to make him break his hold, then followed up with the heel of his hand under the squat nose. They thrashed over and over on the grass, and Craig smelt on the man's gleaming body the scent Yasmin had been using. He tried to knee the other in the crotch but the other man sensed the move and bent his whole body convulsively. The knee cracked him squarely under the jaw, and he flopped back.

In an instant Craig was on his feet, crouching, seeking the mislaid gun. Then he saw it in Yasmin's hand, finger on trigger, pointing at his head, and there was a ring of men watching impassively. Craig rose stiffly to his feet and raised his hands.

'Thank you,' said Yasmin, and turned to look at the man on the ground. He was sitting up, but still dazed. She threw the Colt to one of the gunmen, who caught it neatly. Then, with eyes blazing, she bent down and slapped the man's dark face viciously, left and right. The great diamond on her finger tore his cheek, but he sat with head lowered, unflinching, expecting more. She raised her bare foot, lazily curled the toe into the thick, fuzzy hair and pushed him over. The spurt of savage violence had passed.

She stood up, regal in the loosened bath robe that showed the swell of her breasts, and turned to Craig. 'I don't lose my temper as a rule,' she explained, in a soft, society voice, 'but you see, just because I allowed him certain liberties he left his gun downstairs. This musclebound cretin is supposed to protect me from intruders like you and your little spitfire.' She smiled. 'I must match you against him again, some time. You were good.'

She might have been the wife of a Roman emperor, assessing talent in a gladiator school.

This was more than Cleo could take. 'If you think you can keep Peter,' she cried, 'you're—'

'What's to stop me? I'm going to keep you both. You and your athletic friend will stay with me as long as I wish, and do as you're told. If not, you'll have some very unpleasant experiences. But first, how did you come here?' She advanced on Cleo menacingly. 'Go on, tell me.' One of the watching men thrust between Craig and the two women.

'Ask me, not the girl,' said Craig. 'It was Frimousse. I told you the truth. The car ran out of petrol and I was trying to find some. The dog was at the entrance and he brought us here. You saw him.' He pulled the dog's lead from his pocket and dropped it on the ground.

Frimousse, who had retreated prudently to the edge of the trees, came up at the sound of his name. Yasmin stared at Craig incredulously, then picked the dog up and kissed him. 'Bad little dog,' she said affectionately, in French. 'It's *your* job too, to keep out vagrants and spies, not welcome them in to interrupt your mistress's private pleasures.' She touched the black man's

shoulder, quite gently, with her foot. *'Va-t'en,*
Ali. *Retrouve ton fusil.'* He got up and went
past the steps and round to the front of the
building.

Cleo joined Craig who was massaging his
neck. 'Are you all right, Peter?'

'Be quiet,' said Yasmin. She turned to Craig.
'So nobody knows you're here, and even if they
come they'll find nothing. It's time I moved on,
and you're coming with me. Where's the car?'

Craig pointed. 'A few hundred yards down
the road. Do you want the keys?'

'Why are you just giving in to them, Peter?'
cried Cleo, with tears in her eyes.

'Because he has some sense,' said Yasmin
sharply. 'The keys.'

He handed them over and she gave orders
to one of the men, who nodded and ran off
down the path through the shrubbery. Another
came and tied Craig's hands with a rope, while
Yasmin kept his own automatic pointing at his
stomach. He was led round the side of the
wooden building, with Cleo following. They
came out onto a terrace facing the sea. Glass
doors gave access to the interior of the house,
which consisted of a large room, with showers
and changing compartments at one end and a
spiral staircase, leading downwards, at the
other. The room was furnished simply with a
large glass-topped table, sofas and cane chairs,
a fridge and sink, and a number of cupboards.

Yasmin opened the door of the shuttered

windows facing the terrace and sat down on a sofa. She pointed to chairs. 'You can sit.' She said something to Ali who brought out a jug of orange juice and served it in glasses, with ice from the fridge. Then he took up his gun again and stood on guard by the terrace doors.

Yasmin took her glass and sipped at it, looking at them over the rim. Then she went to a cupboard, brought out a pad and a ball-point pen, and began to write.

'You're drafting another ultimatum, I suppose,' said Craig, 'offering us for ransom?'

'How intelligent you are, Peter. (You don't mind my calling him Peter, do you, Miss Hamilton? I feel I know him so well.) Yes, something like this.'

'The People's Democratic Army,' she read out, 'have taken into custody two enemies of the Republic, who have already attempted to damage our cause. They are: Mr. Peter Craig, a British police officer whom the soi-disant government of Bourguiba called in to help them suppress the people's spontaneous revolt against corruption. And Miss Cleo Hamilton, who in her reports to the London newspaper *Daily News* has so consistently misrepresented the events of the last three days. The terms for their release will follow in our next bulletin.'

She smiled. 'I'll add something about killing you off if there is any attempt to find you.' She finished writing. 'There. I think that'll spread—what's your nice phrase?—alarm and despondency.'

'Don't forget,' pointed out Craig, 'that you've got to kill yourself off, too. You don't imagine the Government is going to release all the detainees, do you? So Yasmin Belcadi has to die.'

'You're quite right. Poor Papa! He'll be so unhappy.'

'I've met some stony-hearted bitches in my time,' said Cleo, 'but you win hands down. And what's the point of it all?'

'Two points,' corrected Yasmin, ticking them off on her fingers. 'One. My father is a man of considerable influence, and his reactions to the situation are important. If any one person can make the ruling clique unpopular, he can. And two, of course, is the fact that I shall have to work full time now, while this revolution of ours is taking the field, and I can't have my father getting in the way.'

'You haven't answered my question—' began Cleo.

'Who gave you the right to ask questions? I'll tell you what I choose, and I don't choose to explain why I—why I joined the movement.' She quickly scanned Craig's face, but his expression did not change, revealing nothing of the thought that slight hesitation in her voice had aroused.

Going out on the terrace, she called one of the guerrillas, who came in with a rope, put a noose round Cleo's neck, did the same for

Craig, and keeping the end in his hand urged them down the spiral stair. Ali with his gun followed.

They emerged in a large boathouse, which communicated with the sea through a channel formed by rocky breakwaters. In the dock a thirty-foot cabin cruiser lay rocking gently. It was painted white, with a blue wheelhouse built high above the flat deck. Through its large windows Craig caught a glimpse of the interior, which was roomy, with the command chair facing the binnacle and control panel, and space for two settees and chaises-longues. He glanced quickly at the bows, but a towel had been hung over the name. Then he was being pushed down a short companion-way to the floor of the cockpit and forward through an open door under the wheelhouse, which gave access first to a space between the galley and store cupboards and then through sliding doors to the saloon.

He was to come to know that saloon well. It had two large settee beds and a long table between them, and was well lit by rise-and-fall windows. At its further end was the lavatory and washroom, and in the bulkhead beyond was a square, dark opening, leading to the forepeak.

Yasmin's voice came from behind them, and the rope was untied. She pointed to the opening. 'There are two bunks in there, but nothing else. The deck hatch is battened down, but there's a ventilator. You'll be safe until we're at sea, when I'll give you more freedom. Don't try anything silly, Craig, or I'll get Ali to deal with you. He'd be glad of the chance.' She was turning away when she said suddenly, 'Empty your trousers pockets. Craig. Inside out, so that I can see. Now your jacket.' She took away his knife, leaving his other minor possessions, but kept his coat. 'Now I'll have that handbag.'

Cleo clung on to it with both hands and Ali made a menacing move. 'Give it up,' said Craig. She threw it down at Yasmin's feet, walked to the forward bulkhead and, stooping down, entered the dark interior of the forepeak.

*　　　*　　　*

The cabin was ten feet long, the width of the boat at the nearer end but curving to a point in the bows. At first they could hardly see each other by the reflected light coming through the two tiny portholes, one on each side of the cabin and both screwed down. Craig felt for the gridded ventilator in the hatch above, and moved it to the open position.

Then he took Cleo in his arms and comforted her. His lips felt the tears on her eyelashes and he kissed them away. Her whole small body was trembling uncontrollably, and she clung to him tightly. He found a blanket, rolled up in a plastic bag, and made her lie down on one of the curved bunks, with the bag for pillow. Then he explored the dark cabin.

There was a light switch, but the lamp fixed to the bulkhead had no bulb in it. There was nothing in the locker under his bunk, and none of the usual clutter of a boat's forepeak—no ropes, fending bolsters, old sou'westers. It had the feel of a hired boat.

Later, when the light faded entirely, someone switched on lights in the boathouse, and through the four-inch porthole he could see men carrying boxes of stores from the spiral stair and passing out of sight to stow them inboard. There seemed to be three of them, Ali and two others. Finally, Yasmin came down the steps, dressed in jeans and a cotton shirt, with a thick sweater loosely slung over her shoulders. The lights in the boathouse went out soon afterwards, and the powerboat's engine fired. The boat began to tremble. It was quite dark now, and the first he knew of having left the harbour was the slow rise and fall as they came into the open sea. For minutes the craft proceeded slowly and quietly. Then the trembling increased and he could hear the slap of water against the hull. Through his porthole a tiny light, far away, came into sight.

Craig looked at his watch. The luminous hands pointed to just after eight o'clock. He pressed his face to the porthole, and in the distance could see the clustered lights of Hammam-Lif and Soliman across the gulf. He went over to Cleo's bunk.

She was still lying, silent, her feet towards the bow. He sat on the other end of the bunk, where it was broader, and felt for her forehead. It was wet. 'Don't come too near, Peter,' she muttered bitterly. 'I'm hot and sticky, and probably smell.' He found her mouth and held her body in his arms.

'We're heading north-east,' he said finally, 'but going very slowly, showing no lights.'

'So we're going to pass round Cap Bon, is that it?'

'I expect so. Then south, I suppose, and down the coast. Listen, darling. This may be the last chance we have of talking without anyone hearing.' He reached up and closed the ventilator. 'Some time I think they'll open up, as she said, and let us into the main cabin, so that we can eat and go to the loo—'

'I want to go *now*,' she said resentfully. 'That's why that sadistic bitch gave us the drinks. She's out to humiliate me.'

'Both of us.'

'No. Me. She's got her man-eating eye on you, I saw it.'

'Oh don't talk nonsense. Listen. This is what I want to say. We've got to get a message to Chaker, or whoever is looking for us, and we've got to do it without being seen.'

'Oh fine! But how?'

'I haven't an idea yet, but I shall.'

'Yes, but Peter, even if you do, what can you say? We don't even know whose boat this is, unless it's hers.'

'That's one thing quite certain; it isn't. But you've got the point. You saw they'd covered up the name? Right. So we've got to provide other information for the security people to identify and trace it. Now this is what you must do to help. Don't show you're looking too closely, but memorize the make and registration numbers of anything big, like the air-conditioner, the loo and the basin—anything that might carry a maker's name. Got it?'

'Yes,' she whispered, sounding more cheerful.

Shortly afterwards they heard the bars being turned and the bulkhead door opened. They came out, blinking, into the saloon. The table was laid for three and Yasmin, her silk shirt provocatively unbuttoned, was sitting on a settee, smoking.

Cleo said, politely but firmly, 'May I have my handbag, please?'

It lay on the settee, and Yasmin picked it up and threw it across. Cleo disappeared back into the space between the saloon and the forepeak, and they heard a door close.

'And I'll take this, too, if you've removed anything you object to.' Craig picked up his jacket and put it on. The air in the saloon was

207

cool and fresh after the stuffy forepeak.

Yasmin nodded and lazily gestured to the place beside her. 'Come and sit here,' she said. 'What'll you drink? Gin and vermouth? Scotch? It's all there.' She pointed to a side table covered with bottles, glasses and an ice bucket. A man with a carbine held in both hands across his chest stood by the after door, which led out to the cockpit.

Craig helped himself to whisky and sat down. 'Is this your boat?'

'No, it isn't. It belongs to a friend of mine, and not the one whose house you found me in, if that's what you're thinking. But I'm not going to identify the boat for you. It's not that you're likely to escape—at least alive—but one can't be too careful. You won't be allowed on deck and there's no record of the name in here, so we'll just keep it secret, for the time being. Once we get to the fort you'll be very closely guarded and escape will be impossible.'

'That's where you're going to immure us, is it? Some fortress in the south, I suppose.' He took a sip of his whisky. 'One of the old Portuguese ones? That'd be interesting.'

'It's just a fort,' she said smiling. 'And there're hundreds of them, as you well know. I really rather like you, Craig. You're a professional; you never let up, do you?'

'I can relax when I want to. The close proximity of a woman like you might give me ideas, for instance, if I didn't remember that

208

you're as trustworthy as a rattlesnake and have the boat stuck full of trigger-happy thugs.' He smiled at her, and she laughed.

It was at that moment that Cleo returned, face made up and hair combed . . . She looked across at the settee sharply, not liking what she saw. Yasmin stood up, slowly and gracefully, and moved over to her place at the head of the table. She didn't offer Cleo a drink, so Craig passed her the rest of his glass, and she drank it thankfully. They sat down.

The food, served by Ali, who came in with a tray from the galley, was quite adequate. Lobsters bisque, presumably out of a tin, followed by lamb cutlets, cheese and fruit. The Tunisian claret was excellent.

'How long are you keeping us on this boat?' asked Craig.

'Until tomorrow evening. You have to go back to the forward cabin to sleep. In the morning you'll be allowed to take showers and you can spend part of the morning in here. I don't want you to suffocate. But for tonight we must lock you up.'

'It'll be cold, and there's only one blanket.'

'I'll see to that. It probably won't be rough, but for all eventualities Ali will put a bucket in for you. I'm afraid that's the best we can do, but it's only for one night. At the fort you'll have all modern comforts.'

'Why can't we sleep in here?'

'Because I'll be here, of course. And also

another passenger. We're picking him up later.' She looked at her watch. 'There are things I must see to. I'll join you again for coffee. Ali will find you cigars and cigarettes.' She went out through the cockpit door, and shortly afterwards they felt the boat heel over as she altered course.

They looked out of the starboard windows. From somewhere ahead the beam of a lighthouse swept across the dark sea and vanished again. There were some lights on the shore, which seemed only a few miles away. Craig crossed to the port side, ignoring the watchful eyes of the guard, and saw another lighthouse directly on the boat's beam. It was a quarter to eleven. 'That must be the island of Zembretta,' he said to Cleo quietly, 'and the other light, ahead of us, is Cap Bon. So we've crossed the Gulf—I suppose about thirty miles to where we are now—in two and three-quarter hours. We must be averaging about ten knots.'

'She's not doing that now,' said Cleo suddenly. The engine was almost inaudible, and they could hear the swish of waves against the boat's sides as she ran forward smoothly through the placid sea.

Craig was watching the shore lights when he saw those of a car being driven slowly along the coast road. It came to a halt and must have half-turned, because the headlights flashed twice across the water. He heard orders being given in Arabic from the cockpit and the sound of feet running overhead. The powerboat turned to starboard, ran towards the shore for a few minutes and slid to a halt. A moment later they heard the rattle of an anchor chain. Yasmin came in, wearing a heavy cashmere sweater. Ali gave her a cup of black coffee.

'You'll have to be locked up again in ten minutes,' she said not looking at them. Her face was ever so slightly flushed, and her eyes were on the dark glass of the window. 'So if you want to prepare for bed you'd better get started. Ali will bring you the blanket, and, oh yes, the bucket. Goodnight.'

'Can we have a light in the forepeak?' asked Craig.

'So that you can signal to the shore?' She smiled. 'No Peter. The moon's rising and that'll have to be enough.'

Ali waited until they had finished with the washroom and made them go into the forward cabin. Then he picked up a bucket, and another blanket wrapped up in a plastic bag, and handed them in. The door was shut and the bars swung into place.

'How I hate that woman!' said Cleo vehemently, as they stood together in the dark.

'She's rather intriguing, though.'

'I suppose you mean because she's as randy as Messalina.' There was a good deal of pent-up feeling in Cleo's voice.

211

'No. As a matter of fact it's her other motivations that interest me,' said Craig, taking off his jacket. He unzipped his trousers and kicked them off. 'I can't make her out.' He pulled the blanket out of its bag and threw it on his bunk.

He heard a rustling noise, and when he reached for Cleo her clothes were all gone. 'Is your berth wide enough for two?' he said.

'It depends,' she whispered. 'Oh Peter!'

*   *   *

It was over an hour later that Craig heard voices calling on the deck, just above the ventilator. Someone replied, faintly, from a distance. He gently removed Cleo's arm from round his neck and knelt on the bunk, astride her, to peer through the tiny porthole.

The beam from the Cap Bon lighthouse flashed across the water, and shone on a yellow rubber dinghy approaching, rowed by two weary men, with another crouching in the stern. A rope was thrown and the boat came alongside. Someone shone a torch.

The first to clamber over the side was a tall man in a dirty jellaba. He was stiff and awkward with cold, and unshaven, but there was no mistaking that aquiline nose and the fierce eyes. Doctor Habib Mahmoud had come aboard.

Craig re-arranged the blankets and lay

212

down by Cleo's side. There *was* room for two, as long as you got close enough, and there was a lot to be said, in the circumstances, for doing just that.

CHAPTER TWELVE

When Cleo opened her eyes it was after seven o'clock. She could hear the water hissing past on the other side of the varnished teak planks by her head, and when she looked across at the porthole opposite there was one moment nothing to see but blue sky, and the next, the horizon bounded into view, giving a glimpse of sun-flecked sea-horses and blue-green troughs. Then sky again. But the rolling was not unpleasant. She suddenly realized that Craig's eyes were open.

She kissed him. 'What are you thinking about?' she asked fondly.

'Those bloody bags,' he muttered, absent-minded.

She propped herself on her elbow and looked down at him, frowning. 'So that's all you can think of after a night of unlicensed passion. I suppose you mean the bags under my eyes.'

'Shall I tell you what I think about your eyes?'

'Yes please.' She lay back contentedly.

He did, and went on to particularise about her other attributes. It was some time later that she recalled what had been his first words. 'What bags?'

The plastic ones the blankets were wrapped in. If we could blow one of them up like a balloon and let it drift ashore, with a message inside . . . It might work.'

'But you can't open the portholes, they're screwed down. And you could hardly take a balloon with you into the saloon.'

'There's a ventilator above the loo. That's the only way.'

'You mean push the bag through, then blow it up with your mouth close to the grill, and tie it? That's smart.'

'Not smart enough, sweetie. There must be several men on deck. In fact, most of them have probably slept there. Some thug would see it floating away and loose a burst of automatic fire at it. Before telling Yasmin. And you know what she'd do?'

'Tie us up.' Cleo added her personal opinion of Yasmin, in pithy terms.

'Yes.' His arms tightened around her shoulders. 'But I think I've found a way of doing it without being detected. Did you open the white box on the wall of the washroom?'

'Yes. But there's nothing there but sea-sick pills and medicines, and a few first aid things like iodine and bandages.'

'Exactly. Including what I want for the Craig

Self-surfacing Message Balloon,' he explained.

'You still need a message.'

'There, my darling, you've put your tiny finger on the nub of the whole problem. We don't know the name of the boat. The air-conditioning is G.E.C., but I couldn't get near enough to read the registration number. The loo and basin are makes sold in millions. No name on the dinghy either, that I could see. We still don't know who owns the boat or where she's going.'

'D'you still think she's a hired boat?'

'She's got the feel of one.'

'Well, wouldn't they mark the blankets, so that they couldn't be pinched too easily?'

'Good God!' He sat up and reached for the blanket that had fallen to the floor, and looked quickly at each corner in turn. Then he found it, *Saliya*, roughly stitched in red wool.

'It's on this one, too,' cried Cleo.

Craig hastily began to pull on his clothes. 'We shall want weights. Have you any coins in your bag?' He thought, 'And soft money?'

'I've got a ten dinar note, as a matter of fact.'

'Just the job. And give me your lipstick. Come to think of it, there's nothing we can do yet, because the on-shore wind won't blow till sunset, and we don't want them to make a search and find the thing.'

'But suppose they steer straight across the Gulf of Hammamet and don't stay near the

215

shore at all?'

'It depends of course where they're headed for, but I rather think they'll stay in-shore. Have you seen the beaches on the Sahel coast at this time of year?'

'No. But I can imagine. Crowded with British tourists for a start.'

'And boats. Lots of them. And so on all down the coast to Jerba. It's perfect cover for Yasmin and her gang, whereas if she keeps well out to sea she might attract attention. After all, the Tunisians must be searching for us pretty intensively.' He looked out of the starboard porthole and could just see, off the bow and far away, the rugged outline of the Kasbah of Hammamet appearing over the morning mist. As he stepped back he heard noises outside the door, and a moment later it opened. By this time Craig was sitting disconsolately on the edge of his bunk. Cleo was covered in blankets, which was just as well.

Ali brought in coffee and brioches and told them they could use the washroom. He handed Craig a battery-powered razor, and when they had finished breakfast stood in the space outside, barring the way to the saloon, until they had finished their toilet. Then he took the razor away and locked them in.

When they were alone Craig pulled his notebook out of his pocket and began to write, using both French and English. Then he took the plastic bags and wrote with Cleo's lipstick

ATTENTION, on both sides. He slipped one bag inside the other.

Cleo was watching him anxiously. 'I thought you said we'd have to wait till the evening, for the wind.'

'I was talking through my hat. There's a proper wind blowing already, and it's from the south. Look at the waves. We're in luck, half-way across the Gulf of Hammamet already and close in. If we stay like this, skirting the beaches, and can get the balloon away within about half an hour, it'll drift north towards Hammamet or Nabeul, or somewhere along that long stretch of *plage*. And all we need then,' he added soberly, 'is a really outrageous bit of luck. It's got to get into the right hands.'

He took out of his pocket the twelve Alka-Seltzer tablets he had looted from the medicine cabinet, crushed them into powder and put in into the bottom of the inner bag, adding some hundred-millim coins, to give weight, and then the bi-lingual message, wrapped up it the aluminium foil from the tablets. Finally, he introduced the ten-dinar note, and leaving the double-skinned bag open stuffed it into his pocket, tightly folded.

It was half an hour later before they were allowed into the main cabin. The settees were under their day coverings, and it was impossible to tell whether one or both had been occupied during the night. The windows had been wound down and the air was fresh after the stuffiness of the forepeak, where the heat had already built up.

Yasmin and Mahmoud were evidently on deck or in the command cabin, but Ali remained on guard in front of the cockpit door. After a decent interval Craig explained that he wanted to go back to the lavatory, and Ali nodded.

Craig wasted no time. He closed the door, whipped out the double plastic bag, shook the contents of the inner one to the bottom and held the opening of the outer bag under the tap. When about half a pint of water was held between the two skins he gently pushed the opening of the inner bag downwards and taking a piece of bandage from the medicine box, tied the mouth of the outer bag tightly, folding it over to make a better seal. Then he twisted the upper part of the double bag, so that the water in the outer skin could not get at the powder until it unwound, and poked the lower part slowly through one of the slits in the ventilator. Finally, the twisted upper half passed through, and he let go.

His theory was that the coins would make the bag sink, and that somewhere below the water the bag would unwind and that at least some of the water would find its way through the opening of the inner bag and reach the powder, combine with it to form carbon dioxide and gradually inflate the whole bag. It ought then to rise to the surface in spite of the small weight of the coins.

He knew that if anyone on deck should happen to look over the side just at that spot he would see the plastic issuing from the vent and sliding down into the water, but this was a risk that had to be run. He listened, holding his breath, but could hear no unusual sounds from above. He worked the lever of the loo, unnecessarily, and went back to the saloon. It was only then that he realized the danger that the bag would get drawn through the propellor and sliced up like salami. Cleo saw him frown suddenly, but with his back to Ali he made a thumbs-up sign, and she relaxed.

In fact the operation worked perfectly. The coins drew the bag down before the stern passed over it, and half way to the bottom. surrounded by inquisitive fish, it began to inflate, while still descending. The boat was nearly a quarter of a mile ahead before the balloon surfaced. It began to drift northwards towards the crowded beaches, pushed by the hot wind that came from the southern deserts.

Then came Craig's 'outrageous piece of luck'. The balloon could have been seen by anyone bathing off the *plage*, and anything could have happened to it. But long before it reached the strand it drifted near to where a young American named Russ Gleeson was skin-diving.

His girl-friend Shirley was rowing the boat, and she was hot and tired. He had speared two fish, which lay at her feet, and she felt that was enough for one morning. Besides, they were nearly half a mile from the hotel beach.

He was threshing along on the surface now, approaching something that glittered blue-white under the burning sun. Oh heck! she thought, he's off chasing a kid's balloon. 'C'mon Russ,' she shouted, wiping the perspiration that trickled into her eyes. 'I want a Coke.'

He waved an arm and raised his gun. He was in the act of firing, just for the hell of it, when he saw something that stopped him. It wasn't a balloon; it was held down by something under the water. He swam closer, and dived to look at it through his mask. Then he began to swim on his back towards the boat, holding the deflated end of the thing with one hand and his gun in the other. He threw them one after the other into the boat and swung himself over the side.

They saw a word printed in big red letters, ATTENTION. Russ undid the strip of bandage, and the balloon collapsed with a puff of gas that made him sneeze. He reached inside and brought the contents out for inspection. Water had got inside the aluminium foil but the first part of the message was clearly legible. IMPORTANT. TREAT AS SECRET. They read through the rest.

Russ scratched his head. 'It sounds genuine, Shirl. Done in French, too. I think I'd better do what it says, and ring the British Embassy.' He looked at the girl severely. 'And in the meantime treat as secret, which means keep our traps shut.'

'Permission to speak, sir?'

'Idiot!' he said, grabbing the oars and sending the boat towards the beach with short, powerful strokes.

'I want two Cokes,' she said dreamily, trailing her hand in the water, 'and a T-bone steak, if they've got one, with French fries, and some of those gooey honey cakes afterwards, with lots of cream. And then you . . .'

CHAPTER THIRTEEN

Sir John Radcliffe stared at Major Chaker, and his voice was cold and formal. 'I must make it clear that Her Majesty's Government takes this matter very seriously indeed. The lives of a senior civil servant and the correspondent of a highly influential newspaper are at stake.' He flicked his finger at the buff-coloured sheet of paper on his desk. 'According to this ultimatum from the so-called People's Democratic Army those two will be *killed*, at midnight tomorrow, unless you release the demonstrators detained yesterday. You say these are the same conditions as for Mademoiselle Belcadi except for the sum of money demanded in her case, and that so far no detainees have been released, although the vast majority cannot be charged with any serious offence. You set free the young people who kidnapped Craig, admittedly on bail. Why can't you do the same for these misguided students who are guilty, if at all, of a far less serious offence?'

'We cannot,' said Chaker stolidly, 'set prisoners free just because a group of revolutionaries ask us to. It would show weakness, and this is the worst possible moment for that. There have been more attacks, and there is the threat of a general strike, as you know. You must appreciate our position, *Monsieur l'Ambassadeur*. Peter Craig is my friend. I would do anything to get his release.'

'Yes, of course,' said his Excellency, in a milder tone. 'I realise your situation, just as I realise that I'm talking out of turn. I should be speaking to the Minister of Foreign Affairs. But I asked you to come and have an unofficial talk with me, Major, so that I could get at the official line of thinking. I had hoped you could make some gesture—release a few students and start arguing about the rest while you discover where Craig and Miss Hamilton are being held. Have you no clues at all?'

'I'm afraid not, *Excellence*. All we know is that Craig and Miss Hamilton left their hotel yesterday at half-past two and were seen carrying swimsuits and towels. They drove away in Craig's car, but we have no idea where they went. The car has not been found. We've made enquiries at all the beaches where they might have been expected to go, but there's no report of anyone having seen either of them.'

'Damn it,' remarked the Ambassador irritably, 'this is the second time Craig has managed to get himself kidnapped, and he's a policeman, for Heaven's sake. What was he doing anyway, swanning around with Cleo Hamilton? I've scarcely met the girl.' He turned to Michael Thorne. 'You saw a good deal of her, Michael. Were she and Craig friendly?'

'That's the odd thing,' said Thorne. 'Whenever I've seen them together they've been quarrelling.'

'Quarrelling, eh? Then what—' His desk telephone rang and he picked up the receiver and spoke to his P.A. 'Who? A Mr. Gleeson? Don't know him. Can't you cope, Sybil? I'm busy.' He was putting back the receiver when he heard something that made him apply it hurriedly to his ear again. 'About Craig? Well, put him through, child.'

He listened for some time, making brief acknowledgements to the man at the other end. Then he said, 'Now Mr Gleeson, I needn't tell you how important this is or how grateful I am for your quick and correct action. I'll take another opportunity. I want you to listen now while I repeat the gist of what

223

you've said, so that it can be taken down.' He gesticulated to Thorne, who already had a memo pad ready. 'The important points are these. (Mr. Gleeson. If I get anything wrong, break in.) Right. Mr Russ Gleeson, a United States citizen, accompanied by a young lady, intercepts an inflated plastic bag floating in the sea off Hammamet. He was not observed by other people at the time, so far as he is aware, since his boat was half a mile from the shore and there were no others nearby. He telephoned to me as soon as he returned to his hotel the Miramar. Inside the plastic bag was a sum of money and a message wrapped up in aluminium foil taken from Alka-Seltzer tablets, which Mr Gleeson thinks may have been used—I don't quite see why—to inflate the bag. The foil had not protected the message sufficiently, and the message is therefore corrupt. (No, Mr Gleeson. It's just officialese for partially unreadable.)

'What was left ran more or less as follows: TREAT AS SECRET. WHOEVER FINDS THIS PLEASE TAKE IT AT ONCE TO THE BRITISH AMBASSADOR OR TELEPHONE CONTENTS TO TUNIS 48596. REWARD WILL BE GIVEN. FROM CRAIG AND HAMILTON. ON POWERBOAT SALIYA PROCEEDING SOUTH TO UNIDENTIFIED FORT REPEAT FORT . . .

'The rest of the message,' continued the Ambassador, 'is increasingly corrupt, but the names Mahmoud and Janus occur, together

224

with the description of the boat, with very few details. Was that right, Mr Gleeson? . . . Good. Hang on a moment.' He caught a vigorous signalling movement by Chaker and handed him the receiver.

Chaker spoke slowly, in heavily accented English. 'Mr. Gleeson, this is Major Chaker— I'll spell that, C-H-A-K-E-R—of the Tunisian Security Service. I shall be with you in less than an hour. In the meantime you may possibly be in danger, because if someone saw you examining the message and later heard you had telephoned the Embassy they might be very inquisitive. You understand? Good. Now I suggest that you and the young lady remain in your room—I mean rooms—until I arrive and establish my identity with you by pushing my identity card under the door. Chaker, remember. What is your room number? . . . I know the Miramar but I don't want to make enquiries at the desk. Tell me where your room is so that I can go straight there . . . In A block. O.K., and thanks.'

Chaker put down the receiver, smiling. 'That boy is either a professional soldier or has at least been through the draft,' he said, switching back to French. 'I could almost see him pulling his tunic straight. Thank God it wasn't some cretin who'd have told the whole beach. We've still got a chance to act without the enemy knowing what we've learned, which is obviously what Craig had in mind when he started his message with "Treat as secret". Incidentally, *Monsieur l'Ambassadeur,* what was the description of the boat? I'll try and get it traced at once, but there'll be dozens of *Saliya*'s.'

'Thirty foot overall, six foot beam, diesel. Then something about General Electric. But all the second part was mutilated by water.'

'Thank you, sir. May I use your P.A.'s telephone?'

'Of course. But what about this fort he's mentioned?'

Chaker spread his hands. 'There are dozens of old forts all the way down the coast. But if there's a connection between any one fort and any one boat called *Saliya* we're in business. Is Mr. Thorne coming with me? He'd be very welcome.'

'Yes, Michael, you'd better go. Make up your mind on the way what we should do about Gleeson—I mean, whether to reward him or make a fuss of him and his girl-friend in Tunis. I'll back up, of course. I liked the sound of that young man.' He looked up suddenly. 'I've heard about that thug Mahmoud, but who or what is Janus?'

Chaker hesitated for a moment. 'I'd rather you kept this to yourself, *Monsieur l'Ambassadeur,* until I've seen the actual message. *Janus* is the code-name for Yasmin Belcadi. I think Craig is telling us that she also is a prisoner on the boat *Saliya*.'

226

Chaker had his car and driver waiting below, by the Bab el-Bahar. He took the wheel himself, with Thorne beside him, and drove fast, leaving the city on the Hammam-Lif road. They passed through the suburbs and the light-industry area came out into the broad valley of the Oued Meliane, between the twin peaks of Bou Kornine and the sea. The wine country followed, with windbreaks of eucalyptus and the sharp scent of maturing must from the white-painted warehouses. The car's speed increased as the pace of life in the village and farmhouses slowed to what was more decent and dignified than in the barren wastes of the cities. The Tunisian has the gift of appearing dignified even when all you can see of him, from behind, is the thin, hairy legs below the striped jellaba, the scuffed, turned up shoes and the grey bathtowel he wears to protect his head from the implacable sun.

The straight, endless rows of vines rushed past. They slowed down to pass through Grombalia, then on, fast, through more vines and olive groves until they came to the turning on the left for Hammamet. A side-road brought them to the Miramar Hotel. It was fifty minutes since they had left the Embassy.

The side-road ran beside lemon groves for a few hundred yards. A train of camels lumbered past, protesting against having to leave the shade of the trees for the hot dusty road. The car came to a stop in front of a long low building, white, with grilled windows. They got out of the car stiffly, and Chaker led the way through dark glass doors into a deliciously cool foyer; then out again through an arched court surrounding a pool into a garden where palms and eucalyptus trees shaded the brushed earth paths. He evidently knew his way well, because without stopping he branched off to the left and came to a terrace of rooms facing the sea.

Chaker stopped at one of the doors and tapped. A voice answered, and he stooped down and pushed his identity card under the door. It opened and the two men went in.

The man who stood looking at them was about twenty-five, with crew-cut hair, very blond, and light blue eyes. The hairs on his brown, muscular arms shone gold. He was dressed in a white sleeveless shirt and blue slacks. He closed the door and locked it.

It was a pleasant room looking out across the covered terrace at the trees of the garden, with a sea beyond. A tall sandy-haired girl, well covered, was sitting in an armchair by the window. She was introduced as Shirley Connors, but said little, although her eyes were sparkling. She had been told to let her man deal with the situation.

'Before we start,' said Chaker, 'may I order

something to drink? For us all, of course.'

'Gee,' said the girl, 'that's a good start to this session. He wouldn't let me have anything sent in, not even lunch.'

'I'll do it,' said Gleeson. 'So you can keep out of the way if you don't want to be seen. Beer and sandwiches for everybody?'

'I want Coke, with ice in it,' said the girl.

'Thanks a lot. We haven't lunched yet either,' said Thorne.

Gleeson went to the telephone and gave the order. 'I've got the message here, sir,' he said to Chaker, and led them to a table where he had spread out two plastic bags and a water-worn piece of paper. It had dried out on the glass top of the table. Chaker and Thorne bent over it.

MOST IMPORTANT. TREAT AS SECRET. PLEASE INFORM THE BRITISH AMBASSADOR, TUNIS 48596, IMMEDIATELY OF THE CONTENTS OF THE FOLLOWING MESSAGE. IF YOU DO THIS AND DO NOT INFORM ANYONE ELSE YOU WILL BE REWARDED.

TRES IMPORTANT—. VEUILLEZ TRAITER LE CONTENT DU MESSAGE SUIVANT STRICTEMENT EN SECRET, EN FAISANT SAVOIR SEULEMENT L'AMBASSADEUR BRITANNIQUE, TUNIS 48596. IL EST ESSENTIEL DE NE PAS INFORMER AUTRE PERSONNE. CETTE ACTION SERA RECOMPENSEE.

All this earlier part of the message was legible, but the rest had been partly washed clean: FROM CRAIG AND HAMIL . . . FOLLOWING FOR CHAKER. IN POWERBOAT SALIYA REPEAT SALIYA PROC . . . SOUTH . . . TIFIED . . . REPEAT FORT. KIDNAP . . . JANUS REP . . . JAN . . . WHO IS . . . BOAT . . . MAHMOUD . . . (a piece of indecipherable smudges) LAST NIGHT. SAL . . . THIRTY FOOT OVERALL SIX FOOT BEAM WITH DIES . . . GENERAL ELECTRIC AIR COND . . . FOUR BERTH.

Chaker took a Minox camera from his pocket and photographed the paper as it lay. 'Was there anything on the other side?'

'No, Sir. Here's the two bags, one was inside the other.'

Thorne stared at the word ATTENTION written large, in bright red, on both bags. He remembered, vaguely, that Cleo had used a lipstick of that colour. Only two days before she had taken it from her bag and touched up her lips.

Gleeson was looking at Chaker. He was a foreigner, of course, in spite of his excellent English, but there was an air of authority about him which was international, something that, in the circumstances, commanded both respect and obedience.

'There were these things inside the bag, sir,' he said, and displayed the coins and the ten-dinar note.

'The coins I don't understand,' said Chaker, 'but the money is obviously intended for you. And of course there will be a further reward

230

from the British Embassy.'

'No, thank you, sir,' said the young man stiffly. 'I don't do this for money.' There was a muffled snort from the armchair.

Thorne broke in. 'I appreciate that very much, Mr Gleeson. I'll give you an official receipt later, on Embassy writing paper, explaining the circumstances. O.K.?'

'Thanks very much,' said Gleeson enthusiastically. He turned to Chaker, producing a map of the area from a drawer in the table. 'I think I've worked out when the bag must have been dropped, very roughly, and where.' He spread the map out on the bed. 'You see, I was skin-diving here,' he pointed, 'just about half a mile from the shore south-east of Hammamet, and there weren't many boats around. Earlier there had been a few going both ways, but by the time I picked up the bag it was mid-day, and very hot, and they'd all gone home for lunch. So it must have been one of the earlier boats, coming from the Cap Bon direction, and it must have passed me quite a way before the bag was dropped overboard but it could only have been inside the gulf. Otherwise, as you go south, you have to veer east to get round the Monastir peninsula.'

'I see,' said Chaker thoughtfully. 'That's well argued. So we're looking for a medium-sized motor cruiser that was passing fairly close in-shore, going south, between eleven and about a quarter to twelve this morning. Could have been earlier, of course.'

There was a knock on the door and when Gleeson opened it the other two men were sitting around as casually as the girl, and there was no sign of the map or the message. Chaker's coat lay on top of them. Gleeson took the tray, which held half a dozen beer bottles, two Cokes and a large plate of chicken sandwiches. It was while they were all occupied in disposing of these things that Shirley spoke. 'I saw it,' she said rapidly, ignoring a reproving look from Gleeson, who had his mouth full and couldn't speak for the moment. 'I saw a white boat with a high blue cabin, like a fishing cruiser we have on the lake at home, and some men lying around on the deck. Yellow dinghy on top of the deck house, or what you call it, and flying a blue flag. It was while Russ was swimming. This boat went round the bay, as you said, and then it turned seawards and off towards that bit of coast that sticks out.'

'When was this?' asked Chaker eagerly. 'And why did you notice it particularly?'

'Why didn't you tell me this before?' asked Russ, reproachfully.

'You were so darn keen to do it all yourself.' She added, more tactfully, 'And anyway, it didn't seem important until you'd explained how the boat must have been moving.'

'When was it?'

'It turned out to sea, to get round the point, just when Russ spotted the balloon.'

'And why,' repeated Chaker, 'were you so interested in that boat?'

She hesitated. 'Well, it looked so like the boats the brothers used. You remember, Russ, the ones with the blue flags.'

'What brothers?' asked Chaker sharply.

'She means the members of a community that lives on an island in the Kerkennahs,' explained Gleeson. 'We were down there, fishing, last week, before we came here. They have boats to go to and from Sfax, and they fly blue flags with a silver moon on them.'

'Did you see the moon emblem?' asked Chaker.

'I can't be certain, but it looked like it,' said Shirley.

Chaker went across to the telephone by the bed. 'May I?' Gleeson nodded, and Chaker rang his office in Tunis. While waiting for the call to go through he put his hand over the mouthpiece. 'I asked my assistant to check on all cabin cruisers named *Saliya*.' Captain Tibaoui came on the line, and there was a long conversation in Arabic. When he put back the receiver he was smiling. ' A motorboat named *Saliya* is owned by the Order of the Divine Moon. Are they your community?'

'Yes, sir,' said Gleeson excitedly. 'They're all crack-pots, though, so it must be a coincidence. They live on this little island about a mile away from Sidi Fraj, towards Sfax. It's in deep water, unlike the rest of the Kerkennahs, and only a couple of hundred yards each way. The brothers live in an old Spanish fort—Jesus! Is that it? The fort?'

'It's a good working hypothesis,' said Chaker dryly. He looked down at the notes he had made during his talk with Tibaoui. 'There are seven powerboats named *Saliya*, all about the size described by Mr Craig, but one of them is owned by Doctor Emanuel Seebogen, the Belgian millionaire. Captain Tibaoui says that Seebogen obtained from our Government a long lease of the island of Sidi Abdallah ten years ago, and set up there the Order of the Divine Moon. The community lives on the island according to rules allegedly laid down by an ancient Egyptian priest whose teachings—I quote—"were revealed to Dr Seebogen by a spiritualist in whom he had complete faith". The brothers remain on the island, which is closed to outsiders, and only their leaders and lay-assistants may travel to the mainland.' He looked up. 'I remember, now. The police investigated the community about a year ago, and came to the conclusion that it consisted, as Mr Gleeson put it, of a bunch of crack-pots. But harmless ones, and all rich. The amount paid to the Government for the lease was very large.'

'All the same,' put in Thorne, 'it's a remarkable coincidence.'

'I agree. It's worth investigating at once. But for the safety of Craig and Miss Hamilton we mustn't let the kidnappers suspect that the hunt is on. So no helicopters just yet.' He paced up and down. 'Mr Gleeson, you said you were fishing in the area last week. Did you have a chance of observing the island closely?'

'No, sir. You're not allowed to land there, because they say the monks are always wandering around, praying. We saw them on the battlements, didn't we, honey?' He started. 'At least, they looked like monks.'

'Sure thing,' agreed Shirley. 'Blue robes and everything.'

'But the whole island's fortified, with the curtain walls rising straight up from the sea in some places. I mean, sir, if you were thinking of raiding it you'd need scaling ladders and a lot of covering fire, with a Bazooka to breach the main gateway. But say,' Gleeson continued eagerly, 'I could have a closer look if you like. There's a lot of skin-diving and scuba-fishing goes on between the island and the mainland, and we're known to the locals already. It wouldn't be at all surprising if we went back. We could say the fishing here was no good.'

'It's very good of you to offer, Mr Gleeson. But you must run no risk of danger to yourselves, so it'd have to be done very carefully. You see, if the island really has been taken over by the insurgents, and they suspect we know it, they'd clear out overnight, or use their three prisoners as hostages. You'd have to attract no attention at all.'

A plaintive voice issued from the armchair. 'Honey, we've only got another week, for land's sake.'

'We could drive there and back in a day, carry out the recce and report.' He turned to Chaker. 'I can look after myself, sir. I'm a Marine. And I've qualified in the intelligence courses.' Shirley groaned.

Chaker smiled. 'The more I think of your idea, the better I like it. You'd attract far less attention than a Tunisian, skin-diving in that area. I'll tell you what we'll do, if you and— er—Miss Connors agree. Pack up enough clothes for a night in Sfax and bring your diving equipment. We'll make a first reconnaissance early tomorrow morning. I'll provide you with operational funds to cover the night at the Mabrouk Hotel in Sfax, meals and any other expenses. I will drive you down there, starting in half an hour, since I've got some telephoning to do first. It's two hundred and thirty kilometres but the road's good and we'll make it in three hours easily. I shall drop you off at the station, and you'll pretend to have arrived by train. You'll arrange your own accommodation and won't see me till half past seven tomorrow morning at the quay. I'll show you where. I shall be looking as much like a man with a motor-boat to hire as I can. There are friends in Sfax who will help.'

'And what about me?' asked Shirey plaintively.

'The invitation is extended to you, Mademoiselle. This will only be a reconnaissance operation and you will make—er—very attractive camouflage. Are you both prepared to do this?'

'Try and stop us, sir, Major Chaker.'

'And I,' said Thorne acidly, 'am expected to get back to Tunis by train, I suppose.'

CHAPTER FOURTEEN

At about mid-day Ali had re-appeared and gruffly ordered Craig and the girl back to their prison in the forepeak, where they had been kept for over an hour. When they were allowed to return to the saloon the long table was laid for lunch, with two places opposite each of the settees. A second guard stood in front of the open doors, through which they could see the short passage and then the cockpit and the stern, over which a blue flag with a silver moon was flying. From the galley came a faint smell of hot olive oil and freshly caught fish.

Ali made them sit down on one of the settees. He took a rope, attached one end to a brass staple in the forward bulkhead, passed it first round Cleo's waist, then Craig's, and secured it to the handle of the sliding door. They waited. Flecks of light thrown up by the sunlit water chased each other across the ceiling. The land was far away on the starboard side, and beyond the straight white wake they could see the headland of Monastir receding into the distance.

Yasmin came into the saloon, followed by Mahmoud. After two days' struggle to escape the closing police nets the guerrilla leader's face was still grey and strained.

Craig had prepared himself for trouble, or at least another piece of teasing cruelty from Yasmin. What he hadn't expected was the over-polite, over-casual way in which Mahmoud nodded to each in turn and asked them in broken English what they would like to drink. He took a bottle of whisky and a siphon from a cupboard, poured out stiffish drinks and called to Ali to bring ice from the galley.

Yasmin sat silently, opposite Craig, raking Cleo with a calculating stare, which the girl returned with a look of demure complacency. Yasmin's finger tapped irritably; her expression was sour. Mahmoud brought her a glass of Campari and sat down, with a whisky in his hand.

'You must agree, Mr Craig,' he said, in French, 'that you are being well treated. I'm afraid your quarters are a little hot at this time of day, but we've let you have your freedom in

238

here as much as possible.'

'Very civilised,' said Craig sardonically. 'But I see no reason to rope us in.'

'That's purely a precaution, Mr Craig. You seem to be a violent man, and I thought we should eat our meal in peace. Ah, here it comes.' Ali came in with bowls of iced soup. 'And you, Miss Hamilton? Have you any complaints?'

'None at all,' said Cleo, with a radiant smile at Craig. 'We passed an excellent night, thank you.'

'Good. We don't wish you or anyone to think we are not civilised people, but in our patriotic fight against oppression and corruption we have to use radical methods from time to time.'

'Like killing those who stand in your way,' suggested Craig.

'Yes, even that. But rest assured that you have nothing to fear, provided the Bourguiba Government accepts our reasonable demands. You were present at the student demonstration yesterday, Miss Hamilton,' he added, after pausing to finish his soup, 'and although your article published this morning in the *Daily News* is most prejudiced and tendentious, according to the B.B.C. bulletin, even you admitted that most of the students were unarmed and did not attack the police, in spite of deliberate provocation.'

'The deliberate provocation,' retorted Cleo, 'came from your own agitators who —'

239

Mahmoud broke in, his face taut with anger. 'That is not true, and you know it. The only shots fired came from police weapons. But you agree that the students were unarmed, so it is wholly unjust to hold them in prison?'

'Well—' began Cleo, but Craig saw the danger and interrupted.

'That is entirely a matter for the Tunisian authorities to decide.'

'But it was you who advised the Service de Surveillance du Territoire, Mr Craig.'

'I did not. They need no help, neither the Service nor the police, in deciding who are the real agitators, and I hope very much that they have them under detention. Like those who deliberately incited the students in front of the Belcadi building. I suppose you will try to provoke a general strike in the same way?'

'The people have already chosen to declare a general strike tomorrow,' said Mahmoud. 'They have every right to protest against incompetent government.'

'The people!' said Craig scornfully. 'How much of the quarter million dinars you asked for Miss Belcadi's release will find its way into the people's pockets? That is, if you get it.'

'But we are getting it,' declared Mahmoud triumphantly. 'Miss Belcadi's father has already agreed to pay the ransom, and she will be released tonight. We have waived the condition about the release of detainees since we have you as hostages.'

240

'*Released?*' cried Cleo. 'But she's part of your revolution. She's here, isn't she?'

Craig saw the look of exasperation on Mahmoud's face and smiled. 'You'll have to cut that bit out, won't you?'

Cleo turned to him, bewildered. 'What on earth are you talking about?'

'The mike he's got fixed up somewhere under the table. I didn't realise it at first. Until I wondered why Miss Belcadi was keeping so unusually mum during this curious exchange.' Yasmin said something in Arabic. It sounded vicious, and as she was looking with blazing eyes at Craig as she spoke he thought it probably dealt with his parents on both sides. Mahmoud put a restraining hand on her bare arm.

'But *why*?' asked Cleo.

'So that they can record our voices and cut up and stitch together the tape and replay it over the telephone to one of their press friends. Like Benoit.' He saw Mahmoud start. 'As I told you, it's publicity they want more than anything, and they could flog that recording all over the world. It'd be hot stuff— the real live voices of their kidnapped prisoners, admitting this and that. But not Mademoiselle Belcadi's voice, oh no! She's probably recorded already a pathetic conversation with her so-called captors, calculated to tug at her father's heart-strings.' He turned to Mahmoud. 'Do you really mean

241

he's given in?'

'He has.' Mahmoud smiled. 'There will be a secret rendezvous at sea, at three o'clock tonight. He will come in his yacht, and when we're satisfied that there's no Government gunboat tailing him and that he has the money ready in cash—he'll get his darling daughter back.'

Yasmin had recovered her temper. 'It will make him very happy,' she said laughing, 'until the next time.' She helped herself to the fried red mullet that Ali had brought in. 'We need the money, you see. And I have a lot to do in Tunis, not least with your friend Chaker.'

'You cold-hearted bitch!' cried Cleo furiously. 'What are you getting out of this?'

'Power,' said Mahmoud.

Yasmin glanced at the Tunisian, who had poured himself more wine and was sipping it thoughtfully. There was something in her expression that Craig could not understand. 'Yes,' she said, 'it is power we want. Why we want it doesn't concern you, but I assure you we shall succeed. The people are already frightened, and furious with the Government, and we don't need more than a few activists in a crowd to make them defy the police, as you saw. The Government will fall, and then our friends in the opposition will take over until we are ready to denounce them and appoint our own nominees. You will see. Nothing can stop us.'

242

'But they're mobilising the Army,' said Cleo. 'You can't take on armoured cars and tanks.'

'They can do nothing against surprise attacks,' put in Mahmoud, 'and every time we carry out a successful coup they will look more foolish.'

Cleo broke out, 'You're a couple of the most—'

'Be quiet!' rapped Craig.

'That's wise,' said Yasmin coldly. 'You must mend your manners, you fool,' she added, turning to Cleo. 'If you don't, it might give me a lot of pleasure to tell Ali to rape you in front of your boy-friend's eyes.' Cleo's hand flew to her mouth. 'Or spoil your looks for ever,' went on Yasmin remorselessly. 'You are *ours*, to do with as we like. If we tell you to record another tape, you'll do it.' She saw the look of cold ferocity in Craig's eyes, and smiled. 'Well, Mr Craig?'

'Peter,' said Cleo shakily, 'tell her—'

He put his hand on her arm. 'She has made her point,' he said grimly. 'She and Doctor Mahmoud are sensitive people. We must treat them tactfully.'

'Tactfully!' She pointed at Yasmin. 'If that perverted nympho thinks she—'

'Be quiet!' shouted Craig, and she subsided.

'That's sensible,' said Yasmin. 'Now we can finish our luncheon like civilised people.'

*   *   *

It was when they were drinking coffee that Yasmin spoke again. 'I will just explain your situation to you, so that there is no misunderstanding. We arrive at a fortified island this evening, and you will be held in separate rooms, some way apart. So Mr Craig, you will know that if you get any ideas for making trouble we can have access to Miss Hamilton whenever we please. And rape is the least of the things that could happen to her. After all, she might enjoy it.'

Craig's grasp on Cleo's arm tightened. 'What is this place?' he asked, putting down his cup.

'I don't see why I shouldn't tell you. It's a small island, fortified by the Spaniards several hundred years ago. It is the headquarters of the so-called Order of the Divine Moon, and there are twelve Brothers who live there, very abstemiously, concerned mainly with their immortal souls. We have taken over the island, temporarily, while the head of the Order is on a world tour. The reports he gets from the Brothers are reassuring, because they write what they're told to write. As you will, too, if it's necessary.'

'So they're still there?'

'They are all there, confined to their cells, which is as they used to be. We are merely continuing the discipline laid down by the head of the Order. The cells are not

244

uncomfortable, if a bit old-fashioned, and have all the essential conveniences. You see, the Brothers are not supposed to have any contact with each other except at specified periods, so communal washplaces and lavatories are taboo. You'll be given the same treatment as the Brothers, and exercised regularly for the sake of your health. But in your case separately, and under guard, wearing the formal robes of the Order. Believe me, you will not have the slightest chance to escape.'

Mahmoud looked up. 'Even if your friends the police sent a helicopter over the island,' he boasted, grinning, 'they'd see nothing out of the ordinary. My guards also wear the robes, which conceal their Schmeissers very effectively.'

'Your guards,' said Craig reflectively. 'I wonder what they think they're fighting for. From what you said it sounded like a straight ticket—Mahmoud for President, Yasmin Belcadi for Prime Minister. But somehow I can't see you overthrowing the Government without some sort of ideological platform. What is it to be, union with Libya, a new foothold for China in Africa, or a good old-fashioned bourgeois revolution?'

'You talk too much.' Mahmoud signalled to Ali, who untied the rope and took Cleo away to the forepeak.

Craig lowered his voice. 'You won't tell me, of course. But in fact you've told me a great

245

deal already, which would harm you if it got out. If we got out, in fact. So you intend to keep us both indefinitely—irrespective of what happens to your ransom demand?'

Mahmoud smiled. 'By all means interpret your situation that way, if you like. While there's life there's hope—isn't that one of your sayings? But in any case, Mr Craig, while you can be of value to us as hostages you may stay alive.'

*   *   *

The afternoon passed slowly. The heat in the forward cabin became stifling, and they were both gasping for air when they were again allowed into the saloon. Mahmoud appeared, and when he saw the state of near-collapse Cleo was in arranged for them to take showers and remain in the saloon until sunset. They sat by the open window, talking about their lives, and what they had thought of each other when they'd first met on the aircraft, and other trivial things that helped to keep their minds off their immediate future.

Then Cleo said, 'Why did you say that about what the insurgents thought they were fighting for? You couldn't expect Mahmoud to tell you.'

'But that's the curious thing. In every case I know of, when hostages have been taken by a revolutionary movement, the first thing that happens is that someone gives them a lecture on the aims of the movement, and thrusts copies of Chairman Mao or Trotsky into their hands, or whoever is the prophet of the insurgents.'

'The Belcadi woman wouldn't give a hoot anyway for ideology,' said Cleo. 'She's in it for him. He's got a complete ascendency over her. Before he appeared she was happy to amuse herself with Ali or even you—'

'Thank you.'

'—but since then she's kept quiet and I can tell from the way she looks at him that she's hooked.'

'That's interesting, and perhaps important.' He thought for a moment. 'The funny thing is, he doesn't look as if he has any feelings at all.'

'Neither do you, sometimes. But I love you all the same.'

*   *   *

It was after eight o'clock, and they had been immured again for some time in the stuffy forepeak, when they heard the engine slow down. Craig got to his feet and looked out of the little porthole. The rush of water along the hull had reduced to a gentle swish.

For a moment there was nothing to see except distant lights, but then the boat heeled over slightly, turning, and the scene was brightly illuminated. Craig called Cleo, and they stood side by side, faces close together, looking out at a small harbour formed by two moles reaching out from the sides of a stone quay. Behind it loomed the entrance to the fort, a great keyhole doorway at the base of a square tower.

As the boat continued turning they could see the walls stretching away on both sides, falling sheer to the edge of the water. They were at least thirty feet high, constructed to withstand siege and reinforced by square bastions built out to facilitate fire against attackers trying to scale the walls. High up in the sandstone face were narrow windows placed at irregular intervals, and the walls above were capped with pointed Moorish battlements, dimly seen against the starlit sky.

Searchlights fixed above the gateway shone down on the water of the harbour, agitated now by the thrust of the powerboat's propeller as she manoeuvred towards the steps leading up to the top of the mole on the starboard side. Men in dark blue robes, with a silver moon embroidered on the back, were ready with ropes to attach the boat to the bollards. There was a slight bump.

They saw Yasmin and Mahmoud jump ashore and climb the steps. They disappeared inside the archway. Then came the sound of the forepeak door being unbarred, and a voice called Craig. Cleo clung to him.

'We shan't see each other.' There was a

catch in her voice.

He kissed her. 'Do *whatever* they tell you. Don't argue about anything. If they tell you to talk lies into a microphone, *do it*. Being brave wouldn't do you any good and would hurt me, d'you understand? I've got to find time to prepare a way out of here, but I'll do it. I love you, little Cleo, don't forget that.' She held him and whispered in his ear while Ali's angry face appeared in the doorway. Craig went out.

He was hustled through the saloon, out into the cockpit and over the side to the bottom of the stone steps. 'Keep moving,' said Ali, prodding him in the back with the muzzle of his gun. He walked quickly along the mole and on to the stone slabs of the quay. Inside the doorway he found himself in a covered entry, leading to an open courtyard. He was urged up a stair cut in the thickness of the wall on the right of the entry. It came out on to a corridor running behind the cells that looked over the harbour. The doors were marked with Arabic lettering that meant nothing to him, but Ali knew which was his cell and opened the door, signalling him to enter first.

As Yasmin had said, it was Spartan, but quite large, with an iron bedstead, desk, two chairs (one of them a fairly modern armchair) bookshelves, and a table. The deep embrasure of the window was protected by a massive grid of iron bars. Off to one side of the cell was a door leading to a dark chamber lit only by a slit in the outside wall. Ali struck a match, and Craig could see a wash basin, a shower and a very old-fashioned toilet. The little room smelled unsavoury.

There was a light sealed into the wall above the desk in the main room, but no switch. Ali saw Craig's glance. 'Turned off at ten o'clock,' he said. Then he pointed to an opening in the door, about nine inches square, closed by a little wicket. It had a broad ledge on the inside. 'When I bring you food I push it through the guichet, which must be left open at all times.' He grinned, adding, 'You will need the draught anyway. It gets very close during the day.'

'Thank you, Ali. I'm sorry if I hurt you,' he added tentatively.

'Next time I shall know where to hit you,' said the man 'and you will remember it.' He smiled, but there was nothing comforting in the flash of white teeth.

*   *   *

Craig stood for some time at the window. The wall was nearly four feet thick, and he had to squeeze his shoulders between the sides of the embrasure to get his head near the unglazed opening. It was about a yard high and eighteen inches across, and the ancient grille was of forged iron, with the verticles passing through holes opened in the horizontals and hammered tight. All very solid and quite immovable.

Pressing his face to the grille he could distinguish dimly the outline of the little harbour below, and the starlit gleam of waves breaking listlessly against the rocks. While he watched there was a sudden change. The lights on the façade were switched on and he saw two people walk across the quay and down the mole where the *Saliya* lay; Mahmoud first, carrying a suitcase, and then Yasmin, in a cloak. Two men in robes followed. They boarded the powerboat and shortly afterwards the shore lines were hauled inboard and the vessel began to move.

The harbour lights were turned off, but Craig could follow the boat's lights as she headed north, towards the rendezvous with Ahmed Belcadi. He wondered when his hosts would return. The later the better, if he was to have any chance of escape.

CHAPTER FIFTEEN

It was nearly seven o'clock when Craig awoke, and the eastern sunlight was streaming into the cell through the barred window, making a square pattern on the stone floor by the bed on which he lay. It was solidly made of iron, with Victorian brass fittings, and stood against the side wall opposite the door. He had left the little guichet open, as ordered; there was no point in annoying Ali. Not just yet, anyway.

He got to his feet, wearing only the trunks he had slept in, and padded across the warm floor to peer through the guichet. There was nothing to see but the opposite wall of the corridor, and further along a window giving on to the inner courtyard. He crossed to his own window embrasure.

With his face to the grille, he could again see the harbour below, and sniff the rank smell of seaweed left by the shallow tide on the foundations of the moles. Beyond, across a mile or so of water, lay a low island, stretching away to the north-east, with a cluster of white-domed roofs and a mosque with a fluted dome and high minaret. It couldn't be Jerba, because that was joined to the mainland by a causeway, but he recalled a group of islands further north, the Kerkennahs, opposite Sfax. Perhaps he and Cleo were confined on one of those. Fishing boats, with coloured lateen sails, were dotted around the island in his view, and nearer at hand was a small motor-boat, steered by a man in a faded kashabia, who had pulled the hood up against the sun. The two passengers, a man and a girl, wore minimal bathing suits.

The boat slowed down and the man dropped overboard backwards, holding something like a gun in his hand. Skin-diving, obviously. Craig saw the flash of goggles as the swimmer surfaced. He turned back to inspect his room.

The door was far too strong for attack, and if all his meals were to be handed to him through the guichet he would have no chance of tackling Ali either, except at exercise times. On a hook near the door was a blue cotton robe with a silver moon on the back. This he'd have to wear when taken for his carefully guarded exercise, so that he would look like one of the Brothers. As it seemed to be clean, he stripped off his trunks, scrubbed them and his shirt with the plain soap provided in the washroom, rinsed them under the shower and wrung them out. Then he put on the robe and took the damp clothes to hang them from the sunlit bars of the window. It was thus that his eye caught the movement of the motor-boat, which had come within a hundred yards and seemed to be making a slow tour of the island.

He watched it idly as it came nearer. The young man with crew-cut hair, still wearing diver's flippers on his feet, sat on the covered-in bow, with his arm round a sandy-haired girl in a bikini. In the stern was the man in the jellaba, holding the tiller. His hood was down now . . . And it was Chaker.

Frantically, Craig searched for something to signal with, but then remembered the guichet, and ran across the room to half close it, so that no one looking through could see the window. Then again the search. There was no mirror in the washroom—vanity was not encouraged in either Brothers or prisoners—and nothing else to reflect the sunlight, unless . . . He snatched off his robe, thrust the back part against the grille, so that the silver moon was showing, and agitated it up and down. It was still within the embrasure, and invisible from directly below. He looked out, his heart pounding, through the side of the grille, trying to will Chaker to look up. But the man gave no sign, and the boat passed slowly out of Craig's range of vision.

Craig sat down on the bed, the blue robe trailing from his hand. It wasn't defeat—not yet. It *was* Chaker, that he was sure about, and it meant that not only had Craig's message got through, miraculously, but they had already identified the fort and Chaker had come himself to investigate, using two others—who were they? Foreigners, obviously—as a cover. He wouldn't risk an armed landing without complete assurance that Craig and Cleo were in the fort, so he'd make more trips round the island until he caught some sign of their presence.

But then, what? Suppose he decided to land with a force of police and a search warrant, what would happen? The insurgents would merely threaten to drop the prisoners over the battlements. For that matter, they were perfectly capable of wiping out the whole search force before they had a chance of getting inside. It would need a full-scale operation to take the place by storm, even if no account were taken of what might happen to the captives. And that would need time, and meanwhile—meanwhile, Craig couldn't wait.

It was the thought of what Cleo might be suffering that gnawed steadily at his nerves. He couldn't trust her not to provoke the guards into teaching her a lesson, especially if Yasmin had anything to do with it. But then he remembered. Yasmin had gone off in the boat for the meeting with her father; the boat had not returned. With any luck he could expect no interrogation until she and Mahmoud, if he was with her, returned. So it was Ali he had to deal with, first and foremost. And Ali was a hard nut to crack. There had to be a way of overpowering and silencing him without any chance of failure. Then if he could signal to Chaker they might be able to devise a plan of escape.

The robe was no use for Morse signalling. All that agitating might be useful for attracting attention, but what was needed now was some clear-cut on-off sign. He got up and put on the robe, belting it together over his naked body. Then he took the damp silk shirt, which had fallen to the floor in his excitement at recognising his friend, and tied the sleeves to the topmost portions of the bars on either side of the grille. The shirt hung down, covering the whole of the window. If Ali came in it would seem natural that Craig should be drying his washing in front of the embrasure. He could twitch the shirt aside, and back again, in longs and shorts, and just let it hang if he heard Ali coming. He peered past it, hopefully, but the motor-boat was still not in sight.

He lay down on the bed. The uprights at the corners by his feet projected a few inches above the rail which joined them, and were capped by hollow brass balls. He let his eyes wander around the room, and they fell on the armchair. It was cheap, of modern construction, with foam rubber cushions. He wondered . . . Jumping from the bed he snatched up one of the cushions. There they were—rows of thick Pirelli elastic bands, stretched between holes in the frame into which the hooks at the end of the elastic were fitted. He detached one, and let it shrink to its natural size. Eighteen inches, roughly. He undid another, linked the hooks together and stretched the double- length spring across the foot of the bed, between the uprights. It twanged satisfactorily when he pulled back the linked hooks in the middle. He smiled. He had a catapult.

But no missile, and no way of making a pouch to hold it firmly on the back pull and fly freely when he let go. Craig prowled around the room once again, visiting the window just in time to see the little motor-boat disappearing out of sight. He swore, hoping desperately that

Chaker wouldn't give up yet.

It was in the washroom that the idea came to him. A missile, and a good heavy one, but a tethered missile. He reached above the lavatory pan and detached the brass chain suspended from the cistern lever. The chain was made of strong links, and the glazed earthenware handle at its lower end was very satisfactory indeed. It was of British manufacture, somewhere near the turn of the century probably, and it had .stamped in the white glaze. That was what it was for, thought Craig, grinning, and that was how he would use it. Or rather . . . He thought of a better idea.

He took a third spring from the chair frame, attached one end to where the linked springs across the end of the bed were joined, and squeezed the hook until it closed. He inserted the other hook into the hole on the china 'pull', detaching the chain. It had occurred to him that by linking the 'pull' to the middle of the stretched elastic by another elastic would increase the speed of the missile. He squeezed the 'pull' hook until the gap closed. Now, with any luck, the missile could not escape and crash into the door while he practised aiming it. He couldn't risk smashing the china weight before it was used against Ali's face or neck or wherever it might be possible to hit him.

He lay on the bed with his feet braced against the corner posts and hauled on the 'pull', leaning back until both the elastic systems were stretched tightly in an extended Y. Then he let go, and at the same time rolled off the bed on to the floor.

The catapult was impressively successful in the trial. The heavy china weight flew out over the end of the bed, well clear of the railing, nearly reached the door, and came whistling back over the rail towards where Craig's head had been a moment before.

There was a sound from the corridor outside, and Craig only had time to scramble to his feet, throw a blanket over the end of the bed and sit on the edge before the little guichet was pushed wide open and Ali's face appeared. *'Petit déjeuner,'* he announced, and pushed a small pot of coffee and a plate of rolls through the opening, to rest on the ledge inside.

'Thank you,' said Craig. 'When can I take some exercise?'

'At ten o'clock. I take the lady first.'

'Is she all right, Ali?' asked Craig anxiously.

There was no reply and Ali's face disappeared.

Craig ate his breakfast and drank the bitter, unsweetened coffee gratefully, while he thought over his problem, making trips to the window from time to time. But there was no sign of the boat.

If, when Ali came to take him out for exercise, he merely stood in the doorway—or worse, outside it—and signalled to Craig to come out and walk ahead of him, plus his machine-pistol, there would be little chance of knocking him out. There would have to be some way of luring him inside and within range of the catapult, not more than three feet at most from the end of the bed, because although the missile would go much further than that its speed would be decreasing as soon as it passed over the railing. In any case, a lethal hit was too much to hope for, unless he could be got to stand plumb centre opposite the end of the bed.

The man was physically immensely strong and tough, but on the other hand he wasn't—as far as Craig could make out—one of Mahmoud's trained guerrillas. Apart from serving Yasmin's sexual whimsy—and that might have been a one-off exercise—he seemed to be used more as a servant than a guerrilla, and from the way he held his machine-pistol he hadn't had much practice in its use. What was more, he certainly didn't possess a great deal of brain.

Finally, from what Ali had said the night before, and the way he had said it, he would welcome a chance of getting his own back on Craig. And in a hand-to-hand scrap, even without his gun, he would be a tough man to disable. At least quietly. And quiet was a very important factor.

Then there was the problem of knowing

where to find Cleo and how to release her. Ali had said he would come for Craig after exercising Cleo, so he would probably have the key on him. But how to know which door was Cleo's? They were not numbered, as he had seen the night before.

He had almost forgotten the motor-boat, and ran to the window. A ferry was passing on its way from the mainland to the long island. And between it and the fort, almost under the walls, was the boat.

Craig ran to the door, listened, and half-closed the guichet again. When he got back to the window the ferry was moving out of sight. He had thought of a better way of making his signals—by lifting up the shirt tail, so that the window space would appear dark, then lowering it to fill the space with white. Long-long. Short-long. Long-short-long. Short. He spelled it out slowly, MAKE SPLASH. MAKE SPLASH. MAKE SPLASH . . .

Every time he lifted the shirt tails he could see the boat. It had stopped. The girl was lying in the bows, sunbathing. Chaker was wearing his hood, but his face was half turned towards the window. The other man was in the water near the boat, and kicked up a fountain of foam with his legs.

Craig saw another boat passing, much further away, and waited until it had disappeared. Then he slowly signalled SHALL TRY TO ESCAPE ABOUT TEN O'CLOCK REPEAT

TEN O'CLOCK PROBABLY FROM BATTLEMENTS IF WATER DEEP ENOUGH FOR DROP DO YOU AGREE?

There was a consultation between Chaker and the young man. Then Chaker raised his hand, as if to point to some low clouds and made gestures towards the other end of the island, as if there was a better place to fish. The other nodded, and Chaker started the engine. The boat putt-putted away round the island, still keeping near the walls.

So there was a better chance on the mainland side, thought Craig. But how the hell could he get there? His shirt was almost dry, but he left it hanging. The less Ali could see the better.

He practised aiming with the catapult, found it reasonably accurate. He closed all the hooks tightly, so that there was no chance of them coming apart, and left the blanket draped over the railing of the bed, where it would hide his body and his engine of war from anyone coming into the room.

But *if* he could persuade Ali to come in—and he had a plan in mind—wouldn't he go to the side of the bed? Of course he would, if Craig was lying there. So he must be stopped. Craig placed the table between the bed and the door and to one side, and arranged his breakfast plate and mug on it, dragging up the chair, its missing springs now discreetly covered with the cushions, to make it look as if he had eaten breakfast at the table. That should deflect Ali to the bedrail when he came in. *If* he came in. That was still the problem.

Half an hour later he heard footsteps outside. He was already in position on the bed, feet braced, the china pull in his hands, when he realised that there were two sets of steps, and they were passing by his door. It was too late to get to the door in time to call out to Cleo, but if they came back the same way he would be ready.

Twenty minutes passed while he waited by the door, burning with impatience. The footsteps had come from the left, so that was where her cell lay. He pressed his ear to the opening.

They were coming back. Just as the edge of a blue robe came into view he cried, 'Cleo. Where's your cell? How many away?'

There was a growl of annoyance from Ali and something struck the other side of the door with a thud. Cleo shouted, 'Third beyond the stair—Ouch!'

'Tais-toi!' cried Ali, and she gave another little scream. Craig saw the two blue figures passing away to the left, with Ali still prodding the girl with the muzzle of his gun. 'Be ready,' shouted Craig. 'Be ready *soon.*' The word was sufficiently unlike the French to be worth risking.

A few minutes later Ali came to Craig's door. He was in a bad temper. He peered through the panel in the door and saw, in the reduced light of the room, Craig's face appearing above the blanket stretched over the bedrail. He appeared to be sitting back against the head of the bed. Ali unlocked the door and threw it open. '*Lève-toi,*' he ordered.

'*Non,*' replied Craig. '*Je veux dormir.*'

Ali had had enough nonsense from Craig. '*Zut!*' he cried. '*Lève-toi et viens, et sur le champ. Entendu?*'

'*Laissez-moi tranquille,*' said Craig, drowsily, '*je ne veux pas sortir.*'

'*Ecoute,*' growled Ali, coming forward a step. '*Tu feras ce que je dis, et sans blague.*' As Craig had hoped, Ali wasn't going to be put off carrying out his orders. He made a gesture with his gun.

'*Ah, fous-moi le camp,*' shouted Craig, insultingly.

'*Merde alors!*' The man took two quick steps forward. The table was in his way and he stepped towards the bedrail, raising the gun butt foremost. Craig let fly, and threw himself on to the floor, crouching and ready to spring.

Ali's reflexes were lightning-quick, and it was only because he was facing the light, such as it was after being filtered through Craig's shirt in the window, that he reacted a split second too late. But he saw something streaking towards him, and ducked. The heavy missile skimmed through his woolly hair. On the return trip, which he couldn't possibly have foreseen, gravity pulled it down, and it struck him hard behind the ear.

Another man would have been knocked out, but Ali's skull was like weathered oak. He turned in a flash to meet the danger from behind, but by this time Craig's stumbling hasty tackle connected, and he fell.

Craig was on his back, one arm thrown round his neck and the other hand twisting his left arm upwards. He roared with pain, but the excruciating pressure increased. He dropped his gun and tried to lever himself over. Craig released his hold on the man's throat, snatched the gun and dragged the butt hard against Ali's ear. Then again, but that was enough. The black man lay on his face, moaning, with a trickle of blood falling from his right ear on to the stone flags.

Craig took no chances. Whatever humane feelings he might have had for Ali had evaporated when he'd heard Cleo scream. He found the china pull, still attached to the spring, near his feet. He picked it up, weighed it in his hand, chose a spot on the back of Ali's head with professional accuracy, and coshed him. The moaning stopped.

Craig stepped over his body and closed the door. Then he forced open the hook on the end of his catapult and slipped the pull into the pocket of his robe. He tore his blanket into strips and used them to gag and tie up the man on the floor and tether him to the end of the bed, so that when he came to he wouldn't be able to bang on the door.

The shirt and trunks were bone dry, and he put them on, with the robe on top, its hood pulled over his head. The machine-pistol he held in his hand, quite openly. Next, he took a bunch of keys from Ali's pocket and went out of the door, locking it behind him. There was no one in the corridor. He walked quickly to the left, passed the narrow stone stair up which he had been brought the night before, and looked through the panel of the third door. Cleo was sitting on her bed, dressed in her robe and holding her handbag in her lap. He called to her, and by the time she had reached the door he was trying one key after another until he found the right one. He held her body against him. She was trembling, and winced when he put his arm round her back. 'That bastard,' he whispered in her ear, 'isn't going to hurt you again. He's tied up.'

'You didn't . . .'

'Yes. Listen. This is our last chance. Chaker—yes, Chaker—is in a boat down below. You've got to pretend I'm Ali, taking you for another walk. Got it?'

She nodded, and he led her out of the room. 'You go ahead and show me the way to the battlements, if you know it.'

'That's where he took me.' She walked past Craig's cell and at the end of the corridor turned into an archway and began to climb a

265

spiral stair. He pushed past her and went up the last few steps very quietly, Ali's gun ready in his hands.

But there was no one in sight when they came out into the square room which formed the top of one of the bastions in the curtain wall. It had windows on all sides, set in the thick stone, and facing outwards over the sea, inwards over the domed roofs of the cells on the floor below, and sideways on to the parapet walk which ran all round the walls of the island, behind the pointed, man-high battlements. These bastions, square towers of immense strength built at intervals along the curtain wall, and projecting beyond it to enable the defenders to enfilade troops trying to scale the fortifications, cut the parapet walk into sections. The only way to pass from one section of the parapet to the next was through the doors set on opposite sides of the bastions.

Through the further doors Craig and Cleo could look along a fifty-yard section of the parapet walk to the next bastion, and beyond that, as the wall curved, to another bastion set in the angle of the rear battlements facing the mainland.

They stepped out on to the walk and went forward, unhurriedly, with Cleo in front. To the right they could glimpse the gaps in the battlements, the sea shining thirty feet below; on their left was a drop from the top of the thick curtain wall to the flattened domes of the cells and other buildings below, which interrupted their view of the courtyard. The door in the bastion they were approaching was open.

'Pete,' muttered Cleo, without turning her head, 'd'you know something? I'm so scared I could—'

'So am I, but it'll soon be over.' One way or the other, he added to himself. 'We've got to get through that next tower, then the one at the corner and we're on the rear wall, with Chaker waiting below. I hope.'

'You mean there, where the men are?' Three robed figures were standing against the rear section of battlements, looking down at the sea.

'Yes. They may have gone by the time we get to the second tower.'

'And if they haven't?'

'Then there'll have to be a confrontation.'

'It's all very well, but I'm the one in front.'

He patted her behind with the muzzle of the gun. 'Not when we get there.'

'I believe you're enjoying this.'

'I'm petrified. Go on, darling. One thing at a time.'

'But how do we get down to sea level, for God's sake?'

'We drop over the battlements. It's deep water, I believe.'

'Like walking off the roof of a house,' she grumbled. 'Suppose I can't swim?'

'You can swim. Don't make difficulties.'

One of the robed men turned, saw them, and waved. Craig waved back. Only another twenty yards to the open door. Cleo quickened her step, and for the last few yards, where the tower hid the men on the rear battlements from sight, Craig walked past her and stepped into the doorway.

It was a room like the one they had left, with a stone staircase leading downwards. And nobody there. It all seemed too easy, so far. They went out by the opposite door and came on to the next section of the walk.

'This is as far as we went,' said Cleo suddenly. 'I think this next tower is locked, because when Ali came to the door he just turned round and we walked back.'

'Oh Christ!' said Craig. 'That's the last thing I wanted to hear. I hope to God you're wrong.' Below, in the courtyard, was a group of men practising unarmed combat on a thick mattress spread over the cobbles. An instructor was shouting exhortations. No one had time or wish to gaze up at the battlements.

'It's no good trying to jump on this side,' said Craig. 'If I understood Chaker's signal the only place where the water comes right up to the fortifications is where those men are. We've got to get into that tower.' They could see that the door was closed.

'You've still got Ali's keys, haven't you?'

'So I have. Let's try.'

268

When they came to the bastion he tried the handle, but the door was locked. Craig looked down at the bunch of keys in his hand and chose one at random. It was useless, and for a good reason. A key had been inserted from the other side, and left there.

From beyond the bastion they heard shouting, and putting his ear to the wood Craig heard the sound of a man running. The footsteps drew nearer, with a loud slapping of sandalled feet. The man had entered the tower room, and was probably just about to run down the stair. Craig reversed the Schmeisser and banged loudly on the door with the butt. The footsteps stopped. Someone approached the door and called out in Arabic, angrily.

Craig tried to imitate the black man's hoarse voice. 'Ali,' he growled. He banged on the door again. The man inside shouted something obviously very offensive, and Craig heard the key turn.

He pushed Cleo behind him, to one side, and as the handle turned charged the door with his shoulder. As it burst open there was a roar of pain from the man on the other side. He fell sprawling to the stone pavement, with one hand to his broken nose. The door behind him was open.

The man's Schmeisser had fallen, and he was grabbing at it when Craig kicked it away and hit him at the side of the neck with the edge of a hand hardened by karate practice.

The man's hand dropped back to the floor.

Craig pushed his machine-pistol into Cleo's hands. 'If he tries to get up, stand away and point it at him. If he does more, pull the trigger and *let go*, immediately.' He ran to the open door. The robed men peering through the battlements were still shouting to the unseen recipient of their abuse below the walls. Craig closed the door quietly, found the right key and locked it.

When he turned round Cleo was standing with the captured gun pointed at the head of the man on the floor, with an expression of grim determination on her face and her finger trembling on the trigger. 'O.K., darling. Don't pull that thing, for God's sake. It's on automatic. You can put it down now.'

The man on the floor was in a bad state, with his nose swelling visibly and blood pouring from it. 'Lock the door we came through,' said Craig. 'We'll have to withstand siege any minute.' He whipped off the man's blue robe, tore off strips and bound his wrists and legs together. Then he removed the thick leather belt from the guerrilla's waist and used it to draw the tied wrists and ankles together behind the man's back. Finally, he took the china pull from his pocket, and used it expertly.

'He'll die,' whispered Cleo, shakily. 'He can't breathe. Look at the blood.'

'We'll get him on his side. There. He'll be all right. He can breathe through his mouth.

270

Listen. We've got to get through one of those windows. They look bigger than the others.' He felt in the man's pockets and found a flick knife sharp as a razor. 'Take this and cut lengths of cloth from our robes. We don't want them any more and it's tough cotton. About a foot broad, not less. I'll do the same. Then we'll twist them into ropes and knot them together.'

'The window's too narrow. I might get out but you couldn't. Try and see.'

He tried, and swore. It was nowhere near broad enough.

'You're to go.'

'Don't be silly, Peter, I'm not going alone. Look. You can get on to the roof.'

There was an iron ladder attached to the wall, and above it a trapdoor secured by a heavy bolt. Craig climbed up. The bolt was rusty and he had a job to open it, but it gave in the end and he raised the cover, climbed higher, and laid it back. He stuck his head through the opening.

Between the battlements that edged the tower roof he could see the two men below. They were talking together, and glancing impatiently at the door he had just locked. Evidently the man Craig had knocked out was expected back, with instructions on what to do about the inquisitive foreigners in the motor-boat. For there it was. From the outer side of the battlements Craig could see the little boat

271

bobbing on the waves twenty yards from the wall of the fortress, which at this point fell sheer into deep water. But that was the rear wall. Where the tower stood there were rocks below.

Chaker was standing up in the stern, shouting and gesticulating, and pointing to the blond young man whose rubber flippers and face mask could be seen nearer the shore. The girl was looking on, but as Craig watched she turned towards him. He leaned through the battlements, extended his arm and waved. The angle of the tower prevented the guerrillas from seeing him.

Shirley behaved very well. If she had pointed or exclaimed the men behind the battlements would have guessed, but she called to Gleeson, who swam to the side of the boat. Craig could hear her voice, 'Oh c'mon, Russ. I'm getting bored. Let's go some place else.' As he came nearer she lowered her voice. Chaker heard, and started the engine, waving apologetically to the men above and gesturing again towards the foreigners. It wasn't my fault, he seemed to be saying, they insisted.

Craig crawled back to the hatch and climbed down the ladder. The man on the floor was still unconscious. Cleo was standing with the Schmeisser in her hands, watching the head of the staircase. 'If anyone starts to come up,' she said, 'I'll pull it and keep it pulled.

O.K.?'

'You do that. I've signalled the boat and we can get down from the roof, I think, before we're spotted.' He picked up the long length of rope she had twisted and knotted together and tested it, standing on the rope and pulling with all his strength. 'That's fine. You first. When you get out of the trapdoor crawl round to the front side, where those men can't see you. And give me the knife.' He closed it, looked down at it for a moment, and pushed it inside one of his socks.

She climbed up as neatly as a cat. Craig unlocked the door through which they had first entered the room, hauled the unconscious man through it and propped him against the wall. Then he went back and locked the door. With any luck, he thought, anyone coming up the stair wouldn't see the spilt blood at once and there would be some delay before he realised what had happened.

The other danger was that the men who had been shouting at Chaker would want to make sure that he left the vicinity of the island completely. They seemed to have no hesitation about acting in a way that hardly seemed compatible with the gentle doctrines of the Order of the Divine Moon. They might come and watch his progress through the windows of the tower. But they would have to shoot out the lock first, or go down to the courtyard and come up that way.

273

He was half-way through the trapdoor when he heard someone rattling at the door. A voice shouted.

He had brought the two machine-pistols with him, and ran across to where Cleo was leaning through the battlements. 'They're just below,' she said breathlessly. 'But there're jagged bloody rocks between the foot of the wall and the boat. If that rope doesn't hold . . .'

'It will.' He kissed her, and she held to him tight for a moment. 'You're a brave girl,' he said. 'Think what a story you've got for your goddamn *Daily News*. Take hold of the end and wind it round your hand. I'll let you down. *Walk* down the wall if you can. I'll help you.'

She scrambled through the narrow opening with the twisted cloth wrapped round her wrist and held tightly in her fist. For a moment he saw her flushed little face staring at him agonised, as she clung on to the sill of the embrasure before letting go. He braced his feet against the edges of the stone and paid out the rope slowly, giving her time to feel for the wall with her feet. It seemed an age before the tension relaxed, and he could haul the rope up. At least, he thought, he'd got her away, with luck. For himself, escape was a more difficult matter.

He ran back to the trapdoor. There was no possible way of securing it on the outside, and there were ominous sounds from below. He poked the muzzle of the Schmeisser through the opening and fired a long burst. The din of the slugs ricocheting off the stone floor and walls was like nothing he had ever heard, and it would certainly give the guerrillas pause for thought. He wanted to keep their minds off the connection between their prisoners and the boat below.

He ran back to the battlements—and stopped short. To the north, about a mile away, he could see a powerboat approaching the island. It looked too much like the *Saliya* for his comfort.

He tied the end of the rope round both the machine guns, holding them tightly together, and laid them across the opening between the battlements. There wasn't much overlap at each end and his mouth was dry as he slid through the gap, got his legs over the edge, and checked the position of the two guns before letting them take his weight.

He lost his footing at one point, and hung spinning as the rope unwound. Then he spread his legs and found purchase. A few seconds later, with his hands clasped on the last foot of twisted cotton, he felt the rock beneath his feet, and let go. A hand grasped his arm. It was the blond young man, who led him to a place where be could drop into the water and swim out to the boat, which was only a few yards away. He clambered over the side and lay on the deck, dripping.

When Craig could get his breath he shouted

to Chaker, pointing at the white hull with the blue superstructure, 'The *Saliya*. It'll have Mahmoud on board.'

The Tunisian swore and peered across the water. 'She's turning this way. You're right. I'll have to go towards her for a bit, or your friends in the fort will see us.' A hundred yards out to sea he moved the tiller over, and the little motor-boat turned westwards towards the mainland. As they came in sight of the rear wall of the fort shots were fired, and they could see the robed guards on the battlements firing at them, all pretence forgotten. Chaker shouted to Gleeson, 'Under the fore deck,' and the young man pulled out of its hiding place an army automatic rifle. Without waiting for further orders he crouched in the stern next to Chaker and opened fire. The rifle had twice the range and four times the accuracy of the Schmeissers, and the heads above the battlements disappeared. By the time they had reappeared at other places and the fire was resumed, the distance was too great. The firing stopped, and through the gaps in the . battlements the men could be seen running towards the corner bastion.

Craig glanced at Cleo. She and Shirley were lying in the stern, too frightened to move. But there was for the moment neither time nor grounds for comforting them. Craig's eyes were on the menacing bow-wave of the *Saliya*, now only a few hundred yards away on an interception course. The gap was closing fast. He turned to Chaker, desperately. 'Can't you wring any more speed out of your engine? They'll riddle us if they get much nearer.'

'Of course I can, and I will. But only when I've kept that boat occupied for a bit longer. Then Tibaoui will get her.'

'Tibaoui? Where's he coming from?'

Chaker pointed forward, past Craig's shoulder. Another craft, low in the water, was coming to meet them, moving very fast. 'It's a coastal patrol launch, with Tibaoui and a half-dozen paras. They were lying out of the way until I signalled that you'd made your escape.' He touched the small receiver in his breast pocket. 'But we've got to give them more time, or the *Saliya* will get away.' He called to Gleeson. 'You were good with that rifle. Try and smash her windscreen.'

The young man stood up, swaying to counter the movement of the motor-boat, and took his time aiming. Then he fired three shots on automatic.

The action was calculated to keep the eye of the *Saliya*'s helmsman from straying, and it succeeded. The man saw the glass in front of him turn suddenly white and opaque as the bullets whipped through it. A man behind him cried out in pain. Mahmoud thrust his gun butt through the glass and cleared a large hole. Then he saw the coastal patrol launch, and bellowed a command.

277

In the little motor-boat Gleeson called out, 'They're turning.'

'*Merde,*' cried Chaker. 'They've spotted her.' He pulled out the radio and spoke into it urgently.

The *Saliya* was slowing down and turning tightly, but by the time she was set on a course to take her back towards the island the patrol launch had her in range. The first 20 mm cannon shell threw up a spout of white foam near her quarter; the second was a direct hit on her stern. Craig heard the American beside him whistle in admiration. There was a cloud of yellow smoke that hid the *Saliya* for a moment, and as it cleared away they saw the powerboat begin to circle helplessly.

'What's happening?' called Cleo. 'I'm missing my first sea engagement.'

'Keep down,' said Craig.

Chaker moved his tiller and followed the launch as she closed with the *Saliya*, now gliding with engine halted through her own wake.

'Taieb,' said Craig urgently. 'I think I know Mahmoud, if he's in that boat. He won't allow himself to be taken prisoner. He'll try anything.' Chaker nodded, and spoke again to Tibaoui. Then he opened the throttle and the little motor-boat surged forward.

'Major Chaker had a forty-five horsepower engine put into this boat during the night,' explained Gleeson. 'She can do fifteen knots if you don't mind springing all her timbers. We tried her out this morning and I'll tell you something, I was scared.'

When they came up level with the launch she was only a hundred yards from the Saliya, moving forward slowly. Tibaoui was shouting through a loud-hailer. A white shirt was held out over the *Saliya*'s stern. The launch moved forward more quickly. One of the paratroopers was lying in her bows with his automatic rifle pointing.

'Mahmoud,' shouted Tibaoui.

They saw the man's long figure emerge from the wheelhouse. He came to the rail and stood looking at the launch as it crept nearer. His hands were in his pockets. He called out something in Arabic.

The launch moved closer. But Craig's warning, relayed through Chaker, had been taken to heart. There were now four men in the bows of the coastal patrol launch, and every foot of the *Saliya*'s deck was covered by their rifles.

Mahmoud saw them, and turned his back. He walked unhurriedly to the other side of the deck and drew a grenade from each pocket. He put one foot on the low rail, drew out the pins with his teeth, stood, poised for a moment silhouetted against the blue sky, and leapt forward.

Those who were watching him heard the double thump of the explosion as his body plunged into the sea. The remains of Habib Mahmoud surfaced in a boiling flurry of crimson foam.

CHAPTER SIXTEEN

Chaker left Tibaoui to deal with the crippled *Saliya* and her crew and guard the harbour at Sidi Abdullah until reinforcements arrived, while he set out for Sfax in the motor-boat.

The two girls and Gleeson were not inclined to talk—Mahmoud's death was still too vivid in their memories—and Chaker's mind was occupied with something he had learned for the first time.

After radioing a report to his newly set-up base in Sfax he had turned to Craig. 'The insurgents on the mainland will have the news, too. We know the fort has radio contact with someone on the coast, because their signals have been picked up. We're still trying to decode them, and D.F. the shore station.'

'I wonder when Yasmin will be told of Mahmoud's death,' said Craig thoughtfully. 'I suppose you've got her inside ...'

'What on earth do you mean, Peter? How could she?'

'But you got my message, didn't you, Taieb? I told you she was in charge when we were captured. She and Mahmoud seem to have run the whole conspiracy, as far as I can make out.'

Chaker stared at him, thunderstruck. Then he said, 'My dear Peter, your precious message was half washed away. It looked as if Yasmin Belcadi was a prisoner with you. She arrived back this morning with her father, and she's as free as air in Tunis. In Allah's name, what happened? But wait a moment.' He pulled out his transceiver. 'Are you absolutely sure? If I order her arrest there mustn't be any mistake.'

'Of course I'm sure. Both Cleo and I heard her say that once they'd got the money from her father she was going to run the Tunis end of the insurgency while Mahmoud remained at the fort. Didn't she, Cleo?'

'She did. She and Mahmoud were lovers.'

'*Merde alors!* That doesn't—'

'And,' continued Cleo coldly, 'she held us both up with a gun. Capturing us was entirely her idea. Mahmoud only appeared afterwards.'

Chaker pressed the bleep button on his radio and spoke for some time in Arabic. As he put it away he said, 'I've sent the message through to the General, and he'll take whatever action he thinks fit. But I know he'll want me in Tunis as quickly as possible so I've arranged for a military aircraft to fly me back. And you too as well, I'm afraid, because we shall need your evidence. No objection, I hope?'

'You'd subpoena me anyway, even if I had. But I agree, and so does Cleo, I expect.'

'All right,' said Cleo, 'but what about Russ

281

and Shirley? From what she's told me we owe them a lot.'

'We've got to get back to Hammamet,' said Gleeson. He sighed. 'It'll seem a bit tame after this.'

'You can have the car, of course,' said Chaker, 'and I'll see that a friend of mine in Hammamet pays all the bills. But I very much hope you will both let us entertain you for a couple of days in Tunis before you leave. As Miss Hamilton says, we have a lot to thank you for.'

'We'd like that, wouldn't we, Shirl?'

'We sure would. I've had skin-diving.'

*   *   *

They had seen Russ and Shirley depart in the hired car and were waiting on the airfield while the transport plane was refuelled. Craig said, 'I'm two days behind with the news. What's been happening to your insurgency?'

'No more attacks. It gave me time to start re-briefing all the agents I had recruited after your previous visit, and when we got your message and I had to leave, the General himself took over. Some very useful reports were coming in, but we promised your Ambassador to make no further arrests until we had made an attempt to release you. There was no whisper of suspicion against Yasmin Belcadi.'

'It's odd,' said Craig. 'It's as if when she and Mahmoud were out of circulation everything came to a stop. You know what I think? I believe all Yasmin told us about the cell system was nonsense. They've got a few well-trained and highly professional commandos who can be sent out from the fort or from hide-outs in Tunis for agit-prop, bank raids and sabotage, and a useful number of agents in politics and the mass media. And that's all.'

'You don't want more than that,' said Chaker soberly, 'to cause chaos. How many hard-core activists were there in Ireland at the height of the trouble?'

'Not more than a few hundred,' agreed Craig. 'And that includes official IRA and Provos on both sides of the border. The others were just persuaded or bullied or blackmailed into co-operation, and they included children of ten or twelve, dozens of well-meaning people in public life, frightened housewives and—' he stopped.

'Journalists, you were going to say,' put in Cleo in a cold little voice.

'*You* said it, darling.'

*   *   *

Chaker's car drew up outside the Belcadi villa in Sidi Bou Said. He spoke to the armed police sergeant at the gate and they were led through the sunlit garden to the interior of the house and into the room with the sea-green floor. Yasmin was seated on one of the sofas, with a young inspector in attendance. She seemed perfectly calm, except for the restless movement of her dark eyes.

'Why am I not allowed to leave my house?' she asked.

'Yasmin Belcadi,' said Chaker, 'I am arresting you on a charge of taking by force and holding for ransom Miss Cleo Hamilton and Mr P. V. Craig, British subjects. Mr Craig, do you identify Yasmin Belcadi as the woman who held you prisoner in the powerboat *Saliya* and afterwards in the fortress on the island of Sidi Abdullah?'

'I do.'

'Miss Hamilton?'

'Yes.'

'Yasmin Belcadi, have you any statement to make? Please stand up.'

She didn't move. 'I was acting under duress. The leader of a group of insurgents was holding me against my will and I was threatened with reprisals if I did not do what he told me.'

'You can't get away with that,' burst out Cleo. 'Why, you held us both at pistol point!'

'I was acting under duress,' she repeated stonily.

Chaker smiled. 'Were you also forced to contribute to the conversation in the *Saliya* that was recorded? You forgot to switch off,

284

you know, and towards the end you expressed yourself very forcefully and even said you were returning to Tunis to carry on the revolution from there.'

'That is another of Mr Craig's stories, I suppose,' she said with a scornful laugh. 'Where is your proof?'

'The tape is in the hands of the police in Sfax,' said Chaker. 'I heard it played through just before we came here. Nobody had destroyed it because, I suppose, Mahmoud still hoped to piece together extracts for propaganda purposes.'

She had jumped to her feet. 'How could they have got it?' she cried desperately.

'Because the *Saliya* is in our hands.'

'If you think Mahmoud will talk —'

'He won't talk. He's dead.'

She stared at him unbelievingly for a moment, then turned away and hid her face in her hands.

They heard the sound of footsteps approaching through the patio. General Farhat appeared; and with him Ahmed Belcadi, who was a very angry man. He stopped when he saw Yasmin and went towards her, but she shook her head and would not look at him.

'I have charged Mademoiselle Belcadi, *Mon Général,*' said Chaker, 'in the presence of two witnesses who confirm that the account I gave you of their kidnapping at her hands is

285

correct.'

The General bowed over Cleo's hand and clapped Craig on the shoulder. 'I am much obliged to you both for your co-operation.' He turned to Belcadi, who was beside himself with rage. 'We have ample proof, Belcadi, apart from what you have just heard. You must accept the fact that your daughter was until now a leading member of the insurgency that has already caused our country so much unhappiness and loss of life.'

'I will accept nothing of the kind.' He seized his daughter by the arm and spoke to her angrily in Arabic. She said nothing, but remained, head bent, her hands over her face.

'What other proof have you got?' asked Belcadi, more calmly.

'Mr Craig and Miss Hamilton can describe the powerboat *Saliya* that had a rendezvous with you last night. Mr Craig saw your daughter and Mahmoud, the leader of the insurgents, leaving the fortress arm in arm. There is the record of a conversation in which she and Mahmoud took part, which shows clearly that she was not in any way acting under duress. But the testimony of Miss Hamilton and Mr Craig, which is detailed and explicit, would leave no Tunisian court in any doubt whatever about your daughter's guilt.'

As his words sank in, Belcadi's legs seemed to give way, and he sat down heavily on the sofa. He thought for a time, then spoke in a low voice. 'I have great respect for you, General Farhat, and I suppose I must believe what you say. With your permission, *I* will attend the hearing before the *juge d'instruction*, and if I can see no reasonable explanation for my daughter's conduct I shall not raise a finger to save her from the punishment she deserves. I have a duty to my country, and she shall not stand in its way.'

The effect of this speech was dramatic. Yasmin whirled round on her father and tried to scratch his face with her pointed, dark-lacquered nails, pouring out a torrent of Arabic. At her first words Belcadi jumped up and seized her long hair with one hand, struck her across the face with all his strength. Chaker and Craig pulled him away, pinning his arms behind his back.

The General spoke to Yasmin, quietly, ignoring Belcadi's protestations.

She held her hand to her cheek and began to speak in a lifeless voice, in Arabic, addressing no one in particular. Mahmoud's name came into it once or twice. Belcadi tried to shout her down, until the General brusquely ordered Chaker to take him outside. Yasmin's monologue went on. Finally, still without raising her eyes, she felt for her handbag and drew out a bunch of keys. She held it out, and the General took it from her limp fingers and, holding out one key after another, gently forced her to select the one she was evidently talking about.

It took some time to search the files and documents in the locked room in the basement, but the evidence which emerged was damning for Ahmed Belcadi. Instruction for the conduct of the insurgency and lists of the principal operatives were in his own hand. And when he was arrested, a duplicate key to the basement room was found in his pocket.

CHAPTER SEVENTEEN

The evening before Craig and Cleo were due to fly back to London Sir John Radcliffe gave a small dinner party for them. General Farhat and his rather formidable wife were there, and the Chakers, the Thornes and the two Americans.

Cleo was radiant. There had scarcely been a let-up since they had seen Belcadi and his daughter taken off in separate cars by the police. Television, radio and press interviews, a wild party at the Press Association, and feature articles to prepare for the *News* and its colour supplement. For her they had been heady days, and she glanced a little apprehensively at Craig, who had earlier been showing signs of restiveness. In his white dinner jacket he looked rather handsome, she decided. She watched the strong lean hand as he played with his brandy glass. Strange that it could sometimes be so gentle.

Chaker was talking. 'We've learned quite a lot about Yasmin Belcadi since the arrests. She seems to have—er—distributed her favours very freely, and some of the high-ranking men in politics and public service admit that was how she influenced them. Once they heard of Belcadi's role in the movement they have been rushing to volunteer information before they are denounced. It's the hard-core insurgents who won't talk, as yet. If you tell them the real leader of the conspiracy was Belcadi they just laugh scornfully. For them, Mahmoud was the boss.'

'One of the trades union leaders says he met him first in Tanzania two years ago,' remarked the General. 'That could explain a lot.'

'Tanzania?' asked Phyllis Thorne.

'The Chinese have poured arms, money and aid into Africa, and Tanzania and Zanzibar are their strongholds. They have training schools there for guerrillas, with senior Chinese army officers to give advice, and most of the rebels in Mozambique and Eritrea are Chinese-trained. And armed. Mahmoud may have been a Maoist agent.'

'But what could the Chinese hope to do in Tunisia, of all countries?' asked the Ambassador. 'It's been a strongly socialist state since independence, but the Tunisians are the last people on earth to embrace the

Maoist form of communism.'

Craig said, 'Ten years ago Chou en-Lai made a tour of African countries and came back with the statement that they offered excellent revolutionary potential. There are at least a dozen African states where the Chinese hope and expect to see national revolutionary governments on their own pattern. They never take no for an answer. After all, they managed to achieve in Albania—the most unlikely country, one would imagine—a very useful beach-head in Europe. To set up another in North Africa wedged in nicely between anti-communist Libya and socialist Algeria, would be something to work for.'

'But Belcadi couldn't have been working for that,' put in Thorne. 'It doesn't make sense.'

'I'm sure he wasn't,' said the General. 'What he wanted was power, in his own hands. He had acquired all the money he needed, and he believed that if the movement created enough chaos he could come in, as the strong man who had always urged harsher measures of repression, and force President Bourguiba to resign. After all, my country is very vulnerable. If the tourists stop coming, we can't pay our bills. Then, if we can believe his daughter, whose only wish now is to see that Ahmed Belcadi gets as long a term of imprisonment as she does—he would have denounced the very people who had done all the hard work. You see,' he added, smiling, 'he knew exactly who they were and where to find them. That was the clever bit.'

'And what did Miss Belcadi want?' enquired the Ambassador.

'Mahmoud,' replied Cleo, succinctly. 'She was completely dominated by him.'

'And if ever I saw a dedicated revolutionary,' Craig intervened, 'it was Mahmoud. Once Belcadi had attained power—and he was the perfect front man—Mahmoud wouldn't have allowed him to survive long. Those two were using each other quite cold-bloodedly.'

'And Yasmin knew it.' Cleo closed her handbag with an angry snap.

The General turned to the Ambassador. 'We owe your country a debt, Your Excellency. Luckily, with Mr Craig's help, we were forewarned and had prepared our counter-measures. The insurgency, even if its leaders were still at large, would have been crushed within a few weeks, but it would have been a bloody, painful business. As it is, the back of the revolution has been broken, and its limbs are powerless. It's our task now to convince thousands of young people who regard us as brutal oppressors that we really have their best interests at heart.' He flicked the ash from his cigar. 'And also assure our friends everywhere that we can offer them a safe and orderly country where they can enjoy a holiday.'

*   *   *

Chaker drove Cleo and Craig back to the Tunisia Palace, and for a time they stood talking in the foyer.

One of the receptionists called Cleo and handed her a cablegram. She came back, white-faced, and passed it to Craig without a word. It was from the editor of the *Daily News* instructing her to leave the following day for Phnom Penh on a special assignment.

Craig growled, 'He can't do this. Tell him to get stuffed. I'm looking after you now.' He thrust the cable into Chaker's hand.

'Oh Peter darling, I can't . . . I can't give it all up, just . . .'

'What d'you mean—just?'

They were still staring at each other angrily, thinking of all they had hoped to do together, sensing the pressures that might force them apart, as Chaker tucked the cable form under Cleo's arm and walked quietly away.